one day
like this

one day like this

LAURA BRIGGS

Bookouture

Published by Bookouture in 2018

An imprint of StoryFire Ltd.

Carmelite House
50 Victoria Embankment
London EC4Y 0DZ

www.bookouture.com

ISBN: 978-1-78681-487-6
eBook ISBN: 978-1-78681-486-9

For all the readers who joined me for my
first wedding book and whose support has continued
to inspire new projects.

Prologue

"You sit here, and Penny sits here," six year-old Tessa said. "Next to Raggedy Ann."

"Do I have to?" said Penny. She was the same age, but only came over to play because Tessa had the biggest collection of glitter ponies in the whole neighborhood.

"You do. I made place cards." Tessa's voice became slightly bossy. "Natalie is next to Mr. Bear and Fashion Girl is across from me." At each place there was a carefully drawn card made with glitter markers, with names printed on them. Froggy, an overstuffed bean bag animal, had fallen forward on his face and squashed it flat, which Tessa noticed and fixed for the eleventh time.

Natalie rolled her eyes. "Just do it," she told Penny. "It's easier than arguing." She sat down at the end of the table in her "chair," which was only a cardboard back drawn with crayons. Next to her, Mr. Bear slumped over his teacup, while Raggedy Ann looked more chipper at her place opposite.

They were in Tessa's playhouse, built out of an old cardboard appliance box with windows and a door cut into it, so, technically, she *could* make the rules for the tea party. As usual, Tessa's tea party couldn't consist of just a toy tea set and some stuffed animals. Her playhouse's crayon-illustrated interior was decorated with lots of old white Christmas twinkle lights she had hauled out of attic boxes, and her mini table had a bouquet of flowers picked from the vacant lot down the street and the next-door neighbor's flowerbeds—she probably hadn't realized yet she was short a few gladiola stalks.

"This one's too tall." Tessa's small fingers trimmed the biggest stalk with a pair of blunt-tipped school scissors. "There, perfect," she said, as she stuck it back in the cracked glass vase. "Don't eat the cookies!" she said to Penny, who had reached for the plate of gingersnaps in the middle of the table. "The party hasn't started yet."

"But I'm hungry," whined Penny. "What are we doing here, if we're not having a party?"

"Everything has to be perfect," said Tessa. "Wait, I'll put on my hostess apron." A pink apron decorated with a cupcake picture was hanging from the plastic yellow stove behind her. "And my hostess crown." It was made from gold paper, decorated with plastic rhinestones.

"Now I'm official," she announced. "We can start the party for Fashion Girl's engagement. Penny, you're the bridesmaid, and so are Raggedy Ann and Natalie. Mr. Bear is giving away the bride, and Froggy is going to be the photographer."

"Fashion Girl isn't engaged," said Penny. "She's a famous worldwide model in the commercials. Plus, she's just a plastic head." She cast a scornful glance at the Fashion Girl at the head of the table, who was only a smiling head with shoulders and a champagne-blonde wig, wearing a dozen barrettes in her hair and too much washable eyeliner.

"It's why we're having the party," said Tessa stubbornly. "It's her engagement party, so we're using special china with roses and having two kinds of cookies for guests to pick, *and* I hung the banner." A very worn vinyl "Congratulations" banner was draped across the cardboard playhouse's wall behind her.

"Big deal. They sell china tea sets for dolls in every store—and this water is *brown*! Ew, ick," said Penny, making a face when Tessa poured her a cup from the little rose china teapot.

"It's real tea," explained Tessa. A long string with a teabag tag hung from the opposite side of the pot.

"Can't we just play house the normal way?"

"No, we can't. We need to have a reason to hold a party," said Tessa. "It has to be a special one, like this one." She held out a scrap page torn from a magazine, showing a big white tent decorated with tiny white star lights, and sprays of white gladiolas and lilies in the gold and cream painted ceramic vases on its buffet table, surrounded by smiling, chatting guests with champagne flutes. In the distance, a little girl chased fireflies. The picture's caption read, *A charming outdoor party celebrates the happy couple's nuptials on a sultry Southern twilight eve.*

"See?" said Tessa, as if holding all the proof anyone needed.

"This is DUMB!"

"But everybody likes gorgeous parties," said Tessa. "I want everything to be extra nice." She looked at the third living person at the table for support.

"Don't look at me," said Natalie. "My mom only brings me over to this house when Gramma has to go to the doctor." She played with the end of one stubby dark braid of hair.

"I'm leaving." Penny seized her glittery pink book bag and crawled out the playhouse's rectangular door opening. "You can have your stupid fancy party without me. You're weird, Tessa Miller."

"Am not!" Tessa shouted back. But she looked crestfallen as she plopped down at her place at the table. The only smiling faces left were those of Raggedy Ann and the guest of honor, which was mostly painted on with real lipstick "borrowed" from Tessa's mom's cosmetic case.

"Are you gonna go home, too?" she asked Natalie. After a minute of quiet pouting, she looked at the only human guest left at her table.

"No. I can't go until my mom comes back for me," Natalie said. "But I'll play." She shrugged her shoulders. "I like weddings okay. Plus, I think playing house all the time is boring anyway."

"Here's your tea." Tessa poured a cup for her. "And a cookie." She passed her the plate. "There are two kinds, because this is a special occasion. You can try both."

"Thanks," said Natalie. "Want me to fix Fashion Girl's makeup? If it's her party, she should look good. I know a lot about makeup—my cousin lets me read all her fashion magazines. She's fourteen."

"Okay," said Tessa. "Her makeup kit is by the grandfather clock." The clock was drawn on the opposite wall, near the chintz curtains created by pink and yellow Crayola markers. The party was suspended for a few seconds as Natalie made the guest of honor a little more fashionable.

"Where'd you get the picture you showed that other girl?"

"From a magazine," said Tessa. "I have lots of them. I put the best ones in a special folder." She pulled it from her Strawberry Shortcake backpack. Marker letters spelled out "Tessa's Big Dreams" between glittery flower stickers.

"Weird," said Natalie. "What's in it?"

"It's all the big celebrations that people want to have," said Tessa. She stuffed the folder back in place behind her history notebook. "That's when people are happiest. I want to make them come true."

"So, like, you have a big book full of parties and fancy dinners and that's what you want to do—plan stuff so other people have fun?"

"It's *my* dream," said Tessa. That stubborn tone returned. "I like it." She tossed a lock of her long, orangey-red hair behind her shoulders in a gesture of indifference to any opinions.

"Can I have another cookie?" Natalie asked.

"Okay. But we're having the party now, so you have to talk to your neighbors too. Mr. Bear, would you like a cookie, too?" Tessa demonstrated. "Don't you think your niece looks *so* pretty? A real fashion expert did her makeup."

"I think she should have been a famous model in Milan instead of deciding to marry that dumb Ninja Turtle." Mr. Bear's voice was a creakier, deeper version of Natalie's real one.

Tessa's pouting lip returned, so her tea party guest stopped making the bear talk and ate another fig cookie bar. "Who's the picture in the frame?" Natalie pointed to the one drawn with gold crayon, apparently sitting on a brown crayon table with stick legs that didn't reach the bottom of the wall. Another magazine picture was pasted inside, of a hunky teen heartthrob who appeared frequently on the cover of TV magazines.

"Him? That's my boyfriend," said Tessa. "When I grow up, I mean." She poured another cup of tea. "Here you are, Froggy. Sugar or lemon?"

"Are you going to marry him in a big tent with star lights?" Natalie asked.

"Maybe." Something dreamy entered Tessa's voice. "When I fall in love, I'll find out." She set aside the teapot. "Time for the special cake," she announced, after ducking under the table and bringing forth a little bakery box with a cellophane top. Inside was an oversized cupcake, generously frosted with vanilla icing and dotted with bright patches of food coloring, whose containers seemed to have exploded horribly in the vicinity. "I made the icing myself."

"I can tell." Natalie wrinkled her nose.

Tessa stuck a birthday candle on top. "Make a wish," she said to Fashion Girl. "All your dreams will come true on your big day that way."

Matches clearly weren't allowed. They waited a moment while Tessa made a blowing noise behind Fashion Girl's smiling head, before she began cutting the cupcake—or decimating it—with the blunt blade of the kitchen's play knife. She smushed the portions back together before serving it, then ate her own with a plastic play fork, while Natalie finished smashing hers to mush, pretend eating.

"I wish I was grown up now," said Tessa.

"Why?"

"Because that's when all the best stuff happens," said Tessa. "That's when all your dreams finally come true." The faraway tone from before was matched by the look in her eyes, as if she was imagining that perfect life right then. Starry hopefulness shone in those bright childish irises, before the party's hostess remembered the guest at hand.

"More cake, anybody?"

Chapter One

With a sigh, Tessa checked her watch as she leaned against the wall beside the bouncy castle. "Ten more minutes!" she called to the kids inside, all of whom ignored her.

"Tess, get those kids out of the castle pronto, will you?" Her boss Bill appeared. "We've got to break down the hotdog table in another twenty minutes."

"Sure," she said. And managed not to sigh again until he turned his attention to the birthday party clown, who was trying to fill his tiny suitcase with magic props. "Come on, kids! Time to go! There's extra cake waiting for you!" She clapped her hands together to get their attention.

Another Saturday afternoon at a rented venue for a kid's birthday party. Despite its name, Party 2 Go actually had four employees. Today, Tessa had drawn the short straw and was stuck with bouncy castle supervision and accidental spills. Lucky June was serving cake and soft drinks, while Tina was decorating ice cream sundaes with sprinkles.

At least she didn't have Steve's job, she reflected. The inside of the T-Rex costume's head had been really smelly as of late.

By now, Tessa was supposed to be one of the top wedding planners in all of Bellegrove, the charming Southern haven where she'd grown up. The city lay on the coast, with a history of rugged sailing ships and willow-lined streets of mansions; it was now a modest metropolis split into sections. The neighborhoods had a cozy, intimate feeling with their old architecture sprawling across the last two centuries, from the waterfront and the fast-growing ethnic districts in historic buildings, to modern office complexes. Stretching from quaint churches and cemeteries in the old town's district to museums in converted antebellum manor houses, chic restaurants in renovated warehouses, and department stores, this was where Tessa had lived all her life—here was the place she planned to make other people's dreams come true: weddings beneath the open sky under shady willows, engagement parties in garden parks, solemn ceremonies in the old stained-glass chapel located mere walking steps from one of Bellegrove's nicest beaches.

That was the plan in her head, anyway. It was one of the reasons she had stayed there after college, rather than moving to a bigger city like Charlotte or Raleigh—or moving to Florida where her mother had chosen to retire. But Tessa loved her childhood home town, with its cozy shops and cafes and sprawling oaks, the magnolia and dogwoods that bloomed in the parks and along the sidewalks every summer, and the distant beach that reminded her the ocean was the gateway to the world. But she might as well be six again, staging parties for her toys—except six-year-old Tessa had been much closer to living her dream than her grownup counterpart seemed to be.

It wasn't as if she hadn't tried. She had graduated with a hard-earned dual business and design degree, and after peddling her résumé to every event planner from one side of the city to the next, she'd snagged a job at the Antebellum, a local tearoom. For five blissful months, Tessa had arranged real tea parties for small occasions instead of dolls, until an economic slump left fewer customers celebrating birthdays and girls' days out with overpriced Darjeeling and macaroons—leaving her jobless again and peddling her résumé anywhere that would take it.

No event planners needed yet another junior drudge at the moment, even with a recovering local economy. Which had landed her here, in the last possible role she ever imagined for herself in dreaming of planning someone's celebration: mopping up soda spills in record time and removing mustard stains from the big T-Rex costume. When she wasn't being forced to wear it, that is.

"Time to pull the plug," said Bill.

You said it, Tessa thought, although not for the same reasons. Her boss had found the release button for the inflated bouncy castle, and its walls began sagging. "Give me a hand, Tess." The two of them folded it, as a crowd of disappointed children booed, then dispersed as one of their mothers intervened.

"This thing is heavier than it looks," said Tessa with a grunt. She struggled beneath the box with the folded castle and the air compressor inside.

"Use those muscles, Tess." Bill thumped her on the back with his clipboard. "We still have to fold tables and clean up that slice of cake somebody smashed over by the emergency exit."

"Great." From the corner of her eye, she saw Steve remove his T-Rex head. A whiny eight-year-old began screaming immediately at the sight of a human head atop the dinosaur body, a group of adults trying to console him.

Bill occasionally needed help planning birthday parties, but not often. Most birthday party clients weren't interested in creativity; otherwise they hired one of the glitzier 'gung ho' planners in the city. Bill advertised the all-in-one package heavily, which included cake, cookies, hotdogs or pizza, with a bouncy castle and two entertainers (one of whom was always dressed as either a dinosaur or a princess). Except for choosing cookies or cupcakes, or picking up new plastic tablecloths, there wasn't much for Tessa to do.

Watching her future slip away was hard. All those classes on hospitality, design, small business budgets—her college years were a hectic collage, with all those bits and pieces helping develop her natural talent for negotiating with people, coordinating their tastes and dreams into a harmonious event, and troubleshooting little setbacks and mistakes for a smooth experience. She had never pictured her degree leading to the same bouncy castle and confetti-print napkins, week after week.

"Hey, Red, you missed a spot." Red was Tina's nickname for Tessa, because of her bright red hair. Her sarcastic coworker pointed to the remains of a hotdog obviously trampled underfoot multiple times, something the broom in Tessa's hands could never possibly clean.

"Thanks a lot," she muttered. She resisted the urge to stick out her tongue, though Tina's back was facing her by now anyway. This was a job for the putty knife in the cleanup supply bucket. Tessa couldn't prevent herself from groaning aloud as she reached for it. She would never crave hotdogs again, she decided, her nose wrinkling in disgust. To top it off, this one had chili sauce on it, making it look a little like someone's barf. That *was* chili, right?

Don't go there, Tessa. She made herself plunge into her latest cleaning task. It was the fifth accidental spill, and they hadn't even finished serving dessert yet—meaning mushy bits of cake and ice cream sundaes were probably in her immediate future.

There were worse lives to live, of course. But there were better ones too—and lately, Tessa found herself thinking of the better kind more and more. The fantasy life where she ran her own event planning firm, creating moments that were both special and personal for her clients.

Portfolios of celebratory concepts both unique and dazzling; digital contact lists of caterers, florists, and suppliers who would provide anything and everything a client wanted. Creating moments that would seem like magic when her clients looked back on them years later, a snapshot of happiness in life's jumbled-up collage—*that* was Tessa's idea of a future.

So what was she doing stuck in the same lackluster job as always? Scraping up squashed bread and Jell-O cake day after day, as chances slipped past her in a world filled with opportunities, all of which had managed to elude her thus far?

She was flicking up the last bit of mess when a pair of stiletto heels crossed her path. Designer, *Devil Wears Prada*-type heels. Instead of moving around her, they stopped in their tracks. The person attached to the sleek legs wearing them exclaimed, "Is that really you, Tessa? Oh my gosh, it *is* you!"

Even before she looked up, Tessa knew it was the last person on earth she would choose to see at this moment. The blast from the past had all the charm of a chilly, damp burst of air from an old window-cooling unit. Even the roommate who left her to pay their part of the year's rent without warning might be more welcome than the owner of these shoes. That was how much she didn't want to see her snobby childhood neighbor turned college frenemy, Penny Newcastle, right now.

Penny had always been infuriatingly superior, entitled, and gifted with perfect luck and perfect timing. She had gone on to greater things after graduating, Tessa had heard through the gossip chain. Which was exactly what everybody believed about Penny's future, which had never been subject to polite *tsk*s of sympathy from those who warned her about the foolhardiness of pursuing *her* dreams.

Penny had probably never eaten a hotdog, much less scraped one off the floor.

"Penny, what a surprise. Great to see you." Tessa tried to sound casual as she jumped to her feet. If she just pretended this whole situation wasn't horribly awkward, maybe Penny would too. *Fat chance.*

"Tessa, I'm in shock. I had no idea you were part of the Hughes's circle of friends," Penny said with amazement. "I mean, I'm *only* their neighbor, of course, but I've been to enough of their parties that I can't believe I haven't come across you before now."

Just then, her glance fell on Tessa's nametag. "Oh…" A polite little *o* formed by a flawlessly lipsticked mouth. "My mistake," she said. "Oopsie. My bad." That awful little smile from their days at college was back—the one that was part pity, part fake sympathy, which Penny always trotted out for people she didn't really like.

"As you can see, I'm part of the event planning staff," said Tessa. "Party 2 Go? We specialize in birthday parties, graduations… pretty much anything involving kids and families. So I'm at work right now, making a client's day feel special." She was trying to sound upbeat. Would Penny believe it, given the fact that she was wearing a t-shirt with a T-Rex in a party hat printed on it, and holding a plastic pail containing the remains of some kid's lunch?

"But how on earth did you end up with this, Tessa?" said Penny, sounding still more amazed—while not being amazed at all, as Tessa well knew. "A kids' birthday party firm just doesn't seem like the you I remember from all those years, who was so into the idea of big weddings, and cozy little intimate ceremonies and all those grownup occasions. I'm *so* surprised to see you doing this instead."

You had such ambition back then. Such big ideas. So why did you pick this dead-end job, Tessa? Why did you fail?

Penny's smile made Tessa want to hurl herself under the nearby fold-out table, where June was laying out a big, green Jell-O cake covered with neon frosting for the Hughes family's noisy guests.

"This is just a temporary position for me." If she said this convincingly, Tessa told herself, then she would believe it, too. "I'm intending to take an opening position at an event planning firm, and work my way up the ladder. It's a plan in progress." Mostly inside her head and in the pages of the five-year business plan she had crafted in her free time. She sometimes took it out of its folder and gave it a wistful flip-through.

"So what about you?" she asked Penny. "It looks like things are going well for you." A massive understatement, since her old classmate was dressed to the nines for a cupcake and hotdog birthday celebration.

Penny gave a modest laugh. "What can I say? Work is positively insane right now. But then you can't accept a promotion from an international firm and *not* expect to lose a few nights' sleep occasionally." She took a sip from her party cup and made a face at its punch. "With the transfer to Florence next year, I'll be busier than ever."

"You're moving to Florence?" Tessa felt envious as she echoed these words.

"I know, I know. My dream job, and I'm only *now* receiving the chance," said Penny. "But it's just for six months or so. I get bored if I stay in the same place too long. Or date the same man." She laughed. "My latest—you should see him. He's a personal trainer named Ashton. Dark, handsome, not too clingy, and he's keeping me firm and fit with a free membership at his gym," she added, resting one hand on her slender hip, flanking her nonexistent stomach.

Penny, who had never been short of admirers, would undoubtedly be surrounded in no time by hunky Italian men as she sipped wine in picturesque villas. Tessa brushed some hotdog crumbs from her t-shirt and tried not to cry.

Things were getting out of hand at the dessert table nearby, with kids shoving ahead of each other for second helpings of the Jell-O cake, rocking the table as June tried to prevent an upset.

"Tessa, could you give me a hand?" she said. A small hand smeared frosting over the plastic tablecloth sporting more smiling T-Rexes, after one kid transformed his slice into play dough by squeezing it.

"Duty calls," Tessa said, pasting on a chipper smile. "Nice seeing you, Penny. Good luck in Florence."

She breathed a sigh of relief as she turned away, dignity intact. Only to walk straight into a comic trap, as the over-exuberant birthday boy made a swipe for an extra slice of cake and shoved the whole thing off the table in the process—all over Tessa's sneakers.

"Oooh, what a shame," Penny sympathized. "At least they weren't real leather, right?" She gave Tessa a consoling pat on the shoulder before moving on to chat with some of her fellow guests.

"Tina! Get the backup cake!" called June. "Tess, when you've cleaned that up, will you grab some extra dessert plates from the truck? Thanks. Hey—did your mom say you could have *all* those cookies, little lady?" June turned on the offending child, who was loading up a plate with a tower of sugar cookie clowns.

It couldn't get any worse than this. Tessa consoled herself with that truth as she finished wiping off her shoes—now stinky and a hideous shade of lime green from the neon food coloring that was saturating the icing. At this juncture, her boss Bill approached, dangling a set of keys from his fingers.

"Tough luck, Tessa," he said. "Justin quit this morning. Looks like you'll have to drive the truck for the next few gigs until I can find somebody new."

"Me? Drive the truck?" Tessa groaned. "I thought I was supposed to work on coordinating cakes and snacks the rest of this month. You promised, Bill." It was better than nothing, being the employee who selected the baked creation for each party—and a thousand times better than driving the truck, which tended to earn honks and snickers of laughter in traffic due its design. The truck's bed was encased in a decorative plastic camper shell that made it look like a dachshund inside of a hotdog bun, complete with a long-nosed head across the truck's cab and a long plastic tail covering the trailer hitch.

Most of the kids referred to it as "the hotdog truck." Whenever it stalled at a light, however, drivers trapped behind her came up with more creative and less polite names for it. Worse yet, the plastic sides of the "bun" created a blind spot in the mirror, making it next to impossible to reverse the truck into the bakery and grocery's tiny little parking spaces.

"Please, Bill," she said. "I'll do any of the other jobs. I'll wear the T-Rex costume for a month—"

"No can do," said Bill. "Tina's had too many tickets, and June has her hands full already. Last time Steve drove, he put a dent in the hotdog's tail. So it's down to you." He tossed her the keys.

At least Bill didn't bring up the time she had crushed the dachshund's plastic nose against a low-hanging supermarket sign. With a sigh of disappointment and despair, Tessa closed her hand around the plastic key ring in the shape of a greasy slice of pizza.

Chapter Two

The Bridal Closet had just decorated its window with its newest wedding gowns for spring. Its mannequins were dressed as ballet brides, evening gown brides, executive brides—all in icy-cold white with fluffy veils, even the one in the tulle skirt. A traditional princess bridal gown was in the middle, the mannequin's plastic hands clutching a bouquet of artificial white roses.

Ama paused outside, admiring the veils that were perfectly placed among the row of brides. Secretly, she pictured herself wearing one of those gowns someday, instead of the traditional red sari she was fated to wear or offend her parents. Maybe if that princess dress were made from embroidered metallic silk in white, and draped over one shoulder... and maybe if the veil over her short dark hair resembled traditional Indian bridal jewelry instead of a little tiara...

Not happening—unless she wanted to break her mother's heart, that is. White was for mourning in India, not marriage, and her mother had her heart set on a traditional Indian wedding, especially since Ama's brothers and sisters had planned their own following those customs. Her romantic fantasy fading with this thought, Ama continued walking, pausing a few windows on to gaze at the sugary treats in the local Italian bakery, Icing Italia, where a young woman was arranging rows of freshly iced gingerbread cookies and the traditional biscotti.

Ama pictured something different this time: rows of her own creations on display. Gingerbread and sugar cookies, and the special glazed almond cookie she'd created, inspired by traditional Indian sweets. In the middle, a big five-layer cake adorned with marzipan birds of paradise flowers circling to its topmost layer. It was her latest sketch, made on the back of one of her dozen or so culinary school brochures, between helping chop ingredients for vegan curry. Brochures she hid from sight whenever one of her parents entered the kitchen.

The girl arranging the desserts noticed her with a brief smile. A moment later, she was replaced by two older women who were setting a basket of twisty bread loaves and a bottle of olive oil in the middle of the display, blocking the spot where Ama envisioned her birds of paradise wedding cake.

Ama's real destination was several blocks from this bakery, giving off a very different aroma from that of yeasty bread and sweet spices. Her family's restaurant, the Tandoori Tiger, was filled with pungent scents of curry, mango powder, garlic, and ginger as she opened its door beneath the big sign featuring a tiger stalking among tall grasses.

The dining room was decorated in red and strung with loads of garish paper lanterns and flower twinkle lights that created the colorful atmosphere her father preferred. He was busy cleaning the plastic menu sleeves by the hostess stand, where Ama's sister-in-law waited for customers in a bright pink sari. From the kitchen came the sound of other relatives, including her mother—they were busy cooking.

Almost everybody in Ama's family worked here, including herself. Her Punjabi father cooked a little, and worked as manager, seating host, and waiter, while her mother cooked a *lot*, along with Ama's widowed auntie, and newlywed sister, Rasha, whose accountant husband did the books for the restaurant. No Bhagut woman ever left the family business unless marriage had other plans for her—case in point, Ama's middle sister Nalia, whose husband was a software programmer on the other side of the country.

As for her brothers, even when they worked outside the restaurant, they chose jobs that benefited it somehow. Her brother Jaidev worked for a spice wholesaler for a while, and Nikil became a butcher.

Even Ama's baking aspirations had been sparked by a need for more desserts to add to the menu years ago, since sweets were not a big part of her mother's background. When Ama first opened an American baking cookbook, she hadn't imagined actually loving the secrets behind making the soft sugar cookies she had eaten at friends' houses, or baking little French cakes as light as a sponge. It was as addictive as the taste of sugar itself, which her American childhood had given her—along with Hollywood movies, and the Western embracing of love at first sight and romances without family approval as real-life concepts.

"Ama! Is that you?" her father called, seeing someone on the other side of the restaurant's glass partition. "Hurry up—we have only a half hour before the customers arrive, and there is no sweet syrup for the *jalebis*!"

"Coming in a moment, Papa," she called back, as she climbed the back stairs to her family's apartment on the top floor. On the desk in her room were several flattened bakery boxes, a big roll of bubble wrap, and butcher's paper and twine for wrapping the outside of packages.

She clicked onto her website. *Sweetheart Treats—Cookies and Cupcakes for All Occasions!* was Ama's own business, an online shop selling sweets of all kinds, including those inspired by different cultures—

delivering treats by mail for birthday parties, wedding receptions, and gifts. Most orders were only novelty cookies, but it gave her the chance to flex her creative muscle outside the restaurant's dozen or so desserts.

Scrolling past pictures of her pearl-studded cupcakes, French cream puffs, and princess cookies, she clicked on the latest purchase button. A new request—two dozen rainbow birthday cupcakes.

Perfect. She printed off the receipt and grabbed the binder notebook containing her best recipes, dessert designs, and recipe cards for her creations, along with lots of pictures that had inspired her, flipping through its pages for her "tips and shortcuts" notes from her last batch of multi-colored cupcake batter.

Someday, she dreamed of selling something bigger than dancing princess cookies—such as the cake she had pictured in the bakery window. Sending a wedding or birthday cake by mail would be a little more challenging than sending an iced menagerie of cookies to a baby shower. But still less challenging than convincing her parents that there was no reason to be suspicious of American views on white weddings, spontaneous kisses, and falling in love with a random stranger who turns out to be your soul mate. The only Bollywood films Ama could ever bring herself to watch—and there were few of them—were ones about spontaneous love supplanting arranged matches; all the classic romance movies in Ama's collection involved magical, perfect connections that happened when one least expects it.

That, however, was an argument best saved for another time. Ama went downstairs to the restaurant to melt sugar for the funnel cake syrup.

Chapter Three

"Hold still," said Natalie, as she slipped a last-minute pin into place in the dress skirt. "No, don't look yet," she said, turning her model away from the mirror fastened to the inside of the bathroom door of her family's bakery. "Wait until I'm done or you won't see the full effect."

"Is this going to be much longer?" asked her cousin, Carrie. "I just told your mom I was stopping for a few minutes to pick up a cream cake for mine and Nick's dinner party tonight. I told my babysitter it'd be an hour's worth of errands, tops."

"I'll be done in ten minutes, I swear," said Natalie. "Hang on. Let me stitch this really quick, then turn around."

She stuck the last pin into her wrist pincushion and turned Carrie's shoulders, spinning her cousin around to face her reflection. In the mirror was a girl in a slinky emerald gown with one careless off-the-shoulder sleeve. With soft and elegant curves, gentle ruching, and a little shimmer in the light, the fabric's clean, natural flow and draping effect were traditional yet modern—in the secret phrase never uttered by Natalie except in her mind: perfect elegance.

"What do you think?" Natalie said. "I call it 'classic and classy.'"

"I like it," said Carrie, with genuine admiration in her voice. "Natalie, this is one of your best. Really—I'm being honest."

"You don't think it's too much?" said Natalie. "The asymmetrical hemline is a little new for me, and I thought maybe it should be a little more modern—"

"Nat. Seriously. I like it," said Carrie. "Stop seeing all the little flaws, all right?"

"You're right, you're right," said Natalie. "I'm psyching myself again. Why do I always do that? You're so right. Okay, you can take it off," she said, unzipping the dress at the back. She checked her watch. "I gotta get going if I don't want to be late to my class."

"Good. Not that I don't love it—but I really have to be back before the babysitter's shift at Old Navy." Carrie stepped out of the dress and reached for her shirtdress, hanging on the bathroom hook. "What's this for, by the way? Are you taking it to class?"

"Nope. This year's classes are more textbook than hands-on. The history of fabric and textiles," said Natalie. "This dress is for the boutique's design rack—if I'm lucky." She folded the dress and put it into the paper gift sack for showing to her boss later that day.

"Hey, if the boutique doesn't buy it, I might be interested," said Carrie, as she shouldered her purse to leave. "Don't forget that, okay?" She smiled, hinting, before she turned toward the door, in pursuit of her cream cake from the bakery's counter.

"You got it. Love to Nick," said Natalie, as she collected her sewing things from the floor. "Tell the kids I say 'hi.' Like they care about me, since Ma's the one who gives them all the leftover cookies whenever you bring them by."

"They love you anyway. And I'm serious about the dress, by the way."

Green thread, retractable sewing tape, funky-handled scissors patterned like a ladybug—the same ones Natalie had used to cut out the fabric for her first design when she was sixteen. It felt like longer ago than eleven years—a hundred or so original dresses, designed and sewn by her, were taking up all the closet space in her apartment, so she was forced to store the rest in her childhood bedroom at home.

"Natalie! Fresh cranberry bread!"

"No thanks, Ma," called Natalie. Her mother loved to feed her, although Natalie did her best to resist some of the tempting treats that came her way at the family bakery.

She snapped closed her metal sewing case, and checked her watch again. If she didn't run, she was definitely going to be late.

"Bye, Ma!" she called again on her way downstairs. "I'm leaving for class now—don't forget that we're out of dried coconut." She let the bakery door swing closed behind her, its little bell jingling. Tossing aside her long mane of auburn hair, she shouldered her bag and crossed the street before the light at the end of the block changed.

Icing Italia disappeared behind her, along with the smell of fresh-baked biscotti and the *beep* of a delivery truck backing up to the bakery's side door. Natalie's fingers flew over the keys of her smartphone, checking to make sure that her professor had received her latest business proposal.

Working at the bakery was a family affair for most of the Grenaldis, but not for Natalie. Her dreams lay elsewhere—cakes and cannoli were less important to her than the current trends in the fashion world. Which was why, despite helping out from time to time, she had traded her bakery apron for textbooks and design classes at the local university, and worked at the boutique designer Kandace's Kreations. She didn't keep Italian cookbooks lying around her apartment—just books on Parisian designers, Italian fashion houses, and fine textiles and sewing techniques. A sewing mannequin was the centerpiece of her two-bedroom place, where the floor tended to be covered with little scraps of colored fabric.

She had thought about trying to sell some of her finished dresses to local boutiques, but had found this was the one sticking point in her courage. After all, she hadn't even sold a design of her own through Kandace's yet. Maybe that was why she hesitated to try it anywhere else, even if Kandace wouldn't see it as a total affront to her label.

Kandace's Kreations was squeezed unmercifully between an empty warehouse space and a used record store frequented by the young hipster wannabes in the neighborhood. It advertised itself by a sign that suggested it sold garments more sophisticated than the designer herself—who considered her work "cutting edge" and "off the path of conventional chic"—had ever managed to create, on paper or with fabric.

"It's just… not acceptable." Kandace sounded dismissive. "Look. I know you're trying. I get that—but it just doesn't speak to the artistic soul. The bustline, the cut of the skirt. It totally doesn't fit with the presentation of our line. It's not the message, Nat. You understand?"

She held Natalie's latest creation at arm's length from her body, as if afraid of being tainted by association with the draped green satin dress supported by the garment hanger. "Our message is one of *defining* the human body by *defying* expectations about lines and symmetry. Look at this thing—it's loose, it's soft. It's totally the opposite of everything we're creating for the collection."

"I thought maybe you'd like it," said Natalie. "It's fluid, and not the conventional fitted style for a dress like this, but it creates definition and contours, no matter what body type a woman has. A woman looking to stand out in a crowd—"

"She could stand in a bed sheet, then, because that's all this is, Nat," said Kandace. "A rumpled sheet gathered a little here, a little there." Her lip curled in disgust. "No—get it away from me. Just take it away, please." She released the hanger into Natalie's possession with a shudder. "Design is not your talent, kid. I've told you before."

"So I remember," replied Natalie. She was trying not to be sarcastic, or upset. "Thanks for the advice, anyway."

"Forget it—we have customers. Coming, coming." Kandace turned her attention to a couple of women entering the boutique, ready to slather on some persuasive charm as they paused to browse the rack of discounted designs. "You would look incredible in that blouse, if you don't mind my saying so…"

It was amazing, in Natalie's opinion, that anybody ever visited this place. Not just because of the obscure business sign advertising its presence, but also because of the atmosphere within: prison-gray walls with stark fluorescent lighting tubes that buzzed and hummed in a mind-numbing drone as they shone upon the interior's mostly empty space.

Kandace called it "industrial modern" and reveled in its blandness, right down to the naked wires from which the light tubes dangled, perhaps because the designer herself screamed with color by contrast with her surroundings. Her short hair was dyed a purplish maroon, and today's outfit comprised a blouse which resembled mismatched scraps sewn together, torn leggings patched by old crocheted doilies, and kitten-heeled lime green sneakers. Completing the look was a nose ring, which appeared to be a small silver corkscrew, through one nostril.

"You would look fetching in that one. It's from my spring line, called 'Nature Web,'" said Kandace, as she lifted down a poncho, seemingly crocheted from strips of garbage bags, hung from a height impossible to reach without a short ladder. Kandace believed garments should be displayed haphazardly on the walls to give them the effect of "works of art"… although more than half of them eventually ended up on the sole metal garment rack in the boutique for "discontinued creations."

Natalie climbed the metal steps to the studio: the loft room where Kandace's creations were cut and sewn by Natalie and her coworker Cal. Pinned on various dressmaker's mannequins were the prototypes of the designer's latest sketches, which Natalie was supposed to finish pinning today—part of the "Twisted Symmetry" collection to be debuted at an upcoming runway show. Or, as Cal referred to it, the "Circus Clown" line of garments; the Cirque du Soleil meets casualwear.

Natalie tossed the dress into an empty gift sack in the corner, and slipped a pincushion onto her wrist as she began working on Kandace's "Harlequin by Fire" gown. It involved pleated strips of red, black, and white fabric, with the skirt's panels ending in points and a series of red diamonds randomly appliquéd on its half-red, half-white bodice. Hence the twisted symmetry of the jarring geometric lines, Natalie supposed.

"I heard what Kandace said," Cal remarked, a note of disdain in his Southern drawl as he worked on cutting the last piece for the dress's sleeve. "She's wrong, though, Nat. Your dress was amazing."

"Thanks," said Natalie with a wry smile. "But Kandace didn't think so, and that's all that matters around here." She pinned a white diamond to one of the red panels after consulting the designer's sketch. "She's the boss. She always says my work is 'too pedestrian' or 'too simple' for the discerning customer."

"Are you kidding? It was sophisticated, not simple," said Cal. "Way better than this nightmare we're sewing today. This thing is, like, the garment version of dogs playing poker. It's not decent, Nat. It doesn't deserve to be seen on the streets."

"It's not that bad," said Natalie, although her lips repressed a smile at this description of the demented harlequin dress, as she privately thought of it. "If you want to look like a mishmash of a pack of cards when you're out on the town."

"We could both design circles around Kandace, given the chance," said Cal, as he cut a length of black trim for the sleeve and began running a needle through all three colored pieces to form a ruffled flounce. "And *I* don't even have an eye for design. I can't believe anybody buys her fashions… then again, we *are* the worst boutique in town."

Kandace's place was located in the seediest part of the town, and the customers who visited it formed a small but elite crowd mostly attracted by the supposed prestige of a Kandace "original." But it had been the only fashion house in Bellegrove hiring when Natalie had been determined to get a job in garment design, and even if she thought the average Asian knockoff dress was a better deal—and a better fashion statement—she couldn't afford to lose the opportunity to work for a designer. Albeit the city's worst designer, with an overinflated ego to boot.

"You know, at the last fashion show, I overheard two people complimenting the blouse you wore," said Cal. "I know they would've been interested in buying one, if Kandace would only let you have a rack downstairs."

"That would take away from her creations," Natalie reminded him. "She's not going to change her mind, Cal. That's why Tracey and Sam both quit, and I ended up here in their place."

"Her line for last winter's fashion show got terrible reviews, though," said Cal. "Honestly, a whole collection of garments inspired by restaurant linens? That napkin bandana bracelet was just bizarre. And who wears a dress with pointed shoulders like a starched tablecloth? You would poke out the eye of anybody short who stood next to you."

Natalie stuck her tongue out as she remembered this fashion item. "At least the boutique scored a couple of sales afterward," she said. "Two fewer garments destined for the half-price rack downstairs, anyway." Someone out there was now wearing the hideous starched tablecloth as eveningwear. And Kandace seriously thought *her* dress was too much like a bed sheet?

"You could probably use some cheering up after Kandace's latest rejection," said Cal. "You know, my roommate bought the complete box set of *That's Entertainment*. And I have chocolate s'more truffles too. You're welcome to stop by tonight and share."

"Thanks, but I'm having dinner at my friend Tess's tonight," she answered. "Not that s'more truffles don't sound fantastic." She shoved another pin into the bodice. "Isn't there another sleeve?" she asked, as Cal handed her the fluffy, tri-striped ruffle, which she pinned to the right side of the dress.

"Only one," he answered. "She changed her mind this morning and altered the design. Just sew a ribbon strap on the other side."

"Actually, I think it's an improvement," said Natalie sarcastically, tucking it in place. "That's a first."

"And that weird little button thing with the clown face in the middle is supposed to be sewn to the top of the strap," said Cal, who shrugged his shoulders at the look on Natalie's face. "She's the boss."

"There goes the improvement." Natalie sighed as she pinned the button in place, noting that the sad clown in the middle resembled a weepy version of a fast food mascot.

"I still can't believe she didn't pay your dress at least *one* compliment," said Cal. "It is pretty great, Nat. She's totally jealous of your talent."

"Whatever," said Natalie, rolling her eyes. "It's no big deal, Cal. I'm tougher than that, I swear." She tried not to glance at the dress's paper sack as she swiveled her rolling chair to face her workstation.

No sigh, no tears, no regrets. It wasn't like she hadn't seen this coming, the rejection of her work *yet* again. But she wasn't a quitter, no matter how many rude remarks came her way... or how many rejected designs were squeezed into her closet, probably never to emerge again, unless Carrie was serious about buying one. In general, however, Natalie hung onto her rejected creations, as if sheltering them from a second failure. Not stabbing Kandace in the back, she always claimed... but was that the real reason? If the closet burst open with fifty dresses, blouses, coats, and other garments she had painstakingly designed, would she keep piling them in boxes in the attic without so much as asking another boutique to consider one?

Above her drawing board were pinned mostly Kreations sketches—including the tasteless line that Natalie was being forced to help assemble. "Sad clowns in drag" was Cal's nickname for its latest additions: a trio of baggy, spotted, tent-like dresses paired with patterned tights. But a few of Natalie's own designs were mixed in with these; lightly penciled color drawings of a gray dress with touches of scarlet embroidery, and a blue suit with harem trousers and a fitted half-jacket.

Cal had dubbed them "timeless" and "chic"—but that was Cal, of course, and he was her friend, after all. That wasn't proof of anything except that she had a winning personality, maybe. Not that it wasn't nice to imagine it was more.

Natalie reached for a chartreuse pencil and gave it a twist or two in her sharpener before she began working on her latest sketch. The tip flew over the paper, the light, feathering strokes framing a drawing of a wedding dress—a ballet-style white one with off-the-shoulder sleeves and a graceful V neckline.

Chapter Four

"So your job sucks," said Natalie. "Join the club." She took a sip from the glass of wine Tessa handed her as she curled up on Tessa's apartment sofa. "I don't love mine, either. Kandace turned me down *again* today, you know."

She reached for one of the pizza slices on the tray—not one of the gluey, cheesy ones like Tessa had cleaned off the plastic party tablecloths, but a crisp sweet tomato one from Natalie's cousin's restaurant, which made authentic Italian pizzas as well as gourmet American ones. Natalie knew all the best little bistros and restaurants in the city that no one had ever heard of—the perk of being Italian, she claimed. Everybody you know is in the restaurant business, or was at one time, or is thinking about trying it before they reach their golden years.

"I'm tired of it, though," said Tessa. "I have to drive the truck now. You have no idea what it's like being stuck in rush hour traffic with that thing. Did I tell you about the time the dog's big plastic nose fell off?" She cringed at the memory of the dent in the truck's hood as it bounced to freedom, and the heckling teenage drivers in the lane next to her. No wonder Justin left to work for a coffee house this afternoon.

"It's just temporary, right?" Natalie asked. "Your boss will find someone else, eventually."

"But it doesn't matter," said Tessa. "My job will still be a dead end in my future career. Half the time, Bill asks June to help him select stuff for the party, and she doesn't even bother to shop around for something interesting that the client might enjoy. She just picks the first convenient name off a review website and orders supplies from them. Cheap plastic trinkets, dry cupcakes—I've seen the lack of quality, Nat. It's depressing."

"Maybe because she doesn't think a nine-year-old's birthday party is a do-or-die event?" suggested Natalie. "For my ninth birthday, I ate cake with a scoop of chocolate gelato and unwrapped a Barbie in between helping my family fill cannoli for my grandmother's Sunday dinner."

"I would do a better job," insisted Tessa. "It's not June's dream to make events special, but it is mine. I watch tiny little opportunities pass me by while I'm dressing up in a dinosaur costume, and I wonder… I wonder if I let bigger opportunities slip away without knowing it."

This was the truth coming home to her. It was the failures of the past talking, and not the glass of wine she was sipping. It was the realization that her future was nothing but a dancing T-Rex and a hotdog truck unless something changed it, both quickly and completely.

"Tell me about it," groaned Natalie. She leaned her head back against the sofa cushion, gazing at the ceiling. It was the perfect sentiment for Tessa's mindset, even though it was also an admission of her friend's agreement about her worry over missed opportunities.

"You really think the same thing, don't you?" said Tessa.

"Of course I do. We all do. It's part of life," said Natalie. "Look at me. I'm stuck being Kandace's chew toy. At least Bill respects your opinion… whenever the rare occasion calls for you to give him one."

Tessa tapped her fingers against the side of her wine glass softly. "But what if," she began, "there was a chance to break free of that vicious cycle? I think I would leap at it at this point," she continued. "You'd take it, right?"

"What? Why?" Natalie lifted her head. "Did you get a job offer?"

"Not exactly. But I've been thinking of doing something different." Tessa stopped toying with her glass and set it aside. She felt a little tingle in her fingers at the thought of what she was about to say. "Maybe opening my own firm. It's a big leap, but I'm beginning to think it might be worth it."

"Your *own* event planning firm?" repeated Natalie. "This, from a career dressing up as a birthday party dinosaur? Tess, I always said you were crazy, but that might be too much, even for you."

"I have a great portfolio," protested Tessa. "So many firms have told me as much; just that pesky 'no real experience' is hanging over my head. Well, I'm never going to get the right experience working for Bill, so I think it's time I do what I was meant to do. And if I have to, I'm going to do it on my own."

Natalie laughed. "Are you being serious right now?" she said.

"You think I'm kidding?"

"It's a big risk," said Natalie, shaking her head. "I've had a few people admire my designs, but I work for an industry professional who treats them like trash. People buy her stuff—at least, she owns her own boutique, and has a reputation in the fashion community. How do I know who's telling the truth? And if I leave—there goes my one connection to the fashion world. Pitiful though it may be." She sipped her wine reflectively.

"The people who admired your work in the past will still notice you," answered Tessa with enthusiasm. "Your dresses are really beautiful, Nat, no matter what your boss tells you. I love the one you sewed for me." For their senior formal in college, Natalie had designed a gorgeous evening gown for Tessa, in a shade of blue that set off her red hair perfectly. Dozens of compliments had come her way that evening, and she felt they were entirely owed to Natalie's magic sewing needle. Even girls like Penny Newcastle, with their designer labels, hadn't been wearing anything near as stunning a statement as Natalie's creation.

"Here's what I'm thinking about." Tessa reached behind her armchair and pulled out a portfolio. "I've been working on this for a little while. I was just playing around at first, but then I realized it could be real. It made sense. Especially if I could find partners to work with."

"Other event planners?" Natalie asked.

"Maybe so. There's a planner at Wedding Wonders who might be interested. You've met him a few times before—at the last New Year's party, remember? And a few other parties at my place, too."

"Who?" asked Natalie.

"Stefan." Tessa braced herself a little for what would follow this casual mention.

"Groeder." Natalie's tone was flat, except for a dash of distaste. "Otherwise known as 'The Wedding Guru.'" She made a face at the wedding planner's pretentious nickname—one he'd given to himself, no less; not that anyone really called him by it except for his personal friends. "Do you think he'll force his clients to call him that, eventually? *I* couldn't say it with a straight face."

"I know he rubbed you up the wrong way a few times—" Tessa began.

"The wrong way?" repeated Natalie. "He calls me 'Natasha,' Tess. He has known me for a *year* now, and he still can't remember my name. Even when I was trapped with him for twenty minutes in that overcrowded apartment, watching him drool all over that partner from E-ventive Wedding Planners."

"Well, at least he's trying to make a name for himself in the business," Tessa replied. "And he told me he hates his work at Wedding Wonders and really wants a change. So a couple of weeks ago, I asked him if he would be interested in a share in a business that would give him more creative control and he sounded excited by it. So then I began thinking... what if he's not the only person in the wedding industry who wants a chance like this?"

Of the three big planners in town and the smattering of little ones, there weren't many opportunities for an aspiring planner hoping to collaborate with others in their career field, as Tessa well knew. It had been logical to think first of the people who had the job she envied most and who wanted more creative freedom than their current work allowed. Stefan was the most obvious choice, really—successful, but not so successful that he had a plethora of options.

"I don't know," Natalie began. Setting her wine glass down, she looked Tessa in the eye. "Are you sure that Stefan is the best candidate for your business partner? Isn't his style a little more... outgoing than yours?"

She was picking her words carefully now, Tessa sensed. Trying to avoid ones like "dramatic" or "over the top." It was an impression Tessa knew all but defined Stefan as a planner... but to agree that her best potential business partner was a less-than-ideal team player would be self-destructive. This dream depended on his support—it required someone who had experience, who could attract clients with a recognizable name in the event planning community, at least in the beginning. Later, that might change, once people trusted their reputation as a group.

"I think we could find a compromise," she answered, fingers crossed under the armchair pillow beside her at the same time. "All of us together."

"Compromise? With a man who threw a hissy fit over the size of an ice sculpture unicorn's horn?" Natalie raised one eyebrow.

"Anyway, Stefan is just one of the people I have in mind," said Tessa, ignoring her friend's remark. "There are others on the list. I have this idea about bringing together different creative forces for a unique event planning firm, see. One, maybe two more partners who would join us."

She held out the portfolio to Natalie. "You've taken a few business classes too, right? Look at it. Tell me if it's such a bad idea."

"I'm no expert," Natalie protested. "Like you said, all I've had are a few classes in small business. You're the one with the business degree."

"Just take a look at it, pretty please? Sugar on top? I'm dying to discuss this with someone and why shouldn't it be my oldest and closest friend?"

"Um, we weren't exactly friends until college," Natalie reminded her. "Before then, I was just the neighbor kid who got babysat at your house and forced to play all your games with weirdly specific rules."

"They weren't weird," Tessa protested. "We both know that Ninja Turtle made a better groom for Fashion Girl than your brother's G.I. Joe. I mean, the tuxedo was too small for Joe—black tie automatically trumps camouflage for a wedding, right?"

"Yes, but tell me again, why couldn't they serve pink lemonade instead of sweet tea for the reception? I had already mixed up that huge pitcher of it just for the occasion and nearly spilled it twice on the car ride there. Eight-year-old me was offended by its rejection," said Natalie, pretending to pout. "My one contribution to your stupid game and it was rejected."

"*Because*, silly, the tea glasses matched the rest of the dishware. I wanted it to be realistic."

"Of course." Natalie rolled her eyes. "Because a wedding for a fashion doll and an action figure really should be as realistic as possible. At least your mother only grounded you for a week after she caught us hauling her vintage glassware back to the house."

"Two weeks," said Tessa with chagrin. "Now, please, will you read this portfolio? For old times' sake." She waved it in Natalie's direction, not giving up.

"Fine, I'll read it. But I don't know how a control freak like you is going to work with an ego as big as Stefan's. You know whose ideas will end up on top every time, no matter who's right." With this warning, she leafed through the folder's contents, glancing over the proposal and its costs. Tessa clasped her hands on her lap, a definite pleading "don't kick me" puppy-dog look in her eyes as she waited for the verdict.

"I don't know. It's a little ambitious, but not impossible." Natalie closed its cover after reading the pages within. "But there are a lot of costs, Tess. How are you going to cover something like this without bankrupting yourself?"

"Well… I have a nest egg of sorts," admitted Tessa. "The money my grandparents left to me, that I held onto with the idea of someday investing in a future business of my own. Plus everything I've been saving since college. It might be nearly enough to cover a down payment on a piece of commercial property… if we could find a good enough deal."

"Meaning a fixer-upper," Natalie replied. "Which means lots of repair costs. You'll probably end up needing more money than a little nest egg, and you'll probably need to invest more in this business than the ex-Wedding Wonders Guru has."

"That's why I need more partners than just me and Stefan," said Tessa. "Like you."

"Me?" echoed Natalie, with a short laugh. "You want me to be one of your business partners? Are you crazy?"

"Yeah, of course you. You always dreamed of having your own workspace," Tessa answered. "Imagine if you were a designer working for a wedding planner whose clients need dresses—bridal dresses, bridesmaids' ones, mother-of-the-bride couture, alterations on funky, eccentric wedding garments of all kinds."

"That'll be the day," snorted Natalie.

"One with extra space for said designer to have her own studio, let's imagine."

"What would I do there?" Natalie asked. "You plan events, not fashion shows. I'm not interested in fluffing flowers, or helping somebody pick out candles for a centerpiece, Tess. Why would your clients pick my clothes?"

"Because of this," said Tessa. From beneath her portfolio of inspirational clippings came a proposal sheet that she had spent hours crafting. "Look. That's my idea. 'A one-stop shop for all your wedding needs.' Not just the perfect planning, but the perfect dress, the perfect cake, the perfect flowers, too—from an exclusive team."

"What?"

"You'd be the dress designer. I'd be the planner, along with Stefan... and we'd find someone else with a completely different skill set to come on board with us, too. Maybe a florist or a caterer."

This was her latest vision for her potential business, the best hope for her future, and maybe that of a friend like Natalie. What if the best way to free her dream from its prison was to join it with others' dreams, and make them all real in one brilliant proposal? In her mind, it sounded perfect... and perfectly sensible, compared to renting a boutique in the new business district and waiting all by her lonesome for customers.

Natalie shook her head curtly. "I'm not ready, Tessa," she answered. "It's a huge risk, pushing your own design on someone for their wedding, maybe ruining their big day if the dress is a flop... I'm not comfortable with that. It's not the same as bringing a blouse to Kandace for the boutique's bargain line."

"That doesn't sound like the Natalie I know," said Tessa, "who's usually brimming with confidence." For anything except her work, of course, but why point that out?

"Touché. Because I have a friend who would *never* be really comfortable taking a back seat to the visions of someone like Stefan," said Natalie. She gave Tessa a look. "You know deep down this idea will bite you later, Tess. The two of you have totally different creative styles. Is that what you want, to work with someone you have to fight all the time just to have an opinion? Believe me, it's no fun. I speak from experience."

Tessa sighed. "It's not that simple anymore," she said quietly. "I want this dream, Natalie. I'm tired of neon frosting and bruises from the piñata pole whenever some kid's swing misses. Compromise is the only way to have the future I want. I know it, and I'm embracing it. This might be my best chance, and I want it, Natalie. I don't want to be on the sidelines, watching other people live their dreams."

The other way was to go it alone. It terrified her just a little, the thought of sitting forlornly, getting passed over for planners with rock-solid reputations and impressive recommendations. But she couldn't say it aloud and still argue against Natalie's closet of secret fashion designs. And if that was her only chance, she might be desperate enough to take it anyway.

"You think I'm a coward." Natalie shook her head. "You would be right. Because I'm not going to sign up to do something I can't handle.

I'd rather stick to my horrible job sewing psychedelic short shorts for Kandace." She poured a second glass of wine from the bottle and took a sip. Tessa's expression was gloomy in response to this.

They were both quiet. Natalie hesitated. "Then again…"

Tessa held her breath.

"…I guess it wouldn't kill me to pick out candles. Sometimes." She gazed reflectively at the proposal lying on the coffee table, with room for multiple partners. "It would be kind of nice to have my own space to work. Come up with some new sketches… maybe for a future fashion line. Some place quiet and atmospheric, maybe."

"I'll bet the loft at Kandace's gets really crowded when she's in a rotten mood after a fashion show," said Tessa. She had read the reviews in the paper, which were often snarky toward the abrasive designer.

"I would be allowed to have my opinions, it's true," Natalie said. "Maybe if I were more like a fashion consultant than a designer, let's say."

"Exactly," said Tessa. "Every bride needs help finding her special gown, no matter who designed it."

"But with plenty of time and space to do my own thing, right? Besides picking out candles and putting those little decorative rocks in vases and stuff." Natalie looked at Tessa for confirmation. "Design work would have to be strictly on the side and not for clients at the start. Just in case I have the opportunity to sell a few garments to local boutiques, maybe. Then we'll talk about garment design for your clients."

Tessa's smile beamed. "You're in," she said. "You're actually in, aren't you? I knew it. It's going to be great, Natalie. Actually living out our dreams instead of letting our lives slip by." She took a generous bite from her piece of pizza, letting out a moan of contentment afterward. "I've been dreaming of telling somebody how I felt about this idea for weeks. Years, if you count all the times I've told myself that something needed to happen since I took the job on the party crew."

"Even if I say yes, that only makes three partners," said Natalie. "I don't know about 'The Wedding Guru,' but I'm not exactly rolling in money. Do you think three people can cover the startup costs?"

"We'll bring in a fourth, just in case," said Tessa. "Maybe my job with Bill wasn't great, but it did give me a chance to meet some other people in the party business. Florists, caterers, entertainers, bakers…" She flipped through a list on her phone. "Tony—he's a pianist. I met him when he played at a *Peanuts*-themed birthday party once, but I know he plays at lots of weddings. And he's probably sick of playing for kids after cleaning all those spitballs out of his sweater." That particular client of Bill's lived on in memory as one of the rottenest kids of Tessa's acquaintance.

"Musicians don't have money, either. Will he need a spot for his piano? That could take up the whole business space."

"How about Felecia? She works for a florist, but she arranges flowers on the side for special occasions and delivers to addresses in the city," said Tessa, reading another name from her list. She had remembered the florist's was overstaffed and Felecia had expressed fears that her job was in jeopardy.

"You met a florist through a kids' birthday party service?" said Natalie.

"No—I ordered a Mother's Day bouquet from her," said Tessa. "Although—she mostly works part-time now that she has a baby." She scrolled ahead.

"Here's one I've considered," she said, pausing again. "A baker who designed cookies for a superhero party we organized. Her website featured tons of creative sweets, good enough for a professional window display. She told me she worked out of her home because that's all she could afford to do, but it looks like her business has really taken off. I mean, look at all these reviews—she must be raking in the customers." On her computer, she had pulled up the website and looked at the long list of happy customers who had purchased cupcakes, cookies, and pastries.

"If she's new at this, then she probably doesn't have much to invest yet, either," concluded Natalie. Her smile wore a skeptical air.

"Maybe she has some money set aside. We haven't got anything to lose but to ask. And if she does, and if the four of us pull together, I think we could find enough to cover the startup costs," said Tessa. "I think we can find a way to make it work, Natalie. Let's think about it, at least."

"You're practically begging for punishment," said Natalie.

"More punishment than neon frosting stains—or your spot in Kandace's torture chamber?" said Tessa. "I don't know about you, but I don't want to spend the best years of my career on my current job. I've had enough of that T-Rex head." Tessa made a face at the memory of the soft drinks, sweat, and halitosis forming the vinyl shell's patented odor.

"Kandace's next fashion line, after the circus clowns one is finished, is going to be a tribute to *Peter Pan*." Natalie shuddered. "The punk version."

"Then I think it's time for us to plan a dinner and invite our prospective partners," said Tessa.

Chapter Five

Redbird Cafe was known locally for dishing up the best of Belle-grove's "soul food," its close proximity to the garden square making it a favorite spot for the crowds who gathered for the outdoors blues concerts in the summertime. It was also the perfect place for Tessa to meet up with her potential new business partners, located halfway between the ethnic-infused restaurant district where Ama lived, and the college campus where Natalie would be coming from her latest classes in design.

The first to arrive, Tessa was seated alone at a corner table. Red-checkered curtains lined the windows that looked out onto the street, and a few old photographs of famous jazz musicians were framed on the wall behind her. A waitress bustled past, refilling glasses of sweet iced tea for thirsty customers. Tessa checked her phone twice for the time, feeling slightly nervous.

Imagining this chance on paper was one thing, but there were tiny butterflies inside her at the thought of actually going through with it. To distract herself, she perused the menu, glancing over pictures of chicken fried steak and barbecued pork ribs, sweet potatoes, collard greens, and fried okra. Blueberry cobbler and a succulent-sounding chocolate-pecan pie caught her eye beneath the desserts section.

If she weren't feeling sick with anticipation, her mouth would be watering.

The seating hostess was pointing someone in Tessa's direction now, a girl with short black hair pushed back from her face by a jeweled headband. She wore a skirt printed with a vintage fabric cityscape and the words "I love New York," a halterneck blouse, and a pair of black sneakers. Her arms balanced a plain flat box that reminded Tessa of the kind you get from a pastry shop. Ama was here, smiling as she recognized Tessa among the restaurant's diners.

She had only met Ama once or twice before, the first time being when Ama had delivered the superhero cookies in the shapes of caped crusaders and magical shields. She remembered three things about that meeting vividly: the scent of unusual, dusky spices from the girl's clothes, the wild print of the paisley blouse-and-culottes ensemble she wore, and the irresistible, casual friendliness of her smile as she chatted about her baking ambitions.

Ama was Indian, from a somewhat traditional immigrant family who ran one of the local restaurants, which was all Tessa really knew about her personally. That, and she really, *really* loved baking.

"Hi. Long time no see. Not since the *Iron Man* birthday party, anyway," Ama said with a quick laugh, taking a seat at the table. "I got your message. Obviously."

"Obviously," echoed Tessa, with a laugh of her own, but one that was equally forced.

"I have to be honest and say, I was a little… well… weirded out by it. Is that the right word for it?" She gave another laugh: she seemed nervous—or unsure—about all of this. "A job offer out of the blue. That was something new for me. I mean, people offer me jobs baking cupcakes and brownies, but not partnerships in new businesses."

"It seemed kind of abrupt, didn't it?" Tessa answered, trying not to be timid in the face of this truth. "I was afraid of that. But I didn't want to lie and tell you that I wanted more cookies for a party. Since we're not yet friends, I wasn't sure you'd come unless I told you the real reason. A crazy one, yes. Still… I thought it might interest you, since you mentioned once wishing you had your own place so you could bake full-time."

"You have me there," said Ama. She sighed. "Sometimes I wish I weren't baking cupcakes at midnight, after my family has gone to bed, just so I'm not working on restaurant time. Of course, there's always the issue of how my family would take this whole idea," she added, and a look between doubt and amusement wrinkled her forehead. "I can see their faces in my head if I told them about this."

No laugh this time, Tessa noticed—and a certain steeliness in Ama's smile, like she was bracing herself for a future battle.

She took the seat across from Tessa, still holding onto the box she carried with her. It rested on her lap somewhat awkwardly, her arms folded across the top in a way that struck Tessa as protective. Before she could ask her about it, though, the third member of their dinner party arrived.

"There's Natalie," said Tessa, waving her hand as the third girl entered the restaurant. Her friend approached, looking causally chic in a pair of tailored black slacks and a white business blouse that Tessa had seen in fashion sketches pinned to Natalie's wall a few months ago. Cherry red heels and a matching belt added a touch of glamour-girl fun to the otherwise professional-looking ensemble. Timeless but modern—maybe only Natalie's friends said it about her work, as she had told Tessa a thousand times, but Tessa knew that someday everybody else would say it, too.

Slinging a heavy book bag under her chair, Natalie sat down across from Tessa. "Sorry I'm late. I had a test today on local business codes and laws for one non-creative class this year. Mr. Hammer's multiple choices are surprisingly tricky for a guy who sleeps in his college office after every class. It's enough to make me wish I had signed up for the history of cotton this semester instead."

"You're practically on time," Tessa assured her. "Join our discussion on the future."

Natalie turned to the girl seated in the chair beside hers, taking her first good look at the talented baker from Tessa's stories. "So," she said. "You're the amazing cookie baker Tess told me about, right? With the online baked goods business?"

"Ama Bhagut." Ama extended her hand.

"Natalie Grenaldi." Natalie shook it politely. "Part-time student and full-time wannabe fashion designer."

"Charmed," said Ama, with a smile more real than the nervous one that had accompanied her previous remarks.

Natalie turned to Tessa. "Where's Stefan, may I ask?" She glanced around for the fourth partner who was supposed to be at dinner. "Don't tell me 'The Wedding Guru' had a tailoring emergency."

The little snort in Natalie's voice was getting to be too much, in Tessa's opinion, since they needed their fourth partner to jumpstart this business. "No," she answered. "He couldn't make it. He texted a half hour ago that he had a prior invitation to a party that he can't escape."

"Who's Stefan?" asked Ama.

"He's an event planner from Wedding Wonders who's partnering with me for the wedding planner side of the business," explained Tessa. "He's a friend of mine… sort of. He's good. And he's used to planning really elaborate and expensive events, so he'll be perfect."

"Perfect," echoed Natalie. "His favorite word for his work. Or is it 'fab'? I forget—there are so many superfluous terms for describing over-the-top glamour, aren't there?"

Ama looked confused. Tessa tried not to cast a warning glance in Natalie's direction. Maybe given time, their fourth partner's personality would grow on her, or at least they would find a decent truce.

"It's just the three of us for tonight," said Tessa.

Natalie and Ama exchanged glances. They were still growing accustomed to each other—and this insane idea, Tessa thought. "I guess we all know why we're here," said Natalie, with a touch of hesitation in her voice.

"Crazy, isn't it?" said Ama. "Four virtual strangers considering opening a business together?"

"You said it," said Natalie.

"It's not as crazy as it sounds," said Tessa. "Natalie's already looked at my proposal and agreed that it's possible, if we all come together and work hard. I've been saving for a down payment on a business for years, so that's one resource we have." Years spent waiting in vain for a big break—and cleaning crushed cookies out of the princess costume's lace net skirt.

"*Your* resource," Natalie pointed out, wryly. "You're putting your whole life's savings into this, Tessa. The rest of us won't be taking nearly that big of a leap, much as it pains me to part with some of my monthly paycheck to cover bills and sundry expenses. Of course, Stefan may have something more substantial to contribute," she added as an afterthought.

"I have a little saved," piped up Ama. "Not much—but it's something." She shrugged her shoulders.

"It's only fair I take the biggest risk, since it's my dream," said Tessa. "Besides, I think it'll work, so I won't lose anything—one location for four of the most talented people in the event planning business can sell itself," she continued. "We're the people essential to any wedding's success. That's who we are, even if we haven't exactly been given a chance to prove it."

"Essential to someone's success? Me? Speak for yourself," laughed Natalie. "I'm not the most talented designer in the business, believe me."

"Yes, you are," insisted Tessa. "And while you haven't seen Ama's baked goods, I have, and they're amazing enough to be in an issue of *Brides* magazine."

"Hold on," said Ama, holding up one hand in protest. "I think you've mixed me up with someone else. My sole experience is baking cupcakes and cookies for fun, and making desserts for the restaurant. The only cakes I've ever made are for family and friends. I don't think I have the kind of experience that somebody will want for their big wedding cake. Who would trust me?"

"Do you know how to bake one?" asked Tessa. "Do you know how to decorate one?"

"Of course," said Ama. "But I haven't done it professionally. I don't know if I'm all that good—well, let me show you. I brought a sort of 'sampler' of my work," she said, lifting the pastry box she'd been holding onto the table. "These are sort of like showing you my résumé, I guess. Be honest in telling me your opinions."

Smiling shyly, Ama flipped back the lid to reveal row upon row of exquisitely handcrafted cookies and pastries. There was everything from cream cheese Danishes flecked with candied orange peel to decorative cake pops painted to look like poodles and Persian cats; fig cherry bars with a lattice sugar glaze, perfect macaroons in pastel colors... and one third of the space was devoted to twin rows of sugar cookies so ornate that Tessa didn't know if someone could bring themselves to eat something that perfect.

"Wowza." Natalie whistled. She was staring at a selection of sparkling "fashion shoe" cookies—complete with edible buckles, beads, and tassels. A pair of glittering ruby red slippers, like the ones Dorothy wore in *The Wizard of Oz* movie, and a funky sixties purple pilgrim shoe studded with silver nonpareils shimmered up at them.

"Did you make all these just to convince us to partner up with you?" Natalie asked. "Because if you're trying to bribe us with baked goods, I have to tell you, it's totally working."

"Not exactly," Ama confessed. "They were some extras left over from my last few custom orders—an engagement party and three birthdays. Some of these didn't turn out quite right, which is why I still had them. A smudge of frosting here, a crooked line there," she explained, with a sigh. "I hate it when my icing tip slips like that."

"They all look perfect to me," said Natalie. "These are the flawed ones, you say?"

"They *are* perfect," said Tessa, picking up a pink poodle cake pop. "Forget about dinner. Let's just eat these instead," she said, taking a bite from it. Strawberry—and was that a creamy filling in the center, with real fruit jam?

"Uh-uh. These are definitely way too beautiful to eat," Natalie said. She was studying a tiny ballerina figure perched atop a sparkly pink cupcake. "What is the tutu made out of? Cotton candy?"

"Good guess." Ama was blushing, as if embarrassed by all this praise. "The ballerinas are white chocolate—I molded them using this old ballerina ornament from a music box I found at a flea market across town. I used non-toxic clay to make the molds, then poured in the melted chocolate. After they harden—paint and serve."

"Genius," said Natalie.

It was pretty genius. This was even better than the cookies Tessa remembered from the superhero birthday party. She hadn't realized how talented Ama truly was. This girl would have no trouble with wedding cakes—maybe that wouldn't be challenge enough for somebody this clever, actually.

They had to move the box aside with haste as the waitress approached to take their orders for the evening. Tessa chose the smoked ribs for her entrée. Suddenly, she felt hungry again.

"Those treats left me craving more sugar," said Natalie. "Maybe I should just skip dinner and order dessert. Then again, the house specialty is cherry cobbler, which isn't really my favorite. And I'm not sure I've even tried sweet potato pie before. Sweet potatoes don't factor heavily in my mom's cooking."

"Have you never eaten sweet potato pie?" Ama asked. "It's kind of like pumpkin pie. See, this one has a candied sugar and nut top—it would taste amazing with a scoop of brown butter cinnamon ice cream on top."

"Isn't that cinnamon overload?"

"Trust me," said Ama. "Spices are kind of my specialty at home. At least, I really love trying out new combinations with them, making a favorite recipe seem fresh with a dash of nutmeg or paprika, or maybe smoky chipotle, even…" She trailed off with a sheepish grin at their looks of bemusement.

"Sorry. I get a little carried away when it comes to recommending culinary combinations," she explained. "I'll take the batter-dipped chicken and sweet potato fries, please," she told the waitress, when she returned from fetching their appetizer of fried okra. Beside her, Natalie settled on the bourbon barbecue cheeseburger.

"I think your enthusiasm is just what we need," Tessa told Ama. "We need someone with your kind of passion, believe me. Once our customers see one of your works on display, they won't have any doubt about it," she added.

"I'll second that," said Natalie.

"The same for Natalie's fashion sense," Tessa continued, with a pointed glance at her friend. "Maybe we haven't all done these things professionally that many times, but we know what we're doing. We know how it's done. We can show them samples of our best work, and that should win anybody over."

"When it comes to wedding cakes, I have a notebook of potential ideas but not much else," said Ama. "I hope these customers don't mind going on a little faith."

"So maybe our best work was done in our own apartments on our own time," said Tessa. "It's still real. Natalie has a closet full of original designs that nobody has been lucky enough to wear—"

Natalie snorted at this remark.

"—and you've made cakes and designer cupcakes for dozens of satisfied customers already, and have a notebook full of great cakes, probably. As for me, I have invitations I designed myself, wedding themes from roses to literature—whole weddings planned down to the last corsage. I just never had a chance to show them to anybody but event planners who weren't really looking to hire yet another creative mind," said Tessa. And she sighed a little inside, though she hid it on the outside. "But I want that to change."

"Me, too." This, surprisingly, from Ama, who had a wistful look in her eyes.

"And we'll have Stefan," supplied Natalie. "He's experienced. His past clients will probably recommend us to others because they liked his planning style at Wedding Wonders. If you have a self-declared genius, what else do you need?" Her biting tone was unmistakable.

"You seem kind of skeptical about him," said Ama dubiously. "I mean, maybe I'm misreading things"—she glanced from Natalie to Tessa with this remark—"but that's the vibe I'm getting."

"Stefan and Natalie... kind of got off on the wrong foot." Tessa gave her friend a sideways glance as she said this, with a warning scowl. "They met at a bridal fashion show where, let's just say, Natalie had a less-than-great first impression of him."

"It was just his whole attitude," Natalie said. "I'm in design, right? Best of show at Spring Stroll was a designer new to the business, whom everybody agreed privately had brought down the house with that amazing throwback line. They were the best, hands down, but there's Stefan in his Hugo Boss suit, schmoozing the Lang collection's designer who's at the top of the industry pyramid despite having one of the *worst* wedding gowns on the spring runway—and why was he doing it? Because the newbie might have been the best, but they weren't a good 'contact' for someone in his field." She made quotation marks with her fingers. "He spent the whole evening trying to impress the top dogs and never even once congratulated that amazing designer."

Ama looked worried. "Is that how he usually behaves?"

Natalie took another sip of water. "Besides, he practically shoved me out of the way to invade a conversation I was having with one of the designers at the winter fashion review. Someone who actually seemed interested in hearing my ideas, unlike my current boss."

Tessa winced. "Probably it was an accident and he didn't even see you standing there."

"Oh, but it wasn't," Natalie said. "He literally nudged me aside mid-sentence. Before I knew it, he was presenting his card and fawning all over the woman like his next meal depended on getting her to design something for his well-heeled client."

Unfortunately, Tessa could picture it all too well: Stefan elbowing her friend out of the circle of professionals, a sycophantic smile on his face as he handed his card to the designer in question. Stefan *was* self-absorbed, it was true. She pictured Natalie's indignant expression as she watched her chance at making a business connection outside of Kandace's shop snuffed out by Stefan's gigantic ego. It was hard not to grimace as she thought of it.

"The worst part is, he didn't even remember it happened," Natalie was telling Ama. "Later that same night, he interrupts another conversation I'm having to ask me—and get this—if I can *fetch him some mineral water from the beverage station*! He actually thought because I was Kandace's assistant I should just drop everything and find him something to drink! Can you imagine the level of ego it would take to treat someone that way? 'Natasha, do me a favor,' he says, as if I'm not doing anything important with my time, standing around talking to professionals in *my* field. Natasha," she repeated, eyeing Tessa with this reminder.

"He's really bad with names," said Tessa meekly.

"He sounds a little full of himself," Ama answered, her tone conveying that she was unsure why they would want to invite a person like this to join their possible business venture. "And you're sure he's a good potential partner for us?"

"Why not?" Natalie said, but still sarcastically. "His clients think he's the best, and he's planning to leave his job. Creatively outgrowing his cubicle, so to speak."

Since Stefan wasn't there to defend himself, Tessa decided she should probably be nice and find a way to soften this negative image of him a little before it frightened Ama away from the whole idea of the partnership. "Okay, so maybe Stefan's ideas can be a little unorthodox," she intervened. "Maybe he's not to my personal taste in planners... the high-strung, creative type gets a little wearing after a time. But he's professional and focused and makes his clients happy. He *is* considered one of the best rising event planners in the city. And we need that kind of reputation if we want our agency to have a fair chance."

The waitress reappeared, delivering plates of steaming vegetables and smoked spicy meats. "Y'all enjoy," she said with a smile.

"What's his work like?" Ama asked. "I've never heard of him... then again, I've never heard of any event planners from the city. Our family is the self-planning type."

"I remember this medieval-themed wedding he planned for a client who was a regular at Kandace's Kreations," mused Natalie. "She showed us pictures. A groom in chainmail and ushers dressed like pageboys. Real swords for the groomsmen, and 'ye olde' tapestries all over the place—the cake had little edible stained-glass windows all over it, which was actually pretty cool."

"Edible stained glass? Seriously?" said Ama. "Was it simple colored panes? Or are we talking about painted scenes, like in a church?"

"Church," said Natalie. Ama looked extremely impressed. "It was shipped here from the Linder Art Bakery in Charleston. Anyway, it was what we call a 'high concept event'—to put it mildly."

"I still thought it was better than the elves," muttered Tessa.

"Elves?" Ama repeated. "Are we talking about Santa Claus, or, like, live action role-playing or something?" she asked.

"Woodland elves and nymphs," said Tessa. "It was a sort of *Midsummer Night's Dream* thing." She had seen pictures from it on Stefan's LinkedIn profile recently. The bridal party's spangled green tights and flowered head wreaths were more like something out of *Hook*, but at least they were attractive, and not like one of Natalie's boss's designs. Even so, the "Frolic in the Forest" theme had seemed a little *too* fanciful, even for Stefan's gushy taste for sequins, glitter, and sheer bunting.

"Okay. Different," said Ama. "Although, if you're a big Shakespeare fan or really into that Tolkien fantasy series…"

"Or *Peter Pan*," Natalie added. "Which has inspired my boss's latest fashion line, apparently." She gave a little shudder. "Right now, I'm looking at a future of sewing sparkling leggings for guys."

"Give Stefan credit for knowing what his clients like. We need to keep the customers happy, right? Maybe that kind of glitz and fantasy concept is exactly what we need. We'll stand out that way." Tessa was trying to sound convinced by this strategy.

"What about your experience?" asked Natalie.

Tessa's expression went blank, an emotional poker face. "Mine?" she queried. "I don't have experience, remember? I have a business degree and a savings account to invest, and some ideas that deserve to be seen by a few clients, I hope. That's who I am right now—the businessperson who pulls together all the right pieces. I'm sure Stefan and I would share the wedding responsibilities fairly and reasonably," she added. "Event planning is all about the client's vision, so we should be able to find common ground on that subject, right?"

"Right," said Natalie solemnly, with an expression that suggested she was thinking the total opposite.

Tessa found herself wishing Natalie would just admit they needed someone like Stefan on their side. Not only for the additional financial contribution, but also for an artistic reputation, something the rest of them didn't really have at this point. So what if it meant her own role in the creative process would be consigned to the background at the firm's beginning? She was willing to accept that. Starting a business and making her dream a reality was the only important part; everything else would fall into place in the future. Once she was no longer scraping glow-in-the-dark frosting off her shoes in front of snobby acquaintances from her past, anyway.

"We definitely need someone experienced, if none of us have ever run a business," said Ama.

"You're practically running one already," Natalie pointed out.

"It's just a basic webpage template. With pictures of cookies and mailing supplies," said Ama with a laugh. "It's not the same as a bricks-and-mortar shop. Or dealing with people face-to-face, either. I don't even do that at the restaurant, since that's my father's job."

"We'll create the most impressive bricks-and-mortar atmosphere we can," said Tessa. "That way, the moment our clients step through the doors, the four of us will give them an impression of confidence and talent."

"And what doors would those be?" said Natalie.

"Real estate's kind of expensive," pointed out Ama. "And kind of scarce, thanks to all the tech outlets opening up in the business sector. The only place I know is available is that dark little shop in the mall. The one at the west end. A shoe store closed last month and left a gap at the far end by the bail bondsman's office."

"It's creepy down there," shuddered Natalie. "Even the wireless provider with the big neon light display moved as soon as a different space was available."

"I was thinking of something better than an outlet in the mall," said Tessa. "A real building with office space for all of us."

"Is my boss renting her warehouse space again?" joked Natalie.

"Actually," said Tessa, "I already have the perfect place in mind." They both looked at her.

"You do?" Ama's eyebrows lifted skeptically.

"I do," said Tessa. "It has charm, plenty of room, and, most importantly, a great location. Best of all, it's available immediately, since its owner is desperate to get out from under it."

"You're serious about this?" said Natalie. "Stop joking around, Tess. This is important."

"I'm not joking. Believe me," answered Tessa. "You'll see what I mean." She hid a mysterious smile behind her glass of sweet tea, pretending not to notice the glances—both curious and dubious— exchanged by her future business partners.

They drove by after dinner. The real estate agent's sign was affixed to the side of the stately brick building downtown. It had a large window facing the street and its front door was painted red, all visible behind the locked metal railings.

It was an old building, and a narrow one, with crumbling sandstone between the floors of red-brown brick. But that was its charm. It was squeezed between two buildings that were in lesser need of TLC. The big window was perfect, Tessa thought—what had once been a townhouse's dignified picture window or a boutique's display would now be perfect for showcasing examples of their talents.

Three further windows looked down on the sidewalk below from the upper story; their untidy window boxes needed a touch of paint and some new flowers. But even in the dark, the tinted panes of the upstairs windows and the leaded glass of the dormers were still noticeable, along with the intricate brass frames of the letterbox and the address numbers on the front door.

"What do you think?" said Tessa. She spread her hands. "It's really beautiful, isn't it?" It had been love at first sight when she saw it on the real estate webpage, a steal for a building this incredible.

"Tessa, we're on Magnolia Street," said Natalie incredulously. "As in, part of the Bellehaven district—this is the oldest, most historic part of the city, which is why its real estate is parceled off to chic little bistros and custom graphic designers. We couldn't afford a billboard space down here, much less an actual business site."

"She's right, Tessa. How could we afford a place like this?" asked Ama. Her jaw had dropped when she first emerged from the car, lifting her gaze to take in the building's impressive dimensions and its former grandeur. "Look at its size. Renting the first floor alone would be expensive."

"I told you, it's a steal," insisted Tessa. "I've seen the cost on it. It's practically ready for auction, because no one wanted to take it on and its owner wants to sell in the worst way."

"Because it's ready for demolition?" suggested Natalie. Little sprinkles of the building's crumbly upper trim dusted the sidewalk noticeably along the property's edge.

"Natalie's right. Most of these businesses seem to be small specialty types," said Ama, glancing around. "Look, there's an imported wine shop on the corner—and I've seen that restaurant featured in the *Best Eateries for Discerning Palates* guide." She pointed toward an innocuous bistro across the street, lit with soft blue lights. "They're small, and they're costly, and they're only using one little partition of these grand old structures."

"This place *is* a little expensive, compared to renting," said Tessa. "But it's a steal for this part of town."

"You're planning to *buy* this monster?" declared Natalie. "You're crazier than I thought. The down payment alone will take every dime you have and then some—are you going to borrow from your mom? From Stefan?"

"I looked it up. This building is worth five times what they're asking for it," argued Tessa. "They're desperate to unload it. Sure, it needs a little TLC… probably"—she averted her eyes from what looked like a water stain above the picture window—"but nothing that four creative people couldn't improve. Maybe with a good handyman to fix the leaks and patch a few holes. The rest we can do with paint and paper."

"How much is a steal?" asked Natalie.

Tessa hesitated. She pulled a sheet of paper from her handbag and held it out to them. Both Natalie and Ama read it in silence.

"That is a steal," admitted Natalie, after a long pause. Her voice did not betray how impressed she was, but Tessa sensed it nonetheless.

Ama spoke up. "That's definitely a lot of cupcake money, though," she said, drawing a ragged breath.

"How come they are selling it for so little?" said Natalie.

"I told you it was a steal." Tessa shrugged her shoulders.

"Even so," said Ama, with a sigh that said it all.

"Tess, we still won't have enough," added Natalie. "Even with your savings and your nest egg, how can we afford this much?"

"We can come close," Tessa insisted. "I have a few extra resources that will bring in some more cash besides what I already have. Once we're earning money by planning events, the payments will be manageable. Nat, think of it. Chances like this just don't come every day. Look at this place—it's one step away from being sold in pieces to make way for a modern property with some fake historic exterior. That's what's happening to all the old buildings nobody wants."

"It would be a shame to tear down a place like this one," said Ama. "It has definite charm." She gazed up at the sandstone carvings encased between the brick stories.

"It has a list of repairs the length of my body, too," said Natalie.

"So? We'll find an affordable handyman, and be careful to only fix what's necessary," said Tessa. "The rest we can cover up or make over with a little paint and some creative measures."

"A big fat zero would be all that was left in my account," said Natalie. "If we did something like this."

"Not so fast," said Tessa. "I'm not asking anyone but me to drain their bank account for this." The last thing she wanted was anyone else risking all they had for her dream—especially with no guarantee it would land them anything more than unemployment. "All I'm asking is enough so we can make this place client friendly. I won't ask anybody to cough up the kind of money I'm planning to invest."

"What'll you live off, though? You told me you were quitting Party 2 Go as soon as we have an 'open' sign on the door." Natalie's face wore a concerned look in the glass window's reflection.

"I'll figure something out," said Tessa. Secretly, she was wondering if any part of the building in front of them was livable enough that she could move into it once her apartment lease was up again. It would be rough, camping out in her future office space until she could afford another apartment. Really rough, from the looks of this place… but maybe worth it, if it meant they had a location this great.

"Once we have a sign and some business cards, think how many people will notice us in a place like this," said Tessa. It was hard not to sound a little awed whenever she gazed up at the building's grand facade. "It's the perfect location, the perfect chance. When will we ever come across another opportunity this good in our lives?" She paused. "But if it's not what you want, it's okay to say so. Investing in a building like this—it's a risk. Investing in this dream is a risk. You've heard everything I have to say, so it's up to you if anything happens."

She was afraid to hear their answers. If they said no, she knew she could try to start the business on her own with Stefan—not in this building, of course, but out of her apartment or a little space they rented in the mall, like Ama suggested. And maybe she would do it, if that were the case. She had nothing to lose, because she had already lost her dignity and temporarily lost her dreams a long time ago, and not just while mopping up party punch for Party 2 Go. But she had a feeling if she didn't make some kind of leap now, she never would. She would be stuck for good playing a princess one week, a T-Rex the next.

Both girls were quiet. "I know I don't want to work for Kandace forever," muttered Natalie. "I just didn't think I wanted to take a risk this big to escape her."

"I don't even know how my family will feel about me cutting back on the hours I spend at the restaurant," said Ama. "Or being a professional baker for an actual living, for that matter." She bit her lip before she spoke again. "But I guess this might be my only chance to find out."

"Then do we want to do it?" said Tessa. She didn't breathe as they stood on the precipice of this decision, as if doing so would push them one way or the other. The next moment would answer everything.

"You got me. Partner," added Natalie. "Now you'd better make good on these promises about success knocking on our doors."

Natalie held out her hand. Ama's joined it, then Tessa's, linked together in a solemn pact of agreement. Tessa's smile dawned, then Natalie grinned slightly. The same impetuous feeling broke across Ama's face in return.

"We're missing one partner's hand, I suppose," said Tessa. "But I think we're mostly in agreement."

"Future, here we come," said Natalie, a little breathless sounding. "Please, don't let us mess this up."

"Now all we need is a name for ourselves," said Ama. "How about 'Best Weddings'?"

"'Now and Forever,'" suggested Natalie. "Or 'One-Stop Wedding Place'?" she joked.

Tessa wrinkled her nose. "Let's keep thinking," she answered.

Chapter Six

It took several weeks to complete the various credit checks and forms, and negotiations with the building's current owner, whose crushing disappointment over a fallen-through offer from a retail store colored his every remark about the property. In the end, however, the papers arrived completed in a business envelope, along with a set of keys to the front door.

"It's ours. Really, truly ours," Tessa crowed. Well, technically it was Tessa's name on the paperwork, but she knew the others would help cover costs as much as they could. "It's glorious, Nat. You should see the view from upstairs—there's a window overlooking the imported goods market with these gorgeous flower urns in front that would *have* to inspire a designer like you at some point."

"So how did it look inside?" Natalie asked. "Do you think it needs a lot of work?" She hadn't seen the property's interior yet; or, for that matter, read the dire remarks of the inspector, whose words on getting it to meet the building code requirements were grim. That report had lessened Tessa's indignation over the fact the owner had planned to let the place be demolished... but only a little.

"Well, it's an old building," Tessa began, cautiously. "So probably some." *Enough that no one can sue us or condemn us, for instance,* she added silently. "We'll have to hire a contractor or handyman or something. I'll look up a few names and get someone to patch up any trouble spots before we move in."

"Sounds good. I have to go," said Natalie. "Kandace gets nervous if we talk on the phone to outsiders while we're working on a new line. I guess she's afraid the competition will hire us as spies. Or saboteurs." Natalie was sewing at the loft studio today, finishing the last "Twisted Symmetry" ensemble.

"Would it actually be possible for someone to sabotage her work?"

"Do a better job of it than Kandace herself, you mean?" said Natalie. "Not unless they put a blowtorch to some of these synthetic fabrics. Oh, wait; she did that to her 'Dark Dreams' collection already." Other voices were audible in the background at her end of the phone call. "Listen, I really have to go—text me when you have an estimate from the handyman, okay?"

"Will do. I'm sure he'll throw a little plaster around and patch a few holes," answered Tessa brightly.

There was more involved than patching a few holes. Any kitchen they installed would have to be up to the inspection code if Ama was going to bake for their clients. They would need a decent washroom, a waiting area for clients... and the worst damage would have to be repaired in a way that wouldn't repulse anybody who dropped by their headquarters. In short, they needed someone reputable, even if it meant kissing the last little bit of her savings goodbye, and possibly her apartment lease, if all else failed.

Her bank account was empty, mere dollars left, and her nest egg was now nothing except tax fees due in April. Unbeknownst to the others, Tessa had sold her car already, and the only pieces of furniture of any value from her apartment. Every little bit of cash helped, she reminded herself, as she placed an ad for her sofa in the local paper. Pretty soon, there would be only the bare necessities left—but that would only be the case until their business took off.

She left voice messages for Stefan and Ama with the news about the finalized sale, then divided the rest of her afternoon between designing their new website and looking for a building repair service. Right now, their wedding planning services website consisted of a handful of pictures borrowed from Stefan's online portfolio and a few images from Ama's online bakery. It needed a name, though. That was still missing.

Perfect Weddings. Too clichéd. She scratched it out on her list. *Special Vows.* Not right either. Something to do with wedding symbols, maybe. She flipped open her portfolio, looking for popular images. Cakes, flowers, rings—those were things people associated with weddings.

Wedding Bouquets. Her pencil wrote it down, then scratched it out, too. *Bells and Bouquets.* A sample invitation tucked in her portfolio featured pink paper roses above a cluster of white bells.

Wedding Bells. She paused, then added an 'e' between the last 'l' and the 's.' Three bells on the invitation, three 'belles' behind the idea—herself, Natalie, and Ama. How perfect was it, too, that they were launching their business in a Southern haven like Bellegrove? She didn't draw a pencil line through this one. Something about it seemed right.

Of course, it left Stefan out. *Oh, well. Can't have everything,* Tessa reasoned, as she typed the name into the website's new header. Stefan already had a starring role in their new business without sharing in the glory of its name, after all. The rest of them deserved to have some part of it, too. It was technically her dream that started this business.

Wedding Belles. It would look perfect on a business card, above three little bells and some roses.

Now to find a reliable repairman to patch up their building. Scrolling through people under "repair and carpentry" on the local home repair web listings, she paused on a business profile for "Ellingham's Repair & Restoration," third down from the top listings of "Industrial Corporate Contractors, Inc." and "Exclusive Interior Artistry and Design."

Their website's photo gallery of completed jobs featured a Victorian mansion with beautiful bay windows and stained-glass door panels, a historic brownstone, and a series of smaller homes and businesses. "Reasonable rates and first-class service!" gushed the latest client. "A professional who understood both my budget and my needs," proclaimed another.

A quick email later, and a contractor from the firm would be onsite first thing Monday morning. Tessa arranged to leave a spare key hidden for him, since she would be running late that morning—one last trip in the hotdog mobile before she turned in the keys and her resignation.

The handyman's work truck was parked outside the building when Tessa arrived the day of the appointment. At least, she surmised as much from the truck bed, which was packed to the gills with a collection that might have been at home in someone's great-grandparent's attic. Splintered wood, ornate brass, and tarnished pewter peeked out from layers of plaster dust and old tarps.

An antique headboard; a gilded frame from a broken mirror. A gothic cast iron fireplace insert, and a broken carousel horse of all things, its blue and gold paint badly cracked and peeling away from the elaborate carvings beneath. Were these part of the contractor's work or was he just a traveling packrat? Tessa drew herself away from the shabby artifacts and put her key in the lock.

Pushing open the red front door, she stepped inside the foyer. Straight ahead of her was the front room with its faded green and gold flecked wallpaper, and a scarred, carved oak mantel seated proudly against the wall, its white paint flaking away in places; then the badly peeling painted spiral stairs leading to the landing above, where the stained glass glowed in the sunlight.

She climbed the stairs, feeling her anticipation mount despite the dust under her fingers and the smell of mildew reaching her nostrils. Shabby but real—this was the place where her dream was coming true. At the top of these stairs was her future office, where she would dream up amazing details for weddings that would impress clients to speechlessness... that would become memories preserved in photo albums and scrapbooks, just as she had always hoped, ever since she began saving pages torn from magazines—even down to the sample invitations from stationery companies.

Never mind the fact that it was technically Stefan whose creations would be dazzling their clients. At this moment, the downside of her dream turning into reality was less important than the reality itself.

This is really happening. It's amazing. I am finally a wedding planner with my own business, and it's all just beginning. She felt a rush of pride and utter happiness—and surprise as she turned to her right on the landing and encountered a tall ladder in the alcove, and a man standing atop it, prying back the trim beneath an ornate dormer window.

"Hey! Wait!" said Tessa. "What are you doing?" He wasn't hired yet, and, more importantly, he was working on something that looked nonessential to the building's list of code demands from the inspector.

The masculine figure in denim and flannel, with broad shoulders and chestnut brown hair that seemed slightly untamed, turned and looked down, a pair of rich blue eyes meeting hers. His well-sculpted cheek-bones and jawline sported a few days' worth of stubble, Tessa noticed.

"Is there a problem?" he asked.

"I said 'stop.' Please," she added this time. "I'm Tessa Miller. You're the contractor, I trust?" A truly ridiculous question, since he wasn't likely to be a stranger off the streets come to check her building for sound structure and good wiring.

"That's me," he replied. "Blake Ellingham." He came down the ladder and extended a hand to shake hers. "I have to admit, I was excited when I got your email."

Excited? "You were?"

"Absolutely," he repeated, with the dawning of a faint smile at this answer, which gave light to his whole expression. It looked exactly the way Tessa felt inside; the way she thought her enthusiasm would look on the outside.

Maybe it was the light in his eyes, but to her surprise something about his reaction both bewildered Tessa and took her breath away for a split-second. Breathless—she hadn't experienced that in a long time, not even when Stefan had texted "yes" to her offer to share a wedding planner partnership. The heady rush of this new experience must be affecting her brain, even when it came to talking with strangers.

"I guess I didn't expect that reply from anybody," she said.

"The historic old town? The shabby but chic quarter looking for new life in this city? Are you kidding?" he answered. "I haven't had the opportunity to work on one of these buildings, and I wasn't going to pass up a chance to do it. Nice brickwork with a little sandstone, modeled on some of the best brownstone architecture."

"Really?" she said. He had a pleasant voice, with a warmth that stirred again those same feelings inside her as when she had climbed the steps to her future workspace. A strange comparison, a strange reaction—maybe there were some chemicals in this old building that were having an impact on her system.

"There's a hundred and fifty years of history in this place—you can sense it the moment you walk through the doors," he said.

He must really like this place. Tessa's spirits rose with this idea. Maybe he would be kind and give them a decent break on his fees. "So, you've been getting acquainted with the building," she said, glancing around them, at the dusty walls and the decorative window with its cracked lower pane of pink glass. "What do you think?"

He released a breath that resembled a sigh. One that diminished his nice warmth somewhat—in the sense that Tessa knew his words would bring no good news for her pocketbook.

"Dry rot," he said.

"Sorry?"

"That's only the beginning. There's water damage in some of the rooms. This hall probably has a leak around the windowsill. It's possible dry rot has set in, depending on how long it's been there. The material around it will have to come out."

That sounded nasty and kind of expensive to fix. Tessa hoped it hadn't gotten bad enough for him to actually think of ripping out part of the wall, or something dramatic like that. All she could see was a little graying beneath the trim he'd started to remove.

She attempted positive confidence. "The realtor seemed to think it was in pretty good shape for an old building. He told me it housed a couple of stores recently, so it's not as if it's been abandoned forever."

"Abandoned, no. Neglected is probably a better word for it." He descended the stairs, and Tessa had no choice but to follow. "That fireplace—original. Most of the carving, molding, and trim are authentic, too. But the rest—a lot of original fixtures have been torn out. This place is a Frankenstein's monster when it comes to repair carpentry over the years, and most of it's shoddy. Take this staircase: probably added about a century ago when this place changed hands, and a totally different style and craftsmanship than the rest."

"I like this staircase," protested Tessa. They had reached the main foyer again, where the carpenter rapped on the walls.

"Pretty solid down here, but we've got problems upstairs. I may have to take out some of the walls. Those two little rooms on the end by the bath are supposed to be one, anyway."

Take out the walls? Actual walls? "I like the walls, too," said Tessa quickly. "Let's leave them. In fact, let's leave as much as we can, because I'm really pretty attached to things as they are." She touched the wallpaper and grime came off on her fingers. She slipped her hand behind her, and smiled again. "What about the overall structure? It's solid, right?" she asked hopefully.

The handyman had turned his attention to the fireplace and was crouching in front of it, running a hand across the brick inlay, where some coals and ash still remained. "The original surround is gone from its exterior," he said. "Cast iron, early Victorian. I could probably find you something pretty close, maybe with the old torch motif. The mantel's oak needs some help—three coats of paint to cover the original finish, but we can fix that too. If you want corbels for it, I could probably find those too."

Tessa had no idea what corbels were, but they sounded unnecessary when it came to getting an "open" sign hung on the building's door.

"Maybe when I hunt up the stuff for the windows," he continued. "Leaded glass isn't always easy to find, but I can probably match it if I visit a couple of specialty vendors I know. It won't be cheap, but nobody will know it's not original when they look at it, which is exactly what you want with a building this old. But first we need to talk about the walls."

Expensive and hard-to-find leaded glass also sounded nonessential. Wasn't lead dangerous, anyway? Hazardous to one's health and the environment? "Hopefully it's nothing a little paint and wallpaper won't fix," Tessa suggested. Inside, her confidence had begun to waver. She was counting on a little wall color and creativity to transform this place, not expensive antiques and a massive demolition of its interior.

"It's rough. *Really* rough. It needs a lot of work and a lot of capital," he said, looking around him. "I know it's pretty daunting at this point and you must be thinking 'maybe we should just tear it down,' but it'll be worth it in the end."

Tear it down? Tessa's high spirits had completely sunk. No bargain bin hardware paint was going to fix this place in the contractor's eyes. These were statements that implied the whole building was about to fall down from rot—plans for gutting rooms, ripping out whole walls, and turning the building into a skeleton of itself were already turning themselves over in his head, clearly.

How could they possibly pay for any of that? She had been cherishing the impossible hope that they would spend only a few thousand at most to fix up this place—and only a few hundred on decor. He needed to understand this fact. Forget antique corbels, or whatever they were—forget leaded glass and knocking out whole walls, so long as there was a chance they would continue to stand on their own for years.

The handyman was oblivious to her thoughts as he wiped his hand on a rag to remove the traces of soot from the fireplace, then pushed up his sleeves as if in preparation for getting to work. He had strong-looking hands and well-defined biceps, she noticed. Not that it mattered, so long as he was strong enough to hammer a few pieces of plasterboard over some holes.

"As for light fixtures—"

Here, Tessa decided, was the perfect point to stop him.

"We're mostly interested in the basics right now," said Tessa. "You know, electrical problems, holes in the floor and roof... that kind of thing. I mean, how many repairs will it take until you can turn on a light and not burn the building down?" She made it sound like a joke, although it was an honest question.

"You'll need a master electrician and a plumber to answer that," he said. "But I've had a little training in electrics, and I did see part of your wiring through the hole upstairs."

"Rough?" Tessa knew the answer before he even said it.

"We'll get to your priorities, don't worry," he said to her. "I can work on the big stuff like reconstruction while I take care of the smaller stuff, like putting the fixtures and trim back the way they should be."

"Maybe I should have explained things better in the email," she began. "I don't mean I want you to tell me the basics as a starting point. I mean, *just* tell me the basics. Because that's all I'm interested in hiring you to fix right now. Not antique light fixtures or missing corbels, whatever they are. Just the basics."

The handyman's smile dimmed noticeably. "The staircase is fine the way it is," she said. "I like it. I don't care if not every fixture is perfect. Truthfully, we can only afford the essentials. We have a small budget, me and my partners, so if it's not necessary to bring us up to code... well, you get the picture."

The carpenter's smile was now gone, Tessa noted, along with the light in his eyes. In its place was a touch of steel in his blue gaze. "So, holes in the walls, holes in the ceiling," he said. "When you say, 'Don't burn the building down,' you mean you want the bare minimum of work done to hold this place together. Is that it?"

"Pretty much," said Tessa. "So, I think we're on the same page now." She reached into her shoulder bag and pulled out a folder. "I brought the blueprints the realtor gave me. Show me the worst places that need to be fixed, and we'll talk about the essentials."

"You're the customer," Blake replied, in a tone that seemed to imply that the customer was not always right. He actually sighed again, she thought, as he crouched down beside her on the floor while she spread the plans out, for lack of a table. Pencil in hand, the contractor made some notes about the condition of the upstairs—hazardous—and the downstairs—dismal—although he didn't use those exact words to express himself to her.

"But the worst problem is in the second story bathroom, where your tub plans to fall through the floor. I know you might not classify that as an 'essential' but if I were you, I would go ahead..."

He had a certain authority when he spoke: not an obnoxious one, although it was slightly bossy, which was why she was arguing with him on some of these points. Or maybe there was some kind of opposing chemistry between them, working against the obvious rugged appeal and rough charisma of the carpenter that had struck her in those first seconds of meeting him.

Not that he was her type. If she had a type at all, that is—and she hadn't in a long time; thoughts of finding her ideal man had been swept away even before her dreams of being an event planner had been suspended. It was just the scent of paint thinner or something going to her head right now. Fumes from old buildings were bad for the brain's normal processes.

"Will it take long to get the estimate?" she asked.

"I'll need a few more days to assess the damage and come up with a ballpark number for expenses," Blake replied. "Is that a problem for you?"

"No," said Tessa. "That's great. If there's nothing else, I'll just go explore my future office." *And potential future home*, she thought, remembering her backup plan to pay the bills by saving on rent—although she might feel a little like a squatter in an abandoned building if the renovations didn't progress quickly.

Nobody needed to know about that part of the plan yet, especially since her lease wouldn't be up at Bluecrest Apartments for weeks.

She rolled up the blueprints and let him keep them, then lifted her bag from the floor. The office to the right of the stairs on the second story landing would be hers and Stefan's, with an adjoining door between them. His space would have the best window view, because Stefan claimed that his creativity would feel like it was caged without at least two windows through which it could "fly away in fantasy."

His words, not hers.

Her half of the room needed some help, clearly, since the water stains on one side of the wall looked like a hideous malformed monster, and the wallpaper on the opposite side was sagging in a papery mess. It was nothing a little paint couldn't fix, though. The carpenter would see she was right about that.

Chapter Seven

"Wedding Belles" was painted on the front window's glass by Friday, which was when Tessa picked up the first batch of business cards and split them up among her partners, as well as distributing them to as many of her business contacts in town who would take one; from antiques shops, hairdressers and nail salons to fashion boutiques and jewelry stores, and everywhere in between. Any place, in fact, where Tessa imagined engaged people might be, even boldly leaving one at the tearoom where she'd worked before.

She had also printed off several fliers to put up around town, and arranged for an ad in the next issue of *Bellegrove Bridal*, albeit a small one. Its receipt rested atop the big stack of grand opening notices in their box on her borrowed car's passenger seat, as she ran errands all week in anticipation of the Wedding Belles officially moving in.

Stefan didn't object to the business's name, she noticed—not that he had even been to see the building yet, except for a cursory visit on his way to another party. He had texted Tessa to say that he would be out of town for two weeks, along with an observation that their new digs had "great vibes" and he couldn't wait to plan someone's "dream-come-true wedding" with her. *Totes ready to do this*, he wrote in his message. *Finally, I'll have real creative freedom. Wedding Wonders had SUCH a dampening effect on me. We'll talk paint colors soon. Love the office windows!!!!*

Finally, everything was coming together, Tessa told herself, as she drove to meet the others at their new headquarters. It still needed some work—she admitted this as she looked at a drooping wall lamp upstairs, dangling by a few wires—but it would be charming with a little more TLC. Chic, eccentric, and unique—that was their atmosphere. They would wear it like a distinctive style, and not a budget limitation.

Natalie let out a low whistle when she walked into the foyer.

"Look at this place," she said. "Walnut paneling, a spiral staircase… a big mantel in the front room. This place was really something a hundred years ago." She touched the old wallpaper, the dull gold and green that had probably been vibrant a few decades ago.

"Wait until you see the upstairs," said Tessa.

She had been looking forward to showing her other two business partners the house for weeks now. Until this morning, however, neither of them had been able to coordinate their schedules with hers for a proper tour. Bursting with pride for its potential, she told Natalie, "Ama and I have already picked out the office space, and there's a room just perfect for yours, with a huge old wardrobe for fabrics. Plus closets, extra space… this is going to be amazing once we have time to fix it up."

"I knew I should have stopped by sooner," said Natalie. "I would have brought some of my stuff over and tried sewing a dress in peace and quiet. Kandace was raging with some fabric dealer the whole time I was trying to pin one of the skirts at work earlier this morning." She set the mail packages she had picked up at the post office on the table. "What's in these boxes, anyway?"

"Some office supplies," said Tessa, opening a box on the table in the entry room, where they hoped to have a reception area after a little remodeling. "And the rest of the business cards, in case we need extra." Their logo was printed beneath the firm's name: the trio of bells with flowers and a fluttering ribbon at the top of the cluster. *Planning Moments to Remember—Weddings, Vow Renewals, and Other Special Life Occasions* was printed below it, with their office number and website. "I'm thinking of designing a web ad for some of the wedding venue sites, something using our logo, or maybe our website's banner."

"Website?" said Natalie. "When did you have time to set up a website?"

"It's only partly set up," admitted Tessa. "I've been working on it. It's missing some details, like photos and a company email, which I'm filling in—we'll spruce it up after our first client or two. Right now, we're just beginning. We're still at least a week away from hosting any paid events." She opened her laptop on the table and clicked on the website's address, revealing the "Coming Soon!" photo page, and the decorative home page with their new logo and name at the top.

"A week away. That's optimistic, Tess."

"Here's where our names and bios will go. Should we have photos of ourselves?" asked Tessa. "I'm hoping to finish this part by the weekend, so send me a nice photo and some biography details you want included for yours. I'm asking Ama for the same."

"I don't want my photo—" began Natalie, as a shower of dust cascaded from the ceiling above, accompanied by a tremendous thud.

"What's that?" Ama had just entered with a box of kitchen supplies in her arms. "Is someone upstairs?" She glanced above their heads, where the antique light fixture was shaking, little bits of plaster dislodging from around its burnished brass.

"The contractor I hired," said Tessa.

"The contractor?"

"He's here to finish assessing what it'll take to fix up the building," said Tessa. "You know, a few basics. So we can have our separate offices upstairs, a decent restroom or two, a reception area by the sitting room downstairs—and, of course, he'll install the kitchen appliances according to code so you—"

Two more thuds followed, accompanied by the protesting squeal of wood. "Are we sure he's not here to tear this place down?" asked Natalie.

"Relax, I already talked to him about it. He knows we only want stuff done if it's absolutely necessary. Plus he had great recommendations on the help site," said Tessa. "He's just getting a feel for the place right now so he can give us a cost estimate."

"I want to see the upstairs before he destroys it," said Natalie. "Maybe I can spot my former future office among the ruins." She began climbing the steps. "How long is the contractor going to be here?"

"Probably not long," said Tessa. "I told him we planned to paint really soon, and put up the new wallpaper." She closed her laptop's lid as more plaster dust showered down.

The contractor sat down with them in the future parlor, where the broken-down furniture consisted of some worn-out kitchen chairs and a folding table Tessa had borrowed from her former boss's surplus stock. Blake was still sporting the flannel and denim look she had thought of as a handyman's cliché when they first met, except his shirt was green this time—contrasting with the frost in his eyes, she told herself, that she'd created when she crushed his illusions about restoring the building.

"It's rough," the contractor announced. Again. Tessa managed not to roll her eyes.

"The estimate, you mean," said Natalie, as she opened a Diet Coke.

"Everything," he said. "That's what I mean."

"What?" said Ama with a funny smile. "It doesn't look that bad to me. I mean, there's a hole in the floor upstairs, and some water damage on the ceiling, but we could plaster and paint over it. It's part of the historic charm, right? Old buildings look old."

"That's what I thought," Tessa told her. "You expect a few crumbly spots in a building this old."

"Water damage? Holes?" Blake said. "Those are the least of your worries. This building isn't getting any younger. A lot of the wiring is shot, and you have a radiator system that's practically a fire hazard unless its pipes get some attention. There are some busted windows on the top floor, ruined linoleum in the bathroom, and a couple of bad joists in the upstairs floor. You're looking at a month's worth of work, just to begin with those little things. And those are essential repairs, yes," he added, with a pointed look at Tessa.

"How much?" asked Tessa. "We're on a budget, like I told you before. We just need the—"

"The basics. Message received," he finished. "But all of this is necessary, if you don't want your building to burn down or fall down. Ideally, I would close this place up long enough to gut the upstairs walls, at least."

"Gut them?" repeated Tessa. "You're kidding. They look fine."

"Tear out all that walnut paneling upstairs? And the antique fixtures?" echoed Ama.

"I would salvage every piece I could, and put it back the way it was meant to be," Blake replied, holding up his hands as if to fend off an attack. "You have my word on that. But you need new supports and new wiring. After that, you can cover the walls with the salvaged paneling and paint or paper them, as you seem so keen to do." Here, his eye landed briefly on Tessa. "Whatever it is you want."

"But we need this place to be presentable really soon," said Tessa. "I have the paint chips and the wallpaper samples ready to pick from today—I bought the primer already. I have furniture coming in next week."

"I can do it one wall at a time," he said. "When I finish with one, paint it. Just don't get too impatient—not if you want me to reinstall some of those original fixtures. I'll have to tweak the wiring and the connectors before they'll work. Unless you want new ones? Shiny modern gold with plain globes?" He didn't look as if this was the reply he wanted to hear. There might even have been a touch of bitter sarcasm in his voice.

Tessa resented the implication of his words. It's not as if she was deliberately targeting the building's history by making him leave the shoddy old patchwork and weird changes by its past owners.

Besides, she *liked* the spiral staircase, no matter its true architectural background.

"Can we get a second opinion?" asked Natalie, raising her hand.

"What about the plumbing?" said Ama. "Is that any good?"

"I took the liberty of looking at it, and I have some good news on that subject. It's copper, original, and fairly decent," he said. "But I have worse news about your probable kitchen space. Those outlets won't be able to hold a fridge or stove as it stands." He tapped the space on the building blueprint that was open on the table. "It'll take a lot to get that room up to code."

"Let me guess. Roaches and rats," groaned Natalie, whose head lolled ceilingward as she drooped in her chair. "Tessa, maybe we should—"

"We're not giving up this spot," said Tessa. "It's too late. Besides, it's perfect. We'll just have to work around the problems and prioritize, that's all."

"Please," said Ama to Blake. "We're a little desperate. Just for the sake of niceness, give us some hope."

A pause, during which the contractor studied his list of the building's woes and the blueprint, looking deep in thought, judging by the concentration on his face.

"I would start with the kitchen," he said. "That means installing the outlets for your appliances, sealing off any cracks, and taking a look at the vents. Then I could put in some stainless steel fixtures, so we can get you up to code. After that… I'd strip the walls upstairs and start with the wiring up there. Lucky for you, I've got some electrical experience, and a friend who's licensed in it and works for cheap. Then I'd look at those weak joists last. Of course, I'd have to cover the walls again afterward—unless you want to do that yourselves."

"Not really," said Natalie. It was obvious that she was picturing the three of them trying to lift heavy paneling into place and drive nails into it.

He made a note with the pencil tucked behind his ear. Glancing up, he made eye contact in turn with all three hopeful expressions trained on him. "Look," he began, in a gentler tone, "I'll keep costs down for you as best I can. I've got a six-month payment plan, so you won't have to rush to pay me." He tapped his pencil against the list of repairs. "So what do you want to do?"

The three of them exchanged glances. Tessa released a deep sigh. "I guess we'll start with the kitchen, then," she said. Stainless steel counters wouldn't be cheap, even if they could find a restaurant salvage warehouse. How much did it cost to rewire a kitchen?

"I'll go get started," said the contractor, pushing back his chair. "I'll grab some extra tools from my truck. Drill, hammer, saw. We'll have to keep the power to the building shut off before I go near anything electrical. In the meantime, try not to plug in any appliances more powerful than a toaster."

"You have a hammer with you already," pointed out Natalie. "Do you really need a second one?"

"Different hammer," he called over his shoulder.

"Great," groaned Natalie. "Not only will we end up tearing out more of the building than we actually keep, but we'll be paying our repairman for the rest of our lives."

"Maybe it won't be as bad as it sounds," said Ama helpfully. "Maybe we can just avoid walking on the bad spot on the floor. That way nobody takes a shortcut to the sitting room, right?"

"I'm glad you can laugh about this," said Natalie. "Me, I'm not so sure I'm ready. We'd better have some good news soon, so I can feel it was worth it. At least you're not worried about your job, whereas Kandace will probably be impossible to work for as soon as she learns about this little venture."

"Don't envy me too fast," said Ama, half-muttering.

"It'll be fine," said Tessa. "I'm sure he'll do what he says and keep the costs low. We'll just trust that he won't overcharge us, and that our first few clients will bring in enough money to pay for the renovations. Plus a little paint." She reached into her bag. "Speaking of which, who wants to pick out room colors?"

"I do," said Ama. "Just not right now. I still have some more stuff to bring in. Think it'll be safe here?" she asked, as the handyman entered again. He held a giant toolbox in one hand, and a Skilsaw dangled from the other one as he made his way to the kitchen.

"He didn't say he was remodeling the closets," pointed out Tessa. She spread open a series of paint shade strips and a book of wallpaper samples.

"Let me see them," said Natalie, holding out her hands. "I need an inspiring color for my workspace. I'm thinking eggshell on the window wall, with some funky modern art-style squares of color. Sort of like a geometric mural."

Colors would definitely spruce things up. They would use bright colors in the sitting room and the foyer, something that suggested flowers, maybe. Lavender and rose... maybe a soft green... something resembling the old smoke-stained wallpaper's former shade, and fresh ivory paint over the dull white wall trim. All three of them would feel better about this place's future once a few improvements were visible, and they could open the doors for their new clients.

A new message popped up on her phone. The front door slammed closed—not Ama returning with a box of pans, but the handyman with a coil of wire over his arm. Tessa tried to remember if his webpage mentioned an electrician's license as she opened the text on her phone. It was from Stefan.

We need to talk. Changed my mind. Sorry.

About what? Tessa's mind flew over this cryptic text. She texted her question, receiving a reply that sucked away her breath.

The business. So sorry. Just won't work out for me. A frowning face appeared at the end of this statement.

What?!? Her fingers flew over the keypad.

Sorry again. Explain later, swear. Totes busy now.

This *couldn't* be happening. Not now. Tessa closed the message box hastily, as if that would somehow erase the conversation just cut short by Stefan, from wherever he had been this past week instead of moving his things here. Now there were only three of them to share the repair costs—and worse yet, none of them had any official reputation in the event planning world.

Whistling to himself, the handyman strolled by with a sledgehammer over his shoulder.

Chapter Eight

"But why do you want to *do* this, Ama?" Her mother's voice was filled with perplexity.

"It's only part-time right now," said Ama reassuringly. "It's a chance for me to help some friends and do a little extra baking. And free the restaurant kitchen from all my supplies, too."

She could feel her mother's suspicion, although Pashma had not turned around while dicing beef for the curry. The free end of her mother's cotton sari was tucked into the strap of her apron—unlike the rest of the family, her mother refused to wear Western fashions after thirty-two years in America, even for practical purposes. She was still disappointed that Ama had cut her hair short and couldn't be depended upon to wear a sari or salwar kameez on formal occasions.

"It's a chance for me to spread my wings," said Ama. "Meet new people. I'll still be making desserts for the restaurant menu, so nothing will change." *Not right now, anyway*, she added mentally.

"I don't know," said her mother, tossing cubes of meat into the hot skillet, where they sizzled along with some cloves of garlic. She shook her head. "There are more important things to do than bake cakes."

"Yes—there's marriage," said her brother Jaidev mockingly. "You can't forget the age-old custom of *shaadi* just for the sake of having a life." His teasing tone earned him a disapproving look from their mother.

Marriage was the only thing on her mother's mind, now that Ama was over twenty-five. Every eligible young Indian man in their neighborhood had been assessed and considered as a possible husband for her since she was sixteen—Ama had been dodging romantic setups for years now.

"Maybe we should put the ad in the paper," said her mother. "Your father thinks it's time."

Ama groaned internally. "No ads," she said. "Not in the paper, or online, either." Matchmaking ads in Indian papers and journals had long been the favorite reading material of her mother and her aunts, and not just for entertainment. Plenty of arranged-marriage sites had caught her father's eye over the past year, after he finally learned to surf the web. Ama now believed he had learned how in order to widen the pool of prospective sons-in-law for his daughters.

"It's bad enough that you've hinted to every boy in the community that I'm available, without bringing in strangers." She took a bite from a mango in the fruit bowl, as her sister Rasha swatted her hand.

"For the dessert," she scolded.

"Not anymore," retorted Ama. "I'm changing that special as of now."

"Maybe you should think about a matchmaking website. I met Sanjay through one." Rasha pulled an apron over her t-shirt and jeans. "I think we're a perfect match, too."

Their father Ranjit entered the kitchen. "Do I smell *kaara kuzhambu*?" he asked, lifting the lid on a pot. "There will be a full house today. I can feel it. Lots of spiced lentils and *rasam*." He put on an apron.

"Tell Ama that you are going to put an ad in the paper for potential suitors," said Pashma.

"I don't think it's necessary," said Ama. "There's still plenty of time to meet somebody. This city is full of single guys. Sooner or later, I'll meet one. Maybe fall in love and be swept off my feet."

Not all of the city's single men were Indian, of course, much less from the right background and family. That was what her parents were afraid of when it came to leaving things to chance: that Ama would fall in love with someone totally different from the rest of them, and, therefore, totally inappropriate.

"Talk to her. She's going to work for strangers in a bakery," said Pashma. "She wants to meet strangers and go out into the world, she says."

"Ama's not exactly leaving," intervened Rasha, in an attempt to explain.

Ranjit looked dumbfounded by this announcement. "What strangers?" he asked accusingly. "Strangers from nice Indian families are no good to you—but strangers from the street are acceptable?"

Ama managed not to roll her eyes. "I just don't want an arranged marriage," she answered.

"It isn't like marrying a stranger," said Rasha. "It's not as if Sanjay and I never saw each other before the wedding. We were matched, we met, we dated. Now look how happy we are. And look at Nalia—she and Devar are happy, too."

"Why don't you leave Ama alone? She'll get married eventually," said Jaidev, who finished carving the side of beef and removed his stained apron. "So she doesn't want to meet someone right now. Big deal."

"She should have married Vikram," said Ama's aunt, piping up shrilly—Pashma's sister, nicknamed "Bendi" for being the ultimate meddling Indian auntie when it came to everything from matchmaking and careers to choosing what side dishes should be on the menu. "He had a good job. Good prospects, nice family. A little homely, but there are worse things than a boy who isn't handsome."

"Vikram didn't even like me," protested Ama. "We were barely friends. Neither of us was interested in the other one, I assure you. He only went out with me because *you* asked his mother to make him do it."

"Besides, he was dating a girl in my class back then," said Jaidev. "Faye Wilcombe. He married her in Las Vegas a couple of years ago when he took that job designing security software for casinos."

Ama could have predicted her mother's worried mutterings at this statement. Vikram had rejected his whole culture, in her eyes, from choosing a sixth-generation American girl who didn't eat rice or yogurt to marrying in a neon wedding chapel—with no saris, bridal jewelry, vermillion powder, rituals and ceremonies, or families involved at all.

"You could meet a nice boy *this* way," coaxed Ranjit. "Maybe he would even work here instead of in his family's business. You could bake for him, if you want to bake. That would be nice, yes?"

"It's not just about changes," sighed Ama. "It's about doing what I want. Meeting a person that I want to love. I want to make my own decisions, and I don't want to meet someone just because you want me to be married."

Her father shook his head. "I'm putting the ad in the paper," he said. "It's time we began trying to find a good match." A chorus of groans and murmurs of approval from the divided sides of Ama's family followed.

"Fine," said Ama. "But I'm not going on a date with some boy just to make you happy."

"You'll change your mind," said her mother.

"You're wasting your time and your money," said Ama. She reached for a mixing bowl and the bottle of milk from the fridge to begin making *gulab jamun* for the dessert menu. The little milk dough balls needed time to soak in their sugar syrup before they were served.

"Told you," said Jaidev to their father archly.

Clearly, it was going to take some time to persuade them she was right, Ama reflected. But if her parents thought the answer lay in a matchmaking site, they had better think again.

"So. Bad news," said Tessa. "Stefan has dropped out."

The shock on her two remaining partners' faces was every bit as awful as she had expected. All weekend long, she had rehearsed what to say—and how to say it calmly—but the practice was all in vain.

"What?" said Natalie with horror.

"What happened?" demanded Ama.

"Well… as it happens… he got a job in Paris. Some fantastic opportunity he couldn't pass up, apparently," said Tessa. "I tried to change his mind but… he's kind of already gone."

Hurrying through this last part didn't make it better, since both of her listeners were panicking. "Now what are we going to do?" Natalie asked.

"It's not the worst news in the world," said Tessa. "We still have time to find a fourth partner before we open. Stefan can't really be the only wedding planner in this city who's unhappy with their job and is dying for a change."

"But what if we don't find one?" Ama worried. In the background, a terrible crash resounded as the contractor ripped the walls from their future kitchen.

"We will," promised Tessa, trying to sound reassuring and not at all desperate. "I'll call some contacts today, and maybe Natalie can try a few of hers."

"I don't know anybody except some wannabe fashion designers," said Natalie. "Not many event planners call on Kandace's talents, for very obvious reasons."

"What about a florist?" asked Ama. "Or a caterer. What if—" Her next remark was drowned out by a sound resembling a jackhammer shattering concrete.

"Hold on. I'll ask him to stop for a while," said Tessa. As if it made any difference at this point how long it was before they had a kitchen that met the city building codes—both Natalie and Ama were already having doubts about this plan ever succeeding, even before Stefan chose to abandon them. And now Tessa was starting to feel the same way; a lack of confidence that this would ever work out. A lump swelled in her throat, but there was no way she was going to cry about this now. Not in front of the handyman, anyway.

She entered the main foyer, and that's when she discovered they had company. An elderly woman in a sweater and long skirt was wandering around in their future reception room, an uncertain expression on her face. She paused to admire the old mantel, one hand touching it as the other clutched an oversized purse that reminded Tessa of her grandmother's old knitting bag.

The visitor looked small and thin, but not frail—and there was a certain determination in her gaze that made Tessa think this wasn't an escaped invalid happening upon their unlocked front door, but a person who was well aware of their surroundings and their purpose in coming here.

"Hello?" said Tessa. "Are you looking for someone?" With their luck, she would be one of the building's former owners, come to announce they were in possession of its true deed.

The woman turned around. "I am looking for—for—" She hesitated. "I don't remember his name. I don't know him. His name is on this piece of paper, but I have left my eyeglasses at home by mistake."

She fumbled through her purse for either the glasses or the slip of paper—eventually producing the latter—then smiled at Tessa apologetically. "A friend told me that I should talk to him because he is the best at weddings, and I am insisting upon the best." Her accent was foreign, but her English was clear.

The piece of paper in her hand was printed from Stefan's online profile—his real name in a smaller font beneath 'THE WEDDING GURU,' spelled out in giant gilded lettering. It also listed this building's address and its disconnected landline under his contact information. Stefan had apparently forgotten to erase those changes when he interviewed for the Paris job.

So he had considered having clients call him by that nickname after all.

"I see," said Tessa, her heart sinking. "But—the thing is—"

"My friend said he is the very best," repeated the woman emphatically. "Do you know where I can find him? He arranged her son's wedding. She said he was a man, very smart, very... what is the word... artistic? He's expensive, I'm sure, but I can pay—" Here, she dug into her purse and produced a decorative antique cookie tin, painted blue with two birds on the lid. From beneath the lid's edge, part of a folded green dollar bill was protruding.

Those traces of a foreign accent in her voice—maybe they were Italian, Tessa thought at first; or maybe Eastern European, on second thought. The tin rattled, as if it contained both coins and bills.

"I have saved for sixty years," said the woman proudly. "Now I have my chance. My daughter said 'no' when she was young… but I will have my chance now that her son has found the right girl. Paolo's wedding will be the very best." Her smile was bright, brimming with eagerness to begin discussing her plans. "I promised his mother. I promised myself."

Stefan was on the other side of the ocean; there was no way he was coming back to plan the wedding of this woman's grandson. She seemed so desperate, so keen, that Tessa didn't have the heart to tell her the truth.

"Well…" she said. "You've certainly come to the right place." *If it were a few days ago, that is, when Stefan still worked here*, she wanted to add, but didn't. "The planner you're looking for was supposed to be here today—"

"Should I come back?" asked the woman eagerly. "I thought I could talk to him today. I thought—if he had time—I would show him some of the ideas I have saved for the wedding." From the pocket of her sweater came an envelope filled with clippings from magazines, snatches of bright flowers and decorative table settings. "I wanted to surprise Paolo and Molly with some special things."

Tessa's mind was racing for excuses. "I'll tell him, of course," she said. "And I'm sure… if you come back in a day or two, he'll be here. He'd be thrilled to see your ideas."

"Will he?" said the woman. "I am so glad. I want everything to be perfect. I will pay whatever he wants, for it will be only the best for them."

That tin probably only contained a few hundred dollars; maybe a couple of thousand were saved in it at most. Not a single wedding firm in town would take up this woman's offer… although probably her grandson and his fiancée were paying for part of it, too, Tessa reflected.

The grandmother just wanted to contribute some money toward a few special things, like she said.

And if they didn't have a planner yet…

"I'll give you our number so you can call and make an appointment," said Tessa, handing her a business card, and making a mental note to plug in the business phone right away. "We can talk about what you want for your family's wedding."

"Thank you," said the woman, tucking it happily in her purse. She clasped Tessa's hand in both of her own. "I'm so grateful. I will come back. I cannot wait to begin. I knew you would help me. You look so kind." She patted Tessa's hand with one of her own, then released her. "I will call soon." She glanced around the foyer as she opened the door. "You are… not moving away, are you?" she asked, puzzled.

"No. New location," said Tessa hastily. "Just moved in. We haven't finished unpacking yet." She smiled and waved as the door closed behind their would-be client.

"Are you nuts?" Natalie was in the doorway behind her, arms crossed. The steel edge in her voice was unmistakable. She had heard everything—the look on her face was one of scathing disbelief and disapproval.

Tessa sighed. "You saw her, Nat," she said. "No one else is going to take her seriously. She just wants to give her grandson a little something nice. Besides, we could use a client—if the odds are in favor of her grandson and granddaughter-in-law actually picking us."

"But Stefan's gone," said Natalie. "She only wants to talk to him. 'The best,' as her friend informed her, who's now working for some Parisian firm, probably. What are you going to tell her when she makes an appointment and wants to see him instead of us?"

"I don't know," Tessa admitted. "Maybe Stefan could recommend someone else—"

"While he's busy setting up a new life in Paris? Get real, Tessa. That weasel dumped this opportunity for that other job in a heartbeat. There's no way you can depend on him to help us now."

"Right," Tessa muttered reluctantly, even though she knew it was probably true. Her eye wandered toward the hallway in search of a distraction from her worries. She caught a glimpse of the handyman through the kitchen doorway as he unrolled a thick coil of electrical wire.

"Wait a minute," Tessa said to Natalie softly. "Maybe… maybe there's another way to make it work. So she *does* meet our wedding planner extraordinaire—or someone she thinks is him, at least."

"What do you mean?" Natalie asked. But she followed Tessa's gaze and saw the handyman too.

"No—" she began.

"Why not?" Tessa's voice was hushed, for fear of being overheard. "He'll be here. He's here every day. All he has to do is smile and say a few words and this woman will be happy that she spoke to 'the best.'"

"Him?" said Natalie.

"I don't know. I think it could work," said Tessa, tilting her gaze as she studied the contractor anew. He would probably look good in a suit, she reflected. Broad shoulders, nice height. A little help taming that hair, but still…

Knock it off, she told herself. This was business, after all. *Her* business—and if she was going to keep it from shutting down before it even got off the ground, she would need some extreme measures. A Stefan substitute to keep them afloat for one precious job might be the only way.

"If he's not in a tool belt, she won't know the difference," said Tessa. "Besides, she'll be heartbroken if she goes to another planner in town with those clippings and that cookie tin of dollar bills and they turn her away. You know they will, too."

"So we convince her that 'the best' planner in town works for chicken feed?" said Natalie.

"It's not as if Stefan was really the best, was he?" argued Tessa. Stefan had been the junior planner at Wedding Wonders for only a year at most, despite his burgeoning reputation in Bellegrove's wedding community. "We're talking about one afternoon's performance to make someone happy."

"What's going on?" Ama was still in the sitting room, perusing job listings via the wireless internet connection, which she hastily closed when they reappeared. Tessa saw it before the lid of the laptop closed: "wanted" ads for help at local bakeries, as the cupcake pictures made apparent. That was not a vote of confidence in their future.

Tessa and Natalie exchanged glances. "Do you want to tell her about your idea?" said Natalie.

Ama listened with surprise, skepticism, then a look of incredulity, until Tessa's suggestion was fully formed. "You want our handyman to pretend to be an experienced wedding planner?" she said. "For an old lady whose life savings fit in a cookie box?"

"It's one afternoon," said Tessa. "Probably her family will balk at the idea of hiring us and we'll never see her again. But if for some reason they're interested, why couldn't we handle the details? They're not hiring a planner, they're hiring a firm. An affordable firm, obviously. Us, the all-in-one package."

"She said that?"

"She will, after 'the best' of wedding planners tells her to do it, right?" said Natalie, not completely without sarcasm.

"Does anyone here have a better plan?" challenged Tessa. "A better way for us to get a client, now that our only experienced partner is gone? A better way to break it to that sweet little old lady that the event planner recommended to her just moved to France? I couldn't do it, but maybe one of you won't mind disappointing her."

She waited for either of them to volunteer. Ama looked uneasy. "Are you sure she's not just a little mixed up?" she ventured. "Maybe she wandered in by mistake?"

"She seemed sane to me," said Tessa. "A little clueless about how the modern wedding scene works since she's so fixated on having Stefan... but that's just her taste, maybe."

"Ugh. A man who actually created 'cupcake tinsel' for a wedding." Natalie stuck out her tongue as she made a face of repulsion.

"I guess that's why she asked someone to point her in the right direction," concluded Tessa, as if her friend hadn't spoken. "It was just bad luck for her that her friend's raved-about event was planned by Wedding Wonders."

They were all three quiet now. "I suppose it wouldn't hurt to let her think we have a fourth partner who's planned a wedding or two," said Ama reluctantly.

"Like you said, her family probably won't hire us anyway," said Natalie grimly. "As if they can afford to hire anybody with chump change from a cookie tin."

"But we would definitely be cheaper than any other firm in town," said Ama. "Although we *are* a little short on capital right now." To punctuate her statement came the sound of a sledgehammer punching through plaster and drywall in the kitchen. "Not that it matters, since we won't actually be working for her."

The sound of debris crumbing to the floor on the other side of the wall followed.

"What's his name?" asked Ama. "The contractor." They were all looking in the direction of the future kitchen, thinking the same thing right now.

"Blake Ellingham," said Tessa.

"That's a nice name," said Ama.

"Very professional," said Natalie. "Like *Downton Abbey* or something."

"I think the client would like it," said Tessa. "It sounds better than Stefan Groeder, when you think about it."

Another pause. "So who wants to tell him?" asked Natalie.

Blake was whistling as he wove several separate wire strands into the ones sticking out of a wall socket, pausing when he noticed the three of them in the kitchen doorway. He offered them a polite smile.

"Something I can do for you?" he asked. As if sensing something was already amiss, the handyman's smile became both uncertain and slightly suspicious.

"Actually," began Tessa. "There is."

Chapter Nine

By the time Tessa had found a phone and plugged it into the business's landline, the surprise client was ready to phone their number, wasting no time. An appointment for one Bianca Fazolli and family for the next afternoon.

"I can't believe someone is this eager to meet us," said Tessa, as she rushed to make the foyer look more presentable—that is, by removing all boxes from sight and hanging up a few paintings borrowed from her apartment. "Whatever that family friend said about Stefan, it must have painted him to be a genius." She kicked a fake Asian rug over one of the floor's worst spots.

"Is he?" asked Ama, as she pushed a small love seat against the sitting room's wall and tried to disguise its worn cushions beneath a rich, velvety sofa shawl that usually adorned one of Tessa's apartment chairs. "You know him best of anybody here. And you seem to like him, at least a little bit."

"Not really," admitted Tessa. "On either score." Although he would seem brilliant next to his stand-in when it came to flowers and fondant, probably. "Natalie's right in the fact that Stefan is a little... well... showy." His crowning achievement was his Cinderella wedding, which was probably what earned him the Paris opportunity. Pictures of the bride in her glass carriage and her dream fairytale cake had flooded the planner's Pinterest board for weeks afterward. "It wows people, sure. But it also seems a little impersonal. Glittery. Created to impress for the sake of someone's big ego, not their special dreams."

She stopped here, because it sounded ridiculous to talk about Stefan's work this way. It wasn't as if she had done anything better herself, was it? At least Stefan's clients had been happy with the results, even if their big day resembled an over-frosted cupcake.

Natalie bustled through the front door, carrying a garment bag. "Sorry I'm late," she began. "A big garment shipment arrived today, and I was trying to help Cal sort them into the storage room."

Kandace's Kreations' storage room was supposed to serve as a warehouse for the designer's supplies and finished garments for shipment—but not that many retailers were clamoring for a Kandace original, which was why it stood empty. The designer had recently sublet the space to a tuxedo and bridal rental shop undergoing remodeling.

"Did you get it?" Ama asked, tossing a pillow onto one of the stiff chairs circling the little coffee table.

"See for yourself." Natalie unzipped the garment bag she was carrying. "One genuine Armani suit in the latest style. I picked it out myself."

"Nice," said Ama. "It's straight from the cover of *GQ*."

"Will they notice it's missing?" Tessa asked.

"Not if we get it back to the warehouse pronto," said Natalie. "Where's our fourth partner?"

"Upstairs, looking at the drywall situation," said Tessa. "I... didn't exactly tell him about this part."

Blake looked less than thrilled when they ambushed him with the suit upstairs. "You didn't mention anything about changing my appearance for this," he told them, pushing a pair of safety glasses back onto his forehead. "You said I just had to say a couple of nice words to your client."

"What's the problem? It's just a suit," said Tessa. "You have worn one before, right?"

"Believe it or not, yes. I even own one or two, so you didn't have to waste your money on a rental." His gaze bordered on scorn with these words—if it weren't for the fact that Tessa was running on pure desperation at the moment, she might have blushed. Determination kept her from it.

"It wasn't a waste, trust me," said Natalie. "This occasion calls for something a little more refined than an off-the-rack suit. They expect you to look sophisticated. It's only for one afternoon—is it so terrible to humor us for a couple of hours?"

"Not terrible," he replied. "Just not necessary, in my opinion. You told me she's never even met this Stefan friend of yours. Maybe she'll be convinced he's just a casual guy if that's what he appears to be."

"She's seen a picture of him." Albeit not a good one, but Blake could be seen to resemble it a little, to a strong imagination. "She probably *does* know that a wedding planner wouldn't dress like a lumberjack," Tessa pointed out. "Trust me, if she knows anything about Stefan, she'll expect something extra special. It's all about expectations."

"You will look great in this," promised Natalie.

"Just try it on," coaxed Ama.

"Please?" added Tessa. "If you hate it, or it doesn't fit, then we'll talk about an alternative."

A sigh of defeat came from the contractor. "All right," he told them. "I'll agree to try it on. But I'm not making any promises yet." He took the garment bag from Natalie's hand and disappeared into the bathroom.

"Too bad he doesn't have time for a shave," Tessa muttered.

"It could be worse," Natalie muttered back. "Stefan was almost bald last summer after that terrible stylist's cut. Remember how he was all but crying over it at Tonya's party?"

The contractor's unruly mane of hair—would it look too untamed for a professional? Tessa wondered. And what about a quick shave? She was still worrying about these things when the door opened and Blake emerged.

"The tie is a little crooked"—he gave it an apologetic tug—"but is the rest of it what you expected?" He asked this begrudgingly.

Natalie let out a wolf whistle. Ama covered her mouth. "Wow," she said. "That's amazing."

It was amazing. Blake the handyman had been, in a word, transformed.

Gone was the too-casual flannel-clad figure in work boots and denim Tessa remembered—not entirely unpleasantly—from their first meeting. In his place, a man of tall, dark, and handsome sophistication had appeared, in a tailored suit filled out to perfection. Even the stubble on his jaw went perfectly with it, and his dark mane looked sexy instead of scruffy.

Tessa crossed her fingers that their client Bianca's friend had never described Stefan and that she had only his tiny internet photo to identify him by—the event planner was neither tall nor so devastatingly handsome as Blake, though if you counted his dark hair, at least they shared one quality.

"That's not bad," she said to Blake. It was better than that, but she couldn't bring herself to say it, not about the contractor. "It'll certainly do for one afternoon. You—you clean up nicely, I mean." She didn't blush. She wasn't even sure why she almost had. It wasn't as if she'd never seen a guy look handsome in a suit, after all.

Natalie and Ama were looking at her like she was crazy. "Nice—is not the word," said Natalie to him. "I can think of several others. Smoking. Hot. But I don't want to make him blush by saying them aloud."

The contractor's face turned red in response. "I don't know about—" he began, reaching up as if to loosen the tie he was wearing.

"That tie *is* a little crooked," said Tessa.

Moving closer, she refashioned the silk knot and slipped it into place, before he had time to loosen it and pull it off. For a second, their eyes met. Tessa realized the tie's color was a perfect match for his eyes. Amazing what a simple strip of fabric could make someone notice about another person.

She stepped back, putting space between them. "Much better," she declared. "I think we're ready for stage two."

"Stage what?" Blake was suspicious again, glancing from one to the other for an explanation. "Wait a minute," he began. "All I agreed to do was put on the suit. Maybe wave at your client and say hi."

"You didn't think we just needed you to wear the suit and not say anything, did you? You'll have to interact with them a little, maybe answer a question or two. Nothing too hard, really."

"We swear," said Ama quickly.

"I'm not an actor," Blake protested.

"You already look the part," said Natalie. "You just need some background on your character, so to speak. Show him the pictures, Tessa," she suggested. "Just in case they ask any questions."

"Great idea." Tessa pulled her laptop from its bag, flipping it open on the nearby folding table. "These are from some of Stefan's events," she told him, bringing up the digital albums on the website she was building. She hadn't deleted any of Stefan's stuff from its photo page yet, as luck would have it. She put the first album on slideshow, as the four of them gathered around the screen.

Unfortunately, the photos highlighted the most extravagant and outrageous events of Stefan's career. The *Midsummer Night's Dream* wedding party dressed as woodland elves and nymphs proceeded down the aisle of a forest park in autumn, wearing flowered head wreaths and sporting pointy ears touched up with glitter. She thought she heard Blake cough—or stifle a snort—but she didn't dare turn around to see his expression. A similar sound accompanied the photo from a Valentine's Day wedding, with the chorale in red satin robes and glittery makeup, and the twin ring bearers dressed as Cupid.

"These are weddings somebody actually wanted planned, you said?"

"Of course. These had huge budgets. Some of them were almost like… society weddings," she explained, for lack of a better description. One had involved the daughter of a state senator, at least.

That statement was left to sink in as a photo of the six-layer Valentine's heart cake popped up, dazzling in ruby glitter. Maybe they should have warned him ahead of the bride who appeared next onscreen, arrayed in a glittering silver and white princess ball gown and seated in a giant transparent horse-drawn carriage, accompanied by three footmen in gold and white uniforms with powdered wigs.

"Ah, the famous Cinderella wedding," said Natalie. "I've heard about that one. Stefan was fawning over those glass-slipper wedding favors he ordered. The gold coins they're tossing to onlookers are chocolate, right? With Stefan, you can't be sure it wasn't some sort of commemorative piece with the bride and groom's pictures embossed on it." A touch of mockery was in Natalie's voice.

"Is that a diamond crown on the groom?" Ama leaned toward the screen.

"Are those trained white *mice*?" Blake spoke again, and not happily.

"The ring was in the little glass carriage they're pulling," explained Tessa, exasperated. "I know it's a bit over the top—but the bride really liked the idea, apparently." It had taken Stefan weeks to find someone who actually trained performing mice, he had told her once at a party.

"I can't believe someone actually requested that for their wedding," said Ama.

"I can't believe someone actually requested *that* for their wedding." Natalie was pointing to the cake from Stefan's "Italian Romance" wedding: a twelve-layer monstrosity sculpted to resemble the Leaning Tower of Pisa, surrounded by two-toned cabbage roses made from frosting and giant marzipan turtledoves at its base. "I mean, I'm all for celebrating, but why not do it with class? That thing screams like an undignified tourist trap. It looks ready to sink under the weight of its own icing."

Next to her, Blake cleared his throat. "I'm not sure about this," he said.

"You don't have to suggest anything original. Just say a few nice words about whatever the clients like," said Tessa.

"I can't pull this off. I can't make them believe that I was somehow connected with… all this." He was eyeing the computer screen's latest image. "It's not my style. I mean, if I *were* an event planner, or a creative person, which I'm not. Clearly." He added this part with emphasis.

"Can't you just pretend? It's only for one conversation, anyway," wheedled Tessa. "Please." Unless they landed this wedding, somehow. But that was just too crazy an idea to actually happen.

"Just smile and nod a lot," Ama suggested. "And say their ideas are fabulous, or something."

"Fabulous?" Blake spoke it like a foreign word he wasn't sure how to pronounce.

"Maybe just say 'divine' instead," continued Ama. "Isn't that what all the hosts say on TV decorating shows?"

"What *did* Stefan usually say?" Natalie asked. "Besides that everything he did was 'marvelous' or 'fab,' I mean?"

Downstairs, the sound of the door's entry bell jingled. "They're *here*," said Natalie, in a hushed tone of horror, as her joking attitude died a sudden death. "They're an hour early!"

"Quick, go down and stall them," whispered Tessa. Natalie sprinted downstairs. "Where's our official planning binder?"

"Over there," said Ama, who looked nervous as she straightened her dress. "Okay, let's be calm…"

"They're in the parlor," said Tessa, who could hear the murmur of voices disappearing from the foyer. "Time to go." She seized Blake's left arm, with Ama on the right, half-dragging him downstairs before he could escape.

"Wait!" he hissed. "No, I'm not—"

At the foot of the stairs, Ama paused to look at Tessa. "We're keeping the name, right?"

"What name?" Blake asked. He sounded suspicious.

"Sure. It sounds great, right?" said Tessa.

"*My* name? Wait a moment. I never agreed to any—"

Tessa opened the door to the sitting room, revealing three strangers on the love seat, awaiting the wedding planners' arrival. She nudged Blake, who gave her an extremely bitter look—thankfully, with his face averted from their clients.

Maybe it was the pleading in her eyes, a silent begging to save his paycheck and theirs, that caused him to turn toward the parlor again. He forced a smile in place that seemed… well… almost charming. Almost.

Tiny, bird-like Bianca sat directly across from Tessa, clutching her oversized purse on her lap, and adjusting a rather awkward-looking pair of reading glasses on her face. Her hair was cut short and spiky, and had been lightly tinted with a reddish-gingery color, her age betrayed by the deep, wrinkly lines across her face, and over the careworn hands that were undoing the clasps of her bag.

Beside her, her grandson Paolo, a cute dark-haired young man, looked slightly nervous; as did his fiancée, Molly, a fair-haired girl with a shy smile.

"I am so glad that you let us come back," Bianca said. "The young man next to you—he's the one my friend told me about? The one who arranged the beautiful wedding at the big hotel?"

"He's the only male wedding planner at this firm," Tessa answered, keeping her voice bright, despite the nervous beat of her heart.

"I'm sorry," said Bianca. "I forgot your name. What was it again?" She held out her hand to Blake.

"It's… Blake Ellingham," he said. "Call me Blake, please." He shook hands with her.

"That name," Bianca said, looking slightly puzzled. "It doesn't sound right to me. It was… something else, I think." Her brow was furrowed in a worried look as the three wedding planners held their breaths collectively.

After a moment Natalie piped up, saying, "We just call him 'The Wedding Guru.' That's his professional nickname." She shot a smile in Blake's direction, who looked as if he'd just tasted something sour.

Light dawned in Bianca's eyes as she nodded. "Yes, that is the name. I remember it now."

"Just Blake is fine," he repeated. "Please." He adjusted his tie as if it were strangling him.

"My friend's son had such a lovely wedding," continued Bianca. "I saw the pictures. Ooh la la—such a cake, with the big candy doves on the top! Such flowers! And that beautiful carriage with the horses. Just like a fairytale! You must have worked so very hard to make it so good."

That was the wedding Stefan had planned for her friend's son? The Cinderella one? It was Stefan's crowning achievement, and his most expensive, Tessa knew. It was his vision of a fairytale for the daughter of a state senator and the son of a fledgling hedge fund manager for whom lunch at the Four Seasons was a casual dining event.

"There were little chocolates at every person's place at the tables," Bianca informed the bride-to-be—who had probably heard this anecdote a dozen times already. "They were shaped just like little mice, so delicate and pretty. The slipper, too, in the little gift bag. It was real glass, just like in the story."

"It all sounds so impressive." The girl, Molly, sounded a little overwhelmed. No doubt, she was thinking of the cost behind such an event.

Bianca turned to Blake again, asking, "You do remember my friend's son's wedding, don't you? Stella Delveccio?"

"Umm…" A long pause, during which Tessa held her breath, and tried not to clench her hands with worry. "Yes. Of course I remember it," Blake answered, as relief flooded through Tessa.

"It was your best. Wasn't it?" continued Bianca.

"The best?" Blake paused. Prompted by a gentle kick from Tessa beside him, he went on: "The carriage and flowers… were fabulous, weren't they?" He followed this with a smile that seemed polite and bright but also extremely uncomfortable, if you were a good judge of smiles. "And the mice. Definitely the mice." He gave the smile of a man who would never understand the concept of harnessing rodents to a fashion doll's carriage.

At least he hadn't bailed on them, Tessa consoled herself. Yet.

"The mice?" said Molly, confused.

"Cinderella. You know—the mice," said Bianca. "I wasn't so fond of them myself… but you can come up with ideas that are even better, I'm sure." She patted Blake's arm lightly. Tessa saw a gleam in his eyes that suggested he was dangerously close to disowning his role.

"Did you see the crystal-studded bouquet?" asked Tessa brightly.

"Oooh, yes. So pretty." Bianca laid a hand over her heart.

"And the ceremonial crowning before the kiss?" piped up Natalie, who was pretending *very* hard to find Stefan's ideas charming.

"I saw a photo of it," said Molly. "I thought it was kind of romantic. Would you like to exchange crowns instead of rings at our wedding, honey?" she teased Paolo, although her smile was as shy as ever.

"No, thanks. I don't look good in diamonds," he answered, squeezing her hand.

"You have such good ideas for weddings," Bianca marveled to Blake. "So many, too. I listen to my friend talk about this wedding you planned for her and say to myself, 'Where does he get such ideas?'"

"You know," said Blake, "I've wondered that myself. Sometimes it's like they just… pull themselves out of the strangest places." His glance flickered ever so briefly toward the wastebasket. "I guess marvelous details just know what place they belong. Although they sometimes escape it, too."

He might have received a less gentle kick from Tessa for this remark, except for the lack of irony in his voice, which made him sound serious enough… and a little charming… on the outside.

"Blake is very modest, isn't he?" said Tessa. "He doesn't like to take credit for his work."

"See? Then he is the right one," said Bianca. "Good. I can cross it off my list." From her bag, she produced a very wrinkled list and put a big mark through the topmost item using a black marker. "Now we have the best planner," she informed the two young people beside her. "We are done with that step already."

"What?" Blake and Tessa spoke at almost the same moment. Had she really just hired them? Natalie and Ama wore equally surprised expressions—even the bride and groom seemed uncertain what to make of this announcement.

"You all plan the weddings, too?" Bianca asked, looking from one to the next among the three women seated there.

"Yes," said Tessa, who found her voice now. "We're... we're the all-in-one package, like it says on the website. Cake, dress, flowers, music—we provide it all."

"Website?" repeated Bianca. "The internet. I don't know the internet too well." She shook her head. "Too many places. I get lost."

Her accent was getting thicker now, but Tessa still couldn't place it. Paolo patted his grandmother's hand. "Gran mostly heard about you through word of mouth, from her friend who was so happy with her experience," he said. "Actually, Molly and I hadn't really looked at any event planners yet. We weren't sure we could afford one, truthfully."

"I have the money," insisted Bianca. "*I'm* paying."

"Gran—" he began.

"This gentleman and these ladies say they will do it all for us, right?" said Bianca. "They look nice. They look like people who understand that things have to be special."

"Well, I'm one of the event planners," said Tessa. "That's the role of me and—and Blake." She gave him an innocent smile. "We're the ones who generally worry about putting the event together exactly the way you want it. Natalie here knows all about dresses and fashion, and Ama is our in-house cake designer."

"We want a *big* cake," began Bianca.

"Gran, we don't have that many guests," said Molly. "Paolo only has some friends from work, and I have some of my clients coming. We don't need all this fuss."

"We don't exactly have a lot of family—either of us," Paolo explained to the planners.

"And a nice dress for Molly," continued Bianca, who clearly wasn't listening. She laid her hand on Molly's arm. "Something big and beautiful. It must be so perfect that everyone will be staring at you. Like the dress for my friend's daughter-in-law. That is what I want." She looked at Tessa and Blake. "You can do it, I am sure. They need someone to make everything special."

"I don't think you can pay for perfect, Gran," said Paolo gently.

"You'd be surprised," Natalie spoke up. "We're a new firm, so we'll be cutting costs wherever we can. I have a lot of contacts in the garment world, for instance—I got a friend of mine a great deal on a wedding dress only a month ago. Sometimes perfect is all about finding the right thing at the right time."

All of this was technically true—although the bargain she mentioned had been down to Natalie's personal friendship with a bridal shop's manager and not any contacts made through working in the fashion world for Kandace. But Natalie looked confident when she said it, unlike when she talked about her own talent.

"We can find something to fit your budget on any front," said Ama. "Me? I'm a very economic baker. It's definitely possible to find special things that don't cost a fortune."

"I told you not to worry about the money," said Bianca dismissively. "I will pay it. I only want the best. Stella gave me the name of the best planner in the city, and my friend Lucca gave me the name of the best florist..." Here, she began digging through her bag again, no doubt looking for some item related to this other piece of wedding advice.

"Will your friend Stella be coming to the wedding?" Tessa asked, foreseeing a new complication if Stefan's former client should happen to encounter his rather unconvincing stand-in. Bianca, however, shook her head.

"Not Stella. She has moved to a retirement community with her husband now. Such a pretty place by the sea—Venice, Florida, the postcard said that she sent me."

Phew. Tessa breathed a sigh of relief and imagined her business partners doing so as well, though Blake looked as uncomfortable as ever. Bianca had finished searching her bag by now, producing an overstuffed envelope of clippings.

"Here are some things that might look good. Molly, you liked this one in the magazine? The one you bought from the newspaper stand?" She removed a poorly folded clipping from a catalog, featuring a ball gown-style wedding dress bedecked with lots of crystals on its bodice, a definite designer creation. And definitely similar to the "Cinderella" gown for Stefan's client, although without such a pouffy skirt that the bride would have to pass sideways through a standard doorway.

"And here is a fancy table at a hotel that would look so very nice."

"Gran, I think it's really costly," said Molly, sounding hesitant. "And that dress seems a little elaborate, too. I'm not sure it's right for me, really."

"What do you think?" asked Bianca, looking anxiously at the planners. Blake glanced at Tessa, and she could see the discomfort in his gaze. Clearly, he wasn't going to tell Bianca it was all great.

Natalie and Tessa exchanged glances quickly. "Why don't we talk to Paolo and Molly about what they want?" Tessa suggested. "They must have some ideas already, surely." She turned her attention to the bride and the groom.

Paolo shrugged. "I just want to marry Molly," he said. "And not spend all of Gran's money," he added, giving his grandmother's shoulder a gentle squeeze. "I'd rather pay for it myself and save her money."

"And what would I have saved all this money for?" demanded Bianca. Tessa remembered the cookie tin from their last meeting. "It's to give you and Molly a nice wedding and reception."

"I don't really know what I want when it comes to a dress or anything," said Molly. "I didn't really plan on having anything. Paolo and I don't make a lot of money, so I hadn't really been thinking about fancy gowns and reception favors, or anything. It was Bianca's idea for us to have a real wedding."

"Is your retaining fee reasonable?" Paolo asked. "If it's not too much, we'll hire you. If only to make Gran happy." He smiled at them, a grin of surrender as his grandmother pinched him in rebuke.

Tessa hesitated, then wrote a figure on a sheet of paper and showed it to Ama and Natalie—remembering at the last minute to show it to Blake beside her as well. He looked surprised at the figure written on it. A thousand dollars wasn't much, after all. No doubt he was thinking it wouldn't pay for the kitchen he was supposed to be creating out of the building's shambles of a back room.

"This is the fee for hiring us to arrange all the details. Hiring a venue, entertainment, arranging the invitations," said Tessa. "It doesn't include things like the venue, the dress or the food, or additional expenses during the process, but we can help you keep those well under budget. It's basically the cost for us negotiating deals on your behalf—and if you hire us to do the dress or cake for you, we'll give you the best deal possible."

"Look at that! I told you they were nice people," said Bianca, sounding excited. "There will be plenty left for planning the wedding. It will be perfect."

"I guess you guys are hired," said Paolo.

"Come to my home for tea," said Bianca insistently, as she put the clippings back in her purse, where the tin of money clanked noisily. "We'll talk about the big plans there."

"Sounds just great," said Tessa.

Of course, really it sounded more like a possible disaster. But she would never admit that in a million years.

Chapter Ten

"What are you doing with those sketches?" asked Natalie's brother Roberto. "Is Kandace finally letting you design something for her boutique?"

He closed the fridge after removing a bottle of milk. Natalie closed her sketchbook. "It's something for one of my classes," she said. Roberto wouldn't remember that she only had one class in textiles this season and none in design. "I'm supposed to be writing a business proposal for my class on Friday."

"That's gonna be disappointing for Ma. She thinks you have a big date on Friday."

"What? With Jake?" she said dismissively. "He's just a guy who asked me out for coffee. Afterward, maybe a movie. It's no big thing, trust me." She flipped open her textbook and made a pretense of studying. "Besides, I promised I'd come by the bakery after hours and help Aunt Louise with the bones of the dead."

The traditional Italian cookies were delicious, and a favorite in the bakery even when it wasn't All Souls' Day. This month's window display theme at the bakery was Italian holidays and weddings.

"'No big thing' is a big problem for her," he said. "She doesn't understand the whole casual dating routine you're into. Do you really want another family dinner where everybody's asking if you've found 'Mr. Right' yet?" He poured milk over his bowl of cereal. "It'll keep happening unless you get serious about one of these guys, Nat."

"I don't think there's a Mr. Right," answered Natalie. "I'm not a big believer in true love. You know that." She hid a smile as she turned the pages of her textbook. Her brother had a habit of turning the heat on her since he hadn't found 'Ms. Right,' as their mother constantly pointed out. "Why don't you marry Kimmie and make Ma happy? *That* would take her mind off me and my love life."

"Kimmie's not interested in marriage," he said. "Besides, Ma knows she can count on me to do the right thing in the end. It's you she doesn't trust." He pointed at her as he spoke these words. "She's starting to think your only baby will be your college degree."

"There are worse things in the world," she pointed out.

The kitchen smelled of fresh-baked bread and pasta flour; her uncle had been making fettuccine and the noodles were drying all around her. Her brother, who had volunteered to help make cinnamon rolls this morning, was now wearing his firefighter's t-shirt as he prepared to leave for his overnight shift, eating the last of the leftover manicotti in addition to his bowlful of cereal. Natalie rolled her eyes at the sight.

"I hope this Jake isn't like the usual losers you date," said Roberto.

"You won't have to meet him, so don't worry."

The door to the kitchen opened and a deliveryman in a green company uniform struggled inside, wheeling a hand truck from which he deposited two heavy burlap bags of flour in the corner. "Ciao," he greeted them—focusing on Natalie in particular—in Italian, although the deliveryman's heritage lay elsewhere. She pretended to be busy studying too hard to notice. "How's it going, Roberto?" he asked.

"Hey, Brayden," said Roberto. "Is that the pastry flour Ma's been dying for?"

"If you sent for it, I brought it," he said. "You're my last stop of the day, so I'll even stock it in the pantry for you, if you want."

"That would be great," Roberto said. "I'll open up the doors." He pushed the storeroom doors wide for the deliveryman, who brought in two more loads of flour, the organic stone-ground kind her mother preferred for certain special recipes. With a grunt, he lifted them on top of the heap, close to the big automated grinder the Grenaldis sometimes used to make their own flour from imported whole grain.

"So... Natalie. How's classes?" On his way back from the pantry, the deliveryman had paused to linger by the table where Natalie was studying. He looked over her shoulder at the open page of her textbook, which outlined the history of post-war French silk.

"Okay," she answered. *Go away*, she added silently.

"I'll bet you're at the top of the class, aren't you?" he said. "I know you. You wouldn't be happy otherwise. In school, whenever somebody got ahead, you'd work hard to catch up to them, even if you couldn't— even in geometry, and you pretty much hated it."

"Yup." She turned the page in her book.

He waited, and when she didn't say anything else, he added, "Silk fabric, huh?" He studied the page. "That's... what's it... Coco Chanel, right?"

"Mmph," she answered. "Good guess."

Brayden dawdled. "Design any new dresses lately?"

"Not really."

"I remember that one you made for prom. I think of it when I see the ones in the windows on the Avenue all the time when I'm delivering stuff downtown—I went in that big designer's showroom last week to deliver a couple of boxes. Did Robbie tell you? Goodman's. You know it, right?"

"Sure." It was the most exclusive design house in the city, but Natalie's attitude remained one of polite disinterest at this fact.

"They had some of their new clothes on mannequins in the back—" Here, Natalie almost sneaked a look at him, but kept her eyes firmly rooted on the page instead. "It wasn't anything that amazing. Their stuff can't touch yours, and you're still studying how to do it."

"Thanks." Short answers should work, but they were failing once again. Didn't he have to hurry home and shower? Eat dinner? Anything else but bother her while she was so clearly busy?

Brayden shifted his weight from one foot to the other. He cleared his throat. "Did I tell you that I was thinking about taking some night classes?" he asked. A pause, which received only silence in reply. "I know I wasn't that good at it in school, but I thought maybe I would give it a try just for fun…"

"Speech class?" suggested Natalie sarcastically.

Brayden laughed a little. *Doesn't he at least have the decency to be wounded?* she thought.

"I was talking about mechanical engineering," he said. "I used to fool around in shop class, but I always wished I could be good at it. The company pays mechanics pretty good, see—you get promoted faster in mechanics than in delivery. Not that I'm thinking about changing, necessarily. Who knows?"

"Good for you."

"Maybe you could give me some pointers on how I'd get started. Maybe who to talk to at the college?"

"I think you should talk to the registrar's office, not me," pointed out Natalie.

"Forget it, Brayden," said Roberto, who was shrugging on his jacket. "She's not interested. She doesn't have time for average nice guys. I'm thinking maybe she was adopted and she's not really Italian."

"Maybe I just want to be sure I end up with a guy who's nothing like you, brother dearest," said Natalie archly, sticking out her tongue at Roberto.

Brayden laughed at this, too. "Seriously?" Natalie said to him, finally looking in his direction. "That was a terrible joke. You don't have to laugh at it just because I said it, Brayden. Really."

"Guess I just have a bad sense of humor," said Brayden, shrugging his shoulders. He gave her a smile—honest, hopeful, and every bit as terrible and homely as his sense of humor.

His hopefulness was typical, as were the rumples in his uniform, the smell of exhaust from his truck's muffler, and the ink stains from his delivery sheet's pen. Brayden had splattered his fingers and his shirt with his leaky pen again, she noticed. He had the worst luck and the dumbest accidents, marking him as one of karma's biggest losers, but Brayden was a persistent optimist—even after he had given her a handful of dandelions in the second-grade playground and she had left them to wilt on the swing seat as a not-so-subtle expression of rejection.

"I have to go," she said, closing her book and gathering up her things. "I have to pick up my stuff at Kandace's before I go to class. She'll want me out of the studio loft as soon as she knows I'm quitting."

"You're leaving Kandace?" asked Roberto.

"I am," she said. "The business I'm starting got a paying gig, so I've decided to take it as a sign."

"But to quit your job after getting one lousy event," said Roberto, with a half-smile of brotherly concern and sheer amazement. "What if nobody else hires you?"

"They will," said Natalie, grinning slightly. " I could probably get a part-time job at the bridal rental boutique, using her place as storage, if nothing else. So long as they don't know about the suit I borrowed, at least." She could work at a dozen different places in town, from her family's bakery to her cousin's restaurant—none of them were in the fashion world, true, but they would pay the bills.

"You started a business? Robbie, you didn't tell me about this. Hey, congratulations, Nat!" said Brayden. "I always knew you'd do something great. I wish you had said something before. I would have gotten you something for luck, or maybe a congratulatory gift—"

"Not necessary," said Natalie shortly. "I gotta go. Take care." She made her escape with her books and her bag. If Roberto dared to snicker, she would pinch him black and blue later.

Kandace's gaze was neither teasing nor admiring as Natalie packed up her workspace at the studio. The designer was fuming silently, a death glare focused on her now ex-employee, who was reflecting with relief on her lucky escape from having to help Cal put together the latest weird asymmetrical tunics made of shiny Lycra. The one pinned on the mannequin looked like a tight version of Scrooge's nightshirt.

"Two years I've let you work here, and what do you do?" Kandace asked. "You walk out without so much as giving notice. Turn your back on me in my crisis of need so you can go clean tuxedos for a living."

With a snort of outrage, she slammed some random supplies into the box. Natalie's ladybug stapler, and the wobbly fabric cutter that Natalie knew was the studio's, since hers was newer and nicer—and probably now appropriated by her ex-employer, like a million other sewing tools of Natalie's ownership.

"I need a new start, Kandace." Natalie tossed her scissors and her wrist pincushion into the box. "You've never been happy with my work—I thought you'd be thrilled to see me go."

"Lose my seamstress at my busiest time? Nat, listen to me: what you lack in design talent you make up for in technical skill. You're amazing at executing a design. You were *born* to be an assistant. This is because of Eduardo, isn't it? He's been threatening to steal you away since the Street Spirit show, just because his creepy little assistant wanted to be a novelist—"

"I'm not going to work for another designer," Natalie answered. "I need a change. I know what you're saying, but I'm not sure that I'm cut out to be an assistant. I want to try something else for a while. I'm starting my own business."

"Doing what?" Kandace laughed forcefully. "I hope you don't believe you've got what it takes to design, Natalie. I thought we'd finally made some progress on the difference between art and imitations. Really, honey. I didn't think you were *that* stupid." She rolled her eyes as she ripped one of Natalie's sketches off the wall, leaving a piece of it stuck beneath the thumbtack.

Resentment burned inside Natalie. "Actually, design will be a big part of my job at the new wedding planning firm," she replied, seeing Kandace's expression darken even more. "So maybe my style has more potential than you believe. I think the biggest problem is that you and I have different definitions of art," she added. "To be honest—I'd rather clean frosting off bridesmaids' dresses than sew more glitter patches on Peter Pan's tights." She cast an eye in the direction of the designer's sketches, one of which Cal had labeled "demented orphan fairy" fashions.

Kandace's face was red with fury. "Go ahead. Stab me in the back after I gave you a chance," she said. "That's more than anybody else in this town did for you. Just don't try to come back afterward when you regret leaving the *best*! Understood? You're not quitting—I'm *firing* you, you lousy little traitor!" She stuffed Natalie's crushed sketch into the bottom of the box, then swept herself from the loft.

Natalie didn't answer. She dropped her green dress into the box, which held the other designs she'd completed from her own sketches in the past—all of which had failed to meet Kandace's approval and earn a place on one of the random hangers downstairs.

She lifted the box. With one last glance at the loft around her, she released a sigh, although she wasn't feeling regretful. Two years had been a long time to spend in this place, but she was ready to leave in a way. What kind of future did she have in sewing rayon crocodile scales on a corset, anyway? She wouldn't miss it one bit, even if Tessa's plan crashed and burned.

With that thought, Natalie hoisted her box and went downstairs.

"Goodbye and thanks for nothing." Kandace's tone was spiteful. She was tying price tags on the finished "Twisted Symmetry" line at the shop's counter. The short, diamond-patterned dress was among them, to which Kandace had recently added two more weird clown buttons.

Natalie ignored this goodbye. As she walked past the bargain rack, she felt Cal catch her sleeve, a desperate look in his eyes.

"As soon as your business is rolling, hire me," he whispered.

"Oh, no you don't," said Blake Ellingham warningly, holding up his hands. "Not me. Not again."

"We need you, though," said Tessa. "You want us to be able to pay for your services thus far, don't you? How can we do that if we have to close our doors because we rejected a business opportunity?"

"You could find a way," said Blake firmly. "You're very resourceful."

"Not if we declare bankruptcy," Natalie suggested. "It's bad PR for us if we turn down this job."

Blake sighed, hands resting against the wall he was measuring. "I told you I would help you do this one time. You told me that was all you needed."

"That's what we thought," said Ama. "Please. Think of all the things we can hire you to do if you help us out for this job. The dry rot—the leak in the ceiling—the kitchen cabinets…"

"The bathroom floor on the second story," chimed in Natalie.

"Not to mention all the restoration work this place needs," said Tessa. "One happy client can become a dozen more in this business. Like Ama says, we can hire you to remodel our whole building in the future. Think how much you loved the idea—working on a historic old building in this part of town—"

"Bringing back its former glory," added Ama. "Wouldn't that look great on your list of credentials?"

"We'll pay you," said Tessa quickly. "For your work as a fake wedding consultant. We'll give you a percentage of our fees, just like you were part of the business. How's that?"

"Shocking," he answered. "And a little desperate." But he offered no sign of giving in.

"Then help us," pleaded Tessa. "Otherwise, you'll probably never see a dime for your work." This was exaggerated, of course, but she was feeling extra-desperate. "How else are we going to pay you if we've all quit our jobs?"

"Actually, I haven't quit mine," said Ama. "But it would take a lot of months of cookie and cupcake orders to pay the kind of bills we're talking about."

"Who knows when I'll get another job now that I'm free of Kandace," Natalie chipped in, although with a slightly dishonest assessment of her situation, since she could at least pick up extra work at her family's bakery. "Could take weeks, and even then, it'll probably just be part-time."

There was a long pause, then Blake let out another sigh. One hand raked through his dark mane as he leaned against the worktable. Tessa thought he might bury his face and groan in a moment, instead of simply thinking it over. "Just until this client of yours is gone," he said at last. "And only when it's necessary for me to show up. I have other obligations besides this place and your problems, you realize."

"I promise," said Tessa. "We will keep you in the background as much as possible."

Natalie held up the garment bag with a smile. "This one's even trendier than the Armani," she informed him. "It's the latest word in fashion." She unzipped it to reveal a bright blue suit in the fitted, modern tapered leg style that had been at home in closets of the sixties, too. It was too trendy in Tessa's opinion—more like an experimental fashion piece than a suit anybody would wear comfortably, unless maybe they were on *The Bachelorette*.

"Is that fabric electric blue?" asked Ama.

"Wait until you see the tie," answered Natalie.

"We'll be downstairs when you're ready," Tessa said. She didn't wait for Blake's full reaction to his new wardrobe, but instead escaped downstairs.

Bianca's home was an apartment in Little Italy, a block from the big Catholic church and just above a new hair salon. It was a small but tidy space with old furniture, faded wallpaper, and a mantel clock and an antique saint's statue that looked even frailer than Bianca herself. The smell of red sauce and garlic lingered near the kitchen, but the living room smelled like tea, thanks to the tray in the middle of the table, a plate of biscotti beside it.

Natalie took a bite from one. "Delicious," she said. "Did you make these?"

Bianca laughed. "Not me," she said. "Italian cookery—I was never good at it. My husband tried to teach me pasta; I tried to teach him beet soup. But in the end, it was easier for me to buy the sweet treats he liked. Now I eat from frozen boxes mostly—things like he used to cook." Her accent was closer to the Scandinavian accents she'd heard on television, Tessa decided, having watched a whole week's worth of Nordic fishing documentaries. Bianca wasn't really Italian, despite her name.

"Do you take milk or sugar?" Molly asked Tessa, as she sat down in one of the chairs.

"Both, please," said Tessa.

"And Mr. Ellingham?" She glanced at Blake.

"I'll take mine black," he replied.

He was wearing the blue suit that Natalie had "borrowed" from the wedding garment rental, and somehow, he actually managed to pull it off. Tessa was beginning to think he could wear a burlap bag and still look attractive. He held the teacup Molly offered him in both hands, a look of deep, sympathetic concentration on his face that might be his way of avoiding conversation.

"So," began Tessa, setting down her teacup. "Tell us what you have in mind."

Molly glanced shyly at Bianca. "Truthfully, I don't know where to start," she said. "Maybe with the venue? I just moved to the city a year ago, so I don't know much about locations here. There's always a wedding chapel—Paolo's Catholic, after all—but we both like outdoor events. As for the reception, I don't really know."

"Some place nice," said Bianca. "A nice restaurant in the city. I know one…" Here, she opened her ever-present envelope and dug through the clippings. Tessa glimpsed smiling women in evening gowns, vases of flowers, even cutouts of wedding rings. "This one."

It was the NiteLite Lounge, an expensive club near the waterfront, Tessa knew, with a modern dining room that boasted a "starlit" ceiling and an overpriced menu. "This one?" she repeated back.

"It looks just like the big restaurants the movie stars go to," said Bianca. "I thought about the big hotels, but Paolo said no. So I remembered a picture in the paper from this place. It looks just like them, and it's so close! We could walk to it from the church close by, except there will be a limo car for the bridal party, of course." She beamed at Molly.

"I think walking's fine," said Molly gently.

"You deserve a big car, though," said Bianca. "I want you both to have the best. It's important to me." She took Molly's hand in hers. "For you both to have what I couldn't. What Paolo's mother and father couldn't. I was too poor then, but now—now I have saved money, and I want Paolo's marriage to have a big start in the world."

"What do you want this wedding to be like?" Ama asked, as she sampled one of the biscotti. "Do you want something traditional? Your family is Italian, aren't they?"

"I want the best," said Bianca firmly. "These are pictures of the nicest things I could find. And my friends told me some things I should ask about that would make it special. I have the list—it has the dress, the cake, the big place where we will go after the wedding. The limo car, too," she added, checking them off her fingers as she spoke. "I want you to help me find the right ones, so Molly and Paolo have everything they want."

Molly didn't look as if she was comfortable with this idea, Tessa noticed. "We should talk about your budget," Tessa suggested, opening the binder with the Wedding Belles logo pasted on the front—a temporary mockup for jotting down clients' notes.

"Not now." Bianca waved her hand dismissively. "Just tell me what things are important to do. Mr. Ellingham is a planner. He made things beautiful for Stella, so he will know what to do." She was looking at Blake intently. His eyes, for a moment, widened with panic.

Oops. Tessa froze. She hadn't anticipated Bianca point-blank demanding a theme from Blake, their Stefan impersonator. If she jumped in at this point, what would Bianca think? Would it seem like an affront... the kind of affront that would cause them to lose their one client?

All eyes were on Blake, who made himself busy with a long sip of tea, stalling for time, Tessa surmised. She caught his eye. Gently, she tapped her finger against the saucer on her lap, its china pattern exposed. Would he realize this was a hint?

He looked at Bianca. "Roses," he said.

"Roses?" Bianca repeated. She looked ready to be entranced by the idea.

"As a theme," Blake clarified. "It could be... held in a rose garden, maybe. Or the food served on plates with a pattern like this one." He held up his cup. "Very... traditional. But classic and kind of grand, obviously."

At least Natalie and Ama's sighs of relief weren't audible. As for Tessa, her lips formed a smile of admiration only slightly less glowing than that of Bianca. Although, technically, hers was from relief.

"It would be so perfect with the cake," said Bianca. "The one I have a picture of." She rummaged through her pile of magazine clippings and came up with one in her hand. "This one. It's so elegant. I said to Molly, 'You need a cake this beautiful.'"

Sugar doves and roses. Tessa had seen it before, a standard design in the wedding and bakery world. Five layers of cake formed a tower topped with two large marzipan doves and loads of pink sugar roses.

"Maybe you could put some more roses on the sides also?" suggested Bianca. "And some pretty, glittery sugar. Like on Cinderella's cake?" She looked at Blake now.

He cleared his throat. "Um, well," he began. "Don't you think that might be a tad overwhelming?"

"I believe I have just the cake in mind to go with Blake's wonderful suggestion," Tessa said. "I have a picture of it right… here." She pulled one from her portfolio, but Bianca wasn't listening.

"Oh, and the dress! Yes, it must look like that beautiful one, too," she said, clutching Molly's hand in excitement. "You will look so pretty in it, just like a rose in bloom." She took a picture of a multi-layered tulle skirt from the pile. "You can find a dress like this, yes? The skirt should be like petals, I think. Maybe looking more like a big white rose."

It was Natalie's turn. "I could probably find something like that," she answered. "If it was what Molly wanted, of course." She glanced at the bride, who hadn't spoken a word during all of this, letting Bianca take the lead until now.

"I like roses, of course," Molly ventured. "I'm not sure about dressing like one, necessarily," she added, with a gentle laugh. "A garden might be pretty for the reception, though. If we could find one that doesn't have an expensive retainer fee, and is close enough to the ceremony site."

"We could definitely find you an affordable outdoor venue," promised Tessa. "No problem. And a rose garden would be a gorgeous setting." She penciled this idea into her notes, barely able to believe it came from one of Blake's suggestions. That was totally unexpected of him.

"Tea in a rose garden, maybe," Bianca said. "Pretty china like this and tea cakes and cookies—that would be nice. Like that show we like to watch on the television—you know, the pretty English one."

"She means *Downton Abbey*," said Molly.

"I'm a big fan," remarked Natalie. "Gotta love those Edwardian fashions."

Fortunately, Bianca didn't latch onto the idea of an Edwardian-style designer gown in response. She was too busy digging through her clippings in search of a fancy tea garden to show Blake, coming up with something that resembled the lawns of Windsor Castle more than the local botanical gardens.

Tessa edged closer to the bride. "Besides the big and the beautiful, can you think of anything personal for you and Paolo, when it comes to a ceremony or reception?"

"Maybe something from your family history?" Ama suggested. "A tradition that's just yours? My family's big on tradition, so I'm asking out of habit."

"I have no idea if my family had any," Molly explained. "My parents died when I was little. Nobody I grew up with had any real traditions, especially not for weddings. My foster mom wasn't married." She toyed with the china cup beside her for a moment. "Paolo has his Italian heritage, of course. And I have some Irish, on my mom's side of the family."

"Irish," said Tessa. "We could probably come up with some beautiful ideas related to that part of your heritage, if you like."

For a moment, Molly's smile brightened. "I actually went to Ireland on a college trip once," she said. "It was beautiful. I was sort of amazed to think

I was visiting places my family might have stayed, or even lived a long time ago, for all I know. It was fun to imagine, anyway." Her voice held warmth for this memory, Tessa noticed, her smile growing a little less shy beneath her enthusiasm. "I guess I felt connected to it because of that," she said.

"That does sound amazing," Tessa agreed. "Why don't we find a way to honor that heritage for your wedding?"

"I've always meant to learn more about my family's roots but didn't really know where to start. Maybe this would inspire me to actually get serious about my research." Molly laughed. "When I was little, I used to pretend that's why my parents named me 'Molly'—even though it's probably more of a stereotype than a true Irish tradition."

"You never know," Natalie replied. "Maybe you've got an Irish ancestor with the same name a few generations back. Or maybe someone in your family had 'Molly Malone' as their favorite song."

"Well, one of my ancestors did have an Irish necklace," Molly replied. "It got passed down to me along with some other mementos in a cardboard box of family possessions. It's not rare or anything, but it has a really pretty pattern, kind of like two hearts interwoven. I looked it up and it's called a Celtic love knot."

"That's a pretty awesome sounding family heirloom," Ama grinned.

Molly nodded. "I've been thinking about wearing it with my wedding gown. The original chain broke years ago, but I'm going to string it on some green ribbon I bought. I got the idea when Bianca told me that green means good luck in Italy... so, in a way, my necklace would represent both my and Paolo's family heritages."

"Irish and Italian traditions make for a good beginning," Tessa said, making a note of it in her folder. "Maybe for a color scheme or the menu... even the table setting. Irish crystal instead of rose-patterned china, for instance."

"Crystal sounds expensive," said Molly dubiously.

"Expense is no trouble," said Bianca, waving it away.

"It wouldn't be," Tessa promised. "Whatever you choose, we'll find the best bargain possible, from an Italian band to Irish crystal rental."

The word "crystal" had Bianca's attention in a heartbeat. She loved the idea of sparkling dishware almost as much as she liked the idea of English china. "And bagpipes for the wedding march," she told them. "Very dramatic and so different. Maybe you can get bagpipers for the big entrance at the church?"

Tessa wasn't so sure about that one—not only because bagpipes were a Scottish instrument, but also because it seemed so... dramatic... for the simple grace of Molly herself, and the budgetary concerns of Paolo. She looked at Molly and found her struggling to hide a smile at this characteristic flair for the dramatic on Bianca's part. She didn't seem ready to issue an objection if she had one, though. And Blake's thoughts were hard to read at this moment, his gaze directed at the tea in his cup that was probably growing cold by now.

"Maybe the groomsmen could wear traditional tartan if the theme is Irish," Natalie was saying beside her. "You know, kilts."

"That's more of a Scottish tradition, isn't it?" said Ama, frowning. "Or is it both?"

They were getting off track again, Tessa felt. Molly had opened up for a second when talking about her family history, but they needed something more personal than just a fondness for Irish green if they were going to make this wedding memorable for everyone involved.

"Can you think of anything else?" Tessa asked the two of them. "Anything with a special significance for you? A tradition you would like to carry on for your ceremony?" Sometimes there was a moment from the past that couples wanted to recreate—a certain family wedding portrait, a special gift for the wedding favor. Anything would help… if Molly didn't have a tradition, maybe she and Paolo could adopt one from his side of the family.

"Paolo's family must have some," said Molly, glancing at Bianca. "You were married in Europe, weren't you, Gran? Before you came to America?"

"European wedding traditions can be really great," coaxed Natalie. "I'll bet your wedding had a few worth repeating."

Bianca laughed. "Me?" she said. "My wedding? Pah," she added, waving this suggestion away. "It was a poor wedding. We didn't have two coins to rub together, Pietro and I, so we didn't have much. We came to America and didn't make much money. See that photo? Us after we were married. Our first day in America—a stranger took that photo for us."

She wafted her hand toward a framed photo on the nearby side table. Tessa lifted it, seeing a black-and-white image of a young woman in a plain flower-print dress and summer coat, standing beside a young man in an ill-fitting high-waisted suit from the 1950s. They were both squinting against the sun on a street corner; Bianca's face was partly shadowed by the brim of her hat.

"Not like now," Bianca continued. "Paolo has a good job. He went to college and became an architect. He helped them draw some of those new buildings in the banking district. And Molly—she is an artist. People buy her pictures all the time."

"I'm a digital artist," explained Molly. "I design business cards and invitations—I'm making the ones for me and Paolo, for our wedding. That's how we met, actually," she added, with a blush. "I designed some business cards for him." She handed Tessa one from her purse.

"Thanks," said Tessa. "You know event planners—we can always use a new designer to recommend to our clients."

"Or ourselves," said Natalie. "We're bound to run out of business cards sooner or later." They pretended that Tessa hadn't ordered a box of five hundred already.

"I guess we won't have to find you a designer, then," said Tessa, making another note in her binder. She was also noting that the invitations, thus far, were the only wedding detail the bride seemed certain of. "Now, what else would you like to cover?"

"The dress," said Bianca. "I think we should start there, don't you?" She looked at Molly. "Find you something pretty?"

"I guess so," said Molly with a smile. "I probably shouldn't wear jeans and a t-shirt to my wedding, should I?"

"A princess dress," said Bianca, squeezing the hand of her grand-daughter-to-be. "That is what you will have." She beamed expectantly at the wedding planners seated in her living room, who smiled back. "Maybe from the shop where Stella's daughter-in-law found her dress. It was so beautiful—she looked like an angel. She gave me the card for it." She held it toward Blake.

Tessa nudged him, and he accepted it. "It *was* very impressive," he told her, summoning a smile for Bianca's sake, although it wasn't very convincing to the wedding planner seated next to him. He passed the card to Natalie, who gave it an appraisal for possible future reference.

"What was the design's name again?" Molly asked Bianca. "I think we should maybe ask them to look for one a little more affordable."

"I think it was the pumpkin skirt model," muttered Blake; too quietly to be noticed by the two clients in conversation, but not quietly enough to escape Tessa's notice. She gave him a quick jab with her elbow.

"We'll help you find the perfect one," Tessa assured them.

Chapter Eleven

Tessa climbed the spiral staircase, her folder tucked under her arm and her head full of ideas and new thoughts after the day's conversation with their clients. Blake had impressed them with his charms—a surprise given the fact he had been curt and grumbling about it in the moments before. It made Tessa suspect that maybe the contractor possessed a tiny bit of genuine talent for some aspects of the event planning business, regardless of what he might claim if this was suggested.

He had beaten her back to their headquarters as soon as the meeting was over. His tools lay on a worktable formed by a piece of lumber across twin sawhorses, his Skilsaw resting on one side beside a leather carpenter's belt. He was here somewhere, probably, unless he had turned tail and run at the thought of playing Stefan Groeder's replacement anymore.

"Blake?" She pushed open a door to one of the empty rooms that was only half-closed, and discovered the whereabouts of their contractor. He was in the process of changing his clothes—the ones from the meeting were cast aside on an old radiator, with Blake standing a short distance from the doorway in his faded denim jeans, shrugging on his unbuttoned work shirt as the door opened. Tessa released a gasp, and

Blake looked up at the same moment, those intense blue eyes landing on her in surprise.

Washboard abs. A muscular chest, strong shoulders, and the rest of those very promising biceps she'd noticed the first time she had met him, in the alcove of Wedding Belles. Tessa was staring, and didn't even realize it until she had taken a long look that brought to mind certain daydreams she had made an effort to repress since the moment she first saw him; particularly about the two strong hands that were holding their respective sides of his brown flannel button down.

Her face flushed, her cheeks becoming two deep crimson roses, and a very similar shade appeared on Blake's own. Tessa whirled around quickly. "I'm sorry," she said. "I didn't mean— I didn't realize—"

"Give me a second." The shadow on the wall told her Blake was hurriedly buttoning his shirt. "It's safe now," he said. "No further embarrassment if you want to turn around."

Her face grew even warmer. She was embarrassed for completely different reasons than just for seeing him partly undressed. She glanced tentatively over her shoulder—the romance novel fantasy version of Blake had vanished.

"I'm sorry," she repeated, turning around again. She gazed to one side, at the wall of half-peeled vintage floral paper, not daring to meet that steely shade of blue lest he somehow read the truth of the personal attraction in her own eyes.

"No problem." He zipped the suit into its garment bag. "What did you want to see me about?" He stepped past her, entering his workspace again, where he lifted the tool belt from the worktable.

"I… uh… wanted to compliment you on what happened today," she said. "The way they took to you. It was better than I thought it would be. You didn't just fill Stefan's gap… you impressed them. You gave them confidence. It was appreciated—by all of us."

"I did as requested," he said. "I figured that was the deal. I help you get your client, you pay me for fixing up your building, so it all makes sense, as you put it to me beforehand."

"Of course," said Tessa, who was floundering for words of reply. The rest of the speech in her mind from when she had been coming upstairs had flown away upon seeing Blake's chiseled torso. *Be embarrassed for yourself, Tessa. You're not a hopeless romantic, or a college girl with a crush. Get over it. So he's handsome—what does that matter? He's just another colleague, right?*

"I'll let you get back to work," said Tessa. "I just thought I would pay you a compliment, since you deserve it."

She could linger and chat with him more, but between her mixture of mortification and attraction, she only wanted to escape from this conversation now. "Bye." She turned and left with what she hoped seemed only like swift steps and not a rush to hide her confusion behind closed doors in her office.

Natalie checked the time on her phone. So far, the dress-shopping experience was not going well. For the first time, she was beginning to regret leaving Kandace's Kreations a tiny bit, despite believing it would take more than a few minor conflicts to change her mind about this decision. If this was a taste of her work for the business, she was going to be an utter failure in this career.

Bianca had insisted upon visiting the wedding shop that sold the Cinderella dress—a boutique that turned out to have sold its only attractive dress on that day, possibly. The boutique owner's taste sat on the opposite end of the spectrum to Kandace's—kitschy, clichéd wedding garments that screamed "princess," not to mention the overinflated price tags attached to them.

This must be one of Stefan's early contacts, to whom he owed a very big favor.

"I think this one is *so* you," purred the sales clerk as she showed off Molly in her latest selection. Its sleeves were made of pouffy tulle that resembled big tufts of cotton candy, while the skirt was spread wide at the bottom like a feather duster—trimmed with further panels of tulle and actual white feathers.

Molly looked at herself in the mirror. "Really?" she said with skepticism.

"It's one of our most elegant designs," said the sales clerk, who was talking more to Bianca than Molly—Bianca had insisted on seeing "the best," of course, since that was the focus of her dream wedding for Paolo and Molly.

"What do you think?" said Bianca to Natalie. "Is it nicer than the last one?"

"It's certainly more expensive than the last one," said Natalie, who could see the four-figure price tag from here. "But are you sure this is the type of dress that suits Molly? The princess look? What if we consider something that also shows off Molly's great figure?"

Three more pouffy-skirt dresses lay across the fitting room's chair and sofa, each with spread skirts and crystal sequins, and one with Victorian gothic-style black bead embroidery traveling down the bodice and the skirt's upper half like spider webs. Monster dresses, as Natalie thought of them, which swallowed Molly up in fluffy material and glitzy decorations. The bride would be a walking frosted cupcake.

"How about we just *try* something simpler?" suggested Natalie. She lowered her voice. "I know a boutique with something more sophisticated that I think would suit Molly better." She cast a glance in the direction of the sales clerk, who was hustling from the priciest rack with another dress, this one an ivory gown with a giant flamenco skirt and a high, curving off-the-shoulder bodice that would create two wings sprouting from the bride's arms.

"This one is very exclusive," said the clerk. "I think it's a perfect contrast for your color," she said to Molly, as she retrieved the tulle cream puff gown from the previous try.

"But these dresses are supposed to be very fine ones," Bianca answered Natalie worriedly. "I was told they were very fashionable."

"Is something wrong, madam?" The clerk had overheard part of their conversation.

"I was hoping you would show us a little more variety. A few dresses in an evening gown style, for instance," suggested Natalie. "And maybe something a little more affordable. Everything you've shown us has a price tag of three thousand or more."

"Madam wanted the best," said the clerk snootily.

"Are you sure that's how you want to qualify these dresses?" replied Natalie. "The lace trim on that one is clearly nylon. And that ivory gown isn't real satin, as anybody can see in this light."

"We're one of the finest bridal boutiques in town," snapped the clerk. "I resent you suggesting otherwise in front of your client, who *clearly* prefers our designs."

"Do you?" Natalie asked Bianca. *Please say no*, she thought silently. Couldn't Bianca see the dubiousness on Molly's face—and the cheesiness of that mermaid-skirt gown on the clerk's hanger?

Bianca wavered. She considered this for a moment, gazing at the pile of dresses across the chair. She sighed. "What more do you have?" she asked the clerk.

"Our most expensive line," said the clerk thoughtfully. "I haven't shown you any of those yet. They might be just a teensy bit outside your budget, however." She gave Natalie a pointed glance with this remark. "They're not for every customer, clearly."

A stubborn note entered Bianca's tone at this challenge. "Show them, please," she said. The clerk gave Natalie a triumphant glance, then disappeared toward the shop's back room.

"Gran, we can't look at even *more* expensive price tags," objected Molly, as she tossed the latest dress over the doors of the changing stall. "Maybe we should ask for something simpler. Like a dress I can wear to business meetings later on or something."

"No, no," said Bianca, shaking her head. "I want you to pick something special. Just for that day."

Molly sighed. The clerk reappeared with a dress trimmed with shiny metallic lace that resembled plastic to Natalie's eye. "Here we are," the clerk announced. "I think this one will be just right for you."

It wasn't, Natalie knew, and it looked even worse on Molly than the others. Bianca was disappointed that the dress wasn't anything like the pictures she had saved, but perked up significantly when the clerk announced that a new shipment of designs would be in some time next week.

Thus far, not a single dress the bride had tried on had given her a genuine smile when she looked in the mirror. Secretly, Natalie felt that Bianca was only pretending to be pleased by the style of the most expensive one, which had far too much beading and a weird plunging neckline for a ball gown. It was only Natalie's most persuasive efforts that kept the determined grandmother from putting it on hold for the bride-to-be "just in case" the others didn't satisfy.

Natalie sighed. This was almost as bad as sewing Kandace's new "Tinker Bell" blouse, with pointy pleats around its waist.

Ama's experience was almost the same when it came to the cake. Bianca had been eager to see Ama's book of designs, but had quickly fallen in love with pictures of huge bakery cakes that were way too impractical for a small wedding, including Ama's new "Birds of Paradise" design, which surely reminded Bianca of the giant sugary dove cake from the magazine.

"Don't you think this one is a little too much cake?" hinted Ama. "Five layers are designed to feed a lot of people."

"But look how beautiful it is," said Bianca. "It's so grand. How can you miss a cake like that?" She looked at Molly. "Isn't it pretty?"

"It's gorgeous," said Molly. "But it has to cost a fortune, Gran. I think Ama's right, and that it has way too many layers for me and Paolo. Maybe if we only had three... or picked a smaller cake."

"I have smaller designs, of course," said Ama. "Look at this one with the chocolate roses—and this is one of my favorites. It's a little different. A two-layer one decorated with dozens of little fondant wildflowers." She used a technique similar to paper quilling to make them from fondant. Ama loved twirling the little flowers around a wooden skewer to form them, and coiling their little centers like cinnamon rolls.

Bianca looked disappointed. "They look so small, though," she said, studying the picture. "And they look plain. So plain next to those big, pretty ones."

Molly touched her hand. "Small is okay, Gran," she said. "With me and Paolo."

Ama closed the book and laid it aside. "What if we did something unique?" she suggested. "How about a theme that represents you and

Paolo, for instance? I can make a cake topper that looks like almost anything. We could recreate a place that matters to you."

"We met in my apartment," said Molly with a smile. "I can't really see that as a cake topper. We talked about honeymooning in Paris… not that we're actually going there," she added, with a blush. "Maybe on our golden anniversary."

"How about a tiny Eiffel Tower?" said Ama.

"A big one, maybe," said Bianca, smiling. "Can you make a big one from sugar?"

"I could," admitted Ama. She was reluctantly picturing a large candy tower atop a two-layer cake. "But how about something to celebrate your heritage? Paolo's Italian, you're Irish… we could make anything from a Neapolitan cream cake to an Irish mint one."

"I guess," said Molly. "Unfortunately, I wouldn't know an Irish recipe from a French one. Paolo knows a little about Italian cooking. His grandfather and father were both good cooks."

"Can you put the doves on top?" asked Bianca. "How many layers can you make?"

"I think two or three is enough," hinted Ama. "If you want it to be tall, we can put the topmost and middle layers on cake pillars. Or we can make two fake bottom layers for the cake, which would be less expensive."

"Fake cake?" said Bianca. "How is this possible?"

"I cut them out of Styrofoam and cover them in fondant," Ama reassured her. "They would look just like the others, but they're just for show. It would make the cake look bigger… but without actual cake."

"I don't know about fake cakes," said Bianca dubiously. "If someone found out, Paolo and Molly's wedding might be shamed. Not affording real cakes—I can pay for one, so I will." She lifted her chin firmly.

Ama and Molly exchanged glances. "Maybe I can think of something better," Ama said.

"Does anybody besides me feel like this wedding plan is moving in the wrong direction?" asked Natalie.

She curled up on one end of Tessa's sofa, while Ama opened a box of biscotti and laid them out on a platter. Tonight, Tessa was cooking a frozen lasagna and garlic bread at her place so the three of them could spend some time together outside the business. A good way to bond and get work done at the same time, as Tessa put it, although a tempting stack of romantic DVD movies was piled next to her television, begging for a girls' night of fun.

She had made certain to hide her packing boxes in the other room, and hoped that Natalie wouldn't notice that some of her personal things were gone from her shelves. At least her couch hadn't sold yet, so she still had plenty of seats for guests.

"Things didn't go well at the dress shop?" asked Tessa, as she checked the oven's timer.

"It was a disaster," said Natalie. "Every expensive price tag turned Bianca's head. And they were attached to *the* ugliest dresses I've ever seen. Kandace would have been proud of them, believe me." She took a sip from her wine glass. "The way that clerk kept bringing out all those giant, expensive dresses—five minutes with Bianca and the woman knew all the right buttons to push to steer her away from making a smart choice."

"What did you do?" asked Tessa.

"I talked her out of putting a deposit on a hideous dress that Molly would hate," said Natalie. "Molly wasn't crazy about anything the shop had to offer, even the one or two decent designs they showed her. 'Bigger isn't necessarily better,' I kept trying to explain to Bianca, but she's afraid that anything simple equals cheap."

"I agree. Totally." Ama poured herself a glass of wine. "Bianca won't look at any options that aren't the most expensive choices in my book. I kept trying to get Molly and her to think of something special, but it didn't work." She shrugged.

"It doesn't help that Molly doesn't have many memories in her past of special places or experiences," said Tessa. "Neither does Paolo. I think that's why they're letting Bianca's fantasies rule the day. Neither of them had any expectations, but Bianca has this huge wedding in her head that she wants to make come true. It's her special dream for them… and they don't seem to have any of their own."

"A dream complete with a princess ball gown and a giant cake," said Ama. "I think someday they'll look back on the huge wedding with only twenty or thirty guests and wonder why they ever agreed to let Bianca suggest all these impractical things that didn't matter to them."

"Everything that she chooses costs a fortune," said Natalie, sighing. "I've promised to get her a discount on a dress. I'm pretty sure I know a boutique that will be happy to unload some tulle skirt for a few hundred. If I can convince Bianca it's still the best, even with a bargain price tag," she added wryly.

"*You* could sew one better than any of your friends' boutiques," hinted Tessa. "I'll bet there's one somewhere in your closet already." Natalie ignored her and took a bigger sip of wine.

"I'm trying to convince them to choose two Styrofoam layers for the bottom half of the cake," said Ama. "It's a hard sell, though. Bianca's afraid that someone will find out and think Paolo and Molly are cheating their guests or something."

She took a bite from one of the biscotti. "Mmm," she said. "These are better than the ones at Bianca's house."

"Thanks," said Natalie. "They're from my family's bakery. Ma lets family have the day-old stuff, so I have a freezer full of Italian pastries."

"Your family owns Icing Italia?" said Ama. "I didn't realize that. I love that place. I walk by it almost every time I leave the restaurant. I can't believe this—was that you I saw in the window a couple of times?"

"Could be. I help out a lot, especially when my uncle is in his pasta-making phase," said Natalie.

"I used to imagine working there," said Ama with a dreamy smile.

"Believe me, my mother would love to hear that somebody's dying for it," said Natalie. "I may have learned to bake biscotti and fill cannoli, but it never turned into a lifelong love. Not after seeing my first *Vogue* magazine, anyway," she said. "Sometimes I think Ma was a little disappointed that both my brother and I had other plans for our lives than the family business of baking."

"Sounds familiar," said Ama.

"Your family has an Indian bakery?" quipped Natalie.

"No," laughed Ama. "I work at their restaurant—the Tandoori Tiger downtown?"

"I've been there," said Tessa. "The chicken is fantastic."

"And the atmosphere is kitschy, right?" said Ama with a grin. "Anyway, if I quit, they'd probably never forgive me. Everybody works in the family restaurant—unless, of course, they have a husband who moves to another city in a big career move."

"Then it's excusable to leave?" said Tessa.

"Right. Otherwise, you're supposed to stay with the family and do your part. For me, that's being in charge of desserts for the menu."

Ama set her glass on the table and rose to check the garlic bread in the oven as its timer beeped persistently.

"So is that why you run a mail-order bakery?" asked Natalie.

"It let me live out my dream a little," admitted Ama, sliding the bread slices onto a platter. "Of course, not the way the wedding firm could. I've always wanted to make a multi-tiered cake for someone who wasn't family—some great culinary sculpture I could be proud of." She set the hot tray on a trivet by the sink.

"I thought your cupcakes and cookies were perfection," said Natalie. "That's exactly the sort of creativity my mother would love. You know, so we don't turn into a too-authentic Italian bakery."

Tessa lifted out the lasagna from the oven. "I wish that Bianca would agree to let you create something different from a Styrofoam cake for her family's wedding. Cupcakes for a small wedding would be adorable."

"Just imagine what she has in mind for the venue," said Ama, dusting the top of the salad with grated Parmesan. "The NiteLite is way too big for their reception." This was still Bianca's dearest wish for the couple's big day, despite their best attempts to make alternative suggestions.

"Maybe we should have 'The Wedding Guru' talk her out of it," said Natalie. "He is the best, after all." She paused. "That rose garden idea wasn't too bad for a first attempt. He could probably persuade her to do something else if he really tried."

"Blake?" said Tessa. "I think we should have him say as little as possible so he doesn't blow his cover." She served herself a piece of lasagna from the pan, adding a generous helping of salad to the side. "Besides, we promised we wouldn't ask him for extra favors."

"I don't know," said Natalie thoughtfully. "I thought he did pretty well, considering how weird the whole situation is. Besides—he's easy on the eye. It's kind of nice to have someone that handsome around the office," she teased. She accepted the plate Ama handed her, blowing on her first bite of lasagna. "Don't you agree?"

"That the contractor is gorgeous? Absolutely," said Ama. "If he paid attention to me instead of the upstairs wiring, it would definitely be a worthwhile distraction from cupcakes and frosting." She settled on the floor beside the coffee table. "Not that I'm saying I have a crush on him or anything. I'm just admiring him in a purely aesthetic sense."

"I'll grant you that he's good looking," said Tessa. Heat crept into her cheeks. "I mean, he's pretty tolerable in a suit, anyway."

"That's it? Tolerable?" Natalie took on a fake snobby accent, tilting her nose as she said, "He's *tolerable*, I suppose… but not handsome enough to tempt me." She and Ama giggled over this reference to *Pride and Prejudice*. Even Tessa couldn't keep a straight face for long.

"Okay, okay," she admitted with a laugh. "You got me. He's a little bit handsome."

It was usually easy for her to say that a guy was attractive, so Tessa couldn't explain why it was so hard to admit it about Blake. He was certainly easy on the eye, as Natalie said—she had noticed that from the moment she met him. And he was a lot of other things she didn't want to admit right now, too.

There was something about him that she couldn't quite explain, something unexpected and magnetic. He defied the clichés that she had expected from the flannel-clad carpenter whose sledgehammer was tearing into the plaster of their downstairs walls. Maybe that was what made her hesitate to talk about him or think about him in a romantic way, even more than the fact he was handsome.

"He's single. I checked his ring finger," said Natalie.

"And his online profile?" teased Ama.

"No, not me," said Natalie. "I'm not that interested. I have plenty of dates already."

"Nat's never been romantic," said Tessa, glad to shift the subject to her friend's love life and away from her own feelings for the contractor turned fake wedding planner. "She thinks relationships should be fun, not serious. She always says she'll know Mr. Right when she meets him… eventually."

"Exactly," said Natalie, lifting her glass to this statement.

"Lucky you," said Ama. "I'll be fortunate if I escape my parents' attempts to rope me into a marriage with the next nice Indian boy that crosses my auntie's path. My father is threatening to take out an ad for me."

"An ad?" echoed Tessa. "Like—an advertisement for a husband?"

"That's correct," said Ama. "I know it seems weird to you, but it's perfectly normal in my culture. You arrange dates through ads online or in papers. Two people are compatible, they meet, talk, and make a match… or if two people are pushed hard enough by their families, they do it rather than end up with someone worse. That's what I've always been afraid of."

"So do you want that?" asked Natalie. "I mean, I wouldn't. But different strokes for different folks."

"No," admitted Ama softly. "That is… I'm kind of a romantic. I don't know. I just… wish I could fall in love, rather than weigh someone against a checklist of qualities. Not suitability and compatibility, just—impulse." She played with her salad, pushing a tomato to the side. "Mad, passionate impulse."

"Romantics," said Natalie. "They're a different breed. But even a romantic like Tess would never take an impulsive plunge, would you, Tess?"

"Stop it," said Tessa, who was suddenly busy cutting into her lasagna.

"Tess is a romantic?" said Ama. "Are you being serious?"

"Of course," said Natalie. "She's just in denial about it. You should have seen her in college—crushes every other day, always a cute boy on her mind who might be the love of her life—nobody could fall harder than Tess for a potential soul mate."

"Stop it," repeated Tessa, protesting. "That's not true—"

"If she hadn't been such a good student, she probably would have pined away over lovelorn opportunities ages ago," said Natalie. "Not that lots of guys weren't interested in her. But never for the right kind of relationship. The kind of sparks, chemistry, emotions, or passions that Tess longed for. In short—head-over-heels love between two people."

"Okay, I'm going out for a walk now. Text me when you're finished." Tessa tried to rise and was arrested in the act by Natalie seizing her arm. "I'm not listening to this." She covered her ears.

"At least *I* date and pursue options, whereas Tess here hasn't been out with anyone in ages," teased Natalie. "And if you think it's horrible that I'm a serial dater, then meet the woman whose longing for a soul mate connection is *so* deeply buried that she's afraid to ever let it come to life again."

Tessa's face was fire red. "None of this is true," she said. "Natalie's making a mountain out of a little mound of complete exaggeration."

"So you're like a non-relationship romantic?" said Ama.

"I think that's a harsh description," Tessa answered defensively. "I have lots to interest me and keep me busy without a relationship. I like the idea of it, but I have more important things to focus on. Just because someone's a romantic doesn't mean they want to date anybody who comes along."

"My dates are *not* just anybody, thanks," said Natalie.

"I wasn't talking about you, I was talking about me," said Tessa. "Romance is great. I love romantic stories. Look around you; I own a dozen romantic movies and even more books. But those stories don't happen in real life... and I know better than to look for one." She rose and lifted the salad bowl from the kitchen counter, bringing it to the table.

"You could at least go on a date once in a while," said Natalie.

"And waste good working hours?" joked Tessa. "Seriously though, I don't have time for it anyway. Maybe I'll change my mind someday... but right now I know what I should be doing. I'm not interested in my own happily ever after, just other people's."

She lifted the platter of garlic bread and took a slice, then held it out. "Seconds, anyone?" The best way to change the subject from love to regular life was clearly with food.

"So... the handyman's not married, you said?" Ama ventured.

"Not unless he's hiding a wedding ring somewhere," said Natalie.

"He did look pretty hot in that suit yesterday," commented Ama.

"Definitely," said Natalie with a wicked grin. Tessa was busy seasoning her salad, and offered no comment.

"He's probably great with his hands," reflected Ama.

"If only he were my type," sighed Natalie.

"More lasagna, anyone?" said Tessa.

Chapter Twelve

The NiteLite Lounge gave Tessa a complete list of wedding-package prices, and they weren't cheap. One hundred dollars per guest—which might not be much if Paolo and Molly were still planning for a small crowd. Of course, by now Paolo's grandmother might insist on inviting the whole neighborhood to share in her grandson's big day.

"Miss Miller!" A voice called out behind her as she crossed the street from the lounge. She turned to see Paolo catching up with her.

"Hi," she said. "Mr. Fazolli—Paolo. How are you? Call me Tessa, by the way. We try to be on a first-name basis at Wedding Belles."

"Okay," he said. "Listen, I was hoping to catch you and talk to you—you didn't put a deposit on that place, did you?" he asked, glancing anxiously behind them at the club.

"No," said Tessa. "I just picked up a list of quotes for Molly and you to review."

"Good." Paolo breathed his relief. "Do you have time for a cup of coffee? There's something I'd like to talk to you about."

"Sure," she said, checking her watch. "I have time before I stop by a few other venues."

"Then we definitely need to talk," he said.

They got a cup of coffee from a nearby street vendor, and walked along the park. "I'm worried about Gran," said Paolo. "She's obsessed with having this wedding be some big production, and I know she can't afford it. Nothing I say to her makes a difference, because she keeps insisting this is what she wants."

"Is it what you want?" Tessa asked. "That's the most important question when it comes to weddings."

He sighed. "Not really," he answered. "Molly and I... when we decided we were getting married, we knew it would be a small affair. Not that either of us don't dream about a perfect day, but we knew we had to be realistic. Molly wants to save money for her business, and I want to save every dollar I can to put a deposit on a better apartment for the two of us."

"That's why your grandmother insists on paying for it?" guessed Tessa.

"Gran claims it's her dream," he said. "You know, my parents were pretty poor when they decided to tie the knot. They eloped one weekend to a Justice of the Peace, and that was it. Gran never got over the fact there was no big celebration for it. They didn't even tell her in advance so she could make a cake for them. I think she felt like our tiny family didn't have any big moments to bring us together, no milestones that we could cherish. She told me once that it really hurt her that the biggest day in my dad's life was treated just like any other day."

"Hers must have been a lot like that, too," said Tessa. "Judging by the way she talks about it."

"I know. Gran always said her wedding wasn't anything to dream about, either," he said. "So that's why she filled up that old cookie tin with extra money over the years. She has two others just like it, you know. Basically just change she had left over after buying groceries. I used to watch her put it in there when I was a kid. But she's convinced herself that it's enough to pay for some grand event to make up for all the years none of us could afford anything."

"She doesn't have the kind of money to pay for the NiteLite Lounge, does she?" said Tessa. "I figured that was the case when she first hired us. She was just so insistent about having the same planner as her friend." She hesitated before adding, "It's not even the same planner, actually. The one she wanted had moved to France... I didn't have the heart to tell her."

A sheepish smile crossed her lips after this—maybe Paolo was getting ready to fire them, and this admission would give him a good excuse to do it. She couldn't give Bianca what she really wanted, and they both knew it.

"I know my gran's monthly check is pretty small," said Paolo. "I don't think Gramps left her much when he died. I don't want her life's savings spent on my special day, no matter what she says. It'll break her, and I couldn't bear that." He shook his head.

"So you're not angry that we let your grandmother believe she'd found her 'expert'?" asked Tessa.

"Why?" he said. "Anybody Gran insisted on would be in the same boat. That's why I wanted to talk to you—I want you to help me by convincing her to give up these crazy ideas. To choose something sensible for us so she doesn't spend her last dime."

"How?" asked Tessa. "I think if we push away her ideas, she'll fire us and take Molly to another planner instead."

"Anything you can do to help," pleaded Paolo. "I'm afraid she's going to act on impulse and spend all her money before I can stop her. She has no idea how much these things truly cost—she doesn't realize how much some place like that lounge charges, much less caterers or flowers for a venue like that."

"What do you want instead?" Tessa asked.

Paolo paused. "I honestly don't know," he said, leaning against the light post. "We can't afford much. I suppose a small ceremony at a church. Maybe a few friends stopping by for cake at Gran's place. If Molly has a white dress and we hire a limo for a few hours, maybe Gran will be happy. And me and Molly will be married, which is what we both want most."

It didn't sound like his dream wedding to Tessa. But then, maybe Paolo really didn't care about the details so long as he was marrying Molly. He was only afraid that Bianca would be upset if he and Molly held onto their realistic expectations.

"I don't know how much of your grandmother's mind can be changed," said Tessa. "But I'll try. We'll all do our best to make Molly and Bianca happy without spending your grandmother's life savings. Maybe we can find something besides expensive lounges and flowers, anyway." She smiled.

Paolo's features relaxed. "Thanks," he said. "Anything you could do would really help us out." He smiled at her, as his cell phone beeped with a text message.

"My office," he said, checking the screen. "I have to go. But I'm glad we talked. I couldn't bear the thought of Gran leasing that lounge for the big day, or insisting on that giant cake Mr. Ellingham likes."

"Trust me, he's not really that keen on the cake," said Tessa, knowing Blake had no intention of endorsing the sugar doves and roses motif Bianca had shown them. "He'll be happy to forget it."

"Good," said Paolo. "Thanks again—Tessa." He hurried to catch the next train, leaving Tessa to ponder the promise she had just made. How easy would it be to make Bianca see this was what Paolo truly wanted? Especially since she was fairly sure it was more a matter of what Paolo didn't want than anything else… namely, to save his grandmother from spending her final years bankrupt.

The biggest problem of all was that Paolo technically wasn't really her client. It was Bianca who was paying for their services, and that was the person whose wishes she had just promised to sabotage, unless she could find a compromise between the two sides.

"We need a new game plan," said Tessa. "We need to find a way to make this wedding special without emptying Bianca's bank account."

"How?" said Natalie. "Cancel the ceremony and have her grand-kids elope?"

"Be serious," said Tessa, who didn't laugh because Paolo's story was in her thoughts. "It won't be easy to persuade her to look past the big and shiny when it comes to the wedding and reception, but I think it's possible. And it will take all of us to do it. Please, we have to try—for Paolo and Molly's sake at least. They'll never enjoy their big day knowing that it cost Bianca almost everything to give it to them. It'll be meaning-less to them, and that's the *last* thing Paolo's grandmother would want."

"We've known this since the beginning, though," said Natalie. "Why bring it up now, Tess?"

"Because Paolo asked me to help him," said Tessa. "He sees what Bianca has in mind, and it's not something he and Molly can let happen. He told me that Bianca regrets that the weddings in their family's past were always small and understated—no traditions, no family or friends gathered, no real celebrations—and that's why she's so desperate to make his and Molly's the opposite. So I promised him that we would help fix it."

"So we have to find a way to make the wedding truly special," said Ama. "Something that will be memorable for the right reasons?"

"Exactly," said Tessa. "This isn't just about Bianca's regrets from the past—this is about Molly and Paolo turning a new page in their lives. It needs to be about them—their past, their future."

"Maybe we need to find a way to *create* traditions," suggested Natalie. "Make it feel as if we're including things which belonged to their families. Maybe that would help Bianca feel better about her family's past, and give Molly and Paolo something to connect with for their kids' weddings someday."

"First, though, we have to agree to keep the spending costs low," said Tessa. "Anything that we help them choose has to be affordable, so no one in this family loses their money."

"First order of business for me—keep Bianca from putting a deposit on that dress," said Natalie firmly.

"For me, it's persuading Bianca not to choose the NiteLite Lounge," said Tessa. "There must be a less pricey venue I can show her instead. And the photographer—I'll take care of that, too."

"I can take a look at the florist options," Natalie offered. That was awfully generous of her, Tessa thought, given Natalie's warnings about not wanting to "fluff flowers" for clients. "The one Bianca's friend recommended is probably way out of her price league."

"There's always a chapel for the ceremony," said Ama. "But if they want a special spot outside, maybe we can find an inexpensive outdoor location. A park or a public garden that will let a small crowd be present with the right permits."

"Great," said Tessa, jotting these suggestions down. "I'll pull together ideas for Irish and Italian traditions for the wedding—food, decor, ceremonial aspects, wedding favors. We'll find out what kind of music they like and see if we can find a local musician who's affordable."

"And I'll see about catering," said Natalie. "Again, lots of contacts in the restaurant world."

"Shouldn't that be more Ama's specialty?" Tessa wondered out loud. "After all, her family does own a restaurant." Of course, bakers would probably have catering connections too, Tessa knew. Technically, Tessa herself could have handled the catering decision, and flowers were her favorite part of planning a wedding, but right now they needed to divide and conquer to come up with a swift counterplan to Bianca's.

"Not unless the bride and groom want Indian food at the wedding," answered Ama. "I know a nice Bengali restaurant that caters," she added jokingly.

"What about the cake?" said Tessa. "How are your plans for it coming along?"

"I'm working on steering her away from the giant sugar doves," said Ama. "I'm really hoping I can think of something unique... but it's not easy." She bit the eraser on her pencil as she gazed down at her latest sketch, which featured a small wedding cake decorated with French motifs. "It would help if we had the wedding's theme locked down, maybe. I could draw inspiration from it."

"Heritage, traditions, and new beginnings," said Natalie. "That's what it's all about, right? Different cultures coming together, building a future. Paolo and Molly come from different backgrounds, but they're building a life together with pieces of those pasts. That deserves celebration."

"But what would Bianca say?" said Ama. "She sounded less than excited about exploring her family's cultural past."

"This has to impress her," said Tessa. "We have to give it one hundred percent so we can amaze her without the usual pricey choices. We have to show her what she truly wants in this wedding—something unique and meaningful that Molly and Paolo can pass down to the next generation." She glanced from one partner to the other. "We're all on board with this plan, right?"

"I am," said Natalie.

"Me, too," said Ama. "Operation Wedding Surprise, here we come."

"Wedding *what*?" echoed Natalie.

"You heard me. I think it fits," said Ama.

"Come up with a better title than that, will you?" Natalie said to Tessa.

Grinning, Ama tucked her latest cake designs back inside her tote bag, while Tessa checked her phone for new business texts. The baker rose to retreat to her kitchen and her sketches, with Natalie catching up to her in the hall, carrying a flat gift box that she had stowed out of sight when she first arrived.

She held it out to Ama. "This is just… well, something I thought you might like," she said offhandedly. "Something I didn't have a use for, but thought maybe you would." She shrugged to convey that it was totally fine if she didn't.

"What is it?" Ama wore a curious smile as she untied the ribbon holding the lid closed. "Something new for the kitchen? I have a lot of empty shelf space in there still, I know…"

She trailed off at the sight of the garment tucked beneath the layer of tissue paper. She pulled it out, unfurling its candy-stripe fabric to reveal a knee-length spread skirt and sleeveless, ruched blouse. Little vintage, enamel heart-shaped buttons in pale pink cinched either side of the waist to complete a cute, breezy summer style that someone like Ama would pull off effortlessly.

"This is adorable," Ama told her, admiration in her voice as she held the garment in front of her. "Is it vintage? It can't be, it's too perfect and new-feeling. Did you make this?" She lifted her gaze with astonishment.

"I did," Natalie admitted. "A while ago, actually. I found it among some finished projects when I was cleaning out my space at Kandace's shop and thought it would suit you really well. If you like it, that is," she added, with another casual shrug.

"It's definitely my style," Ama said, holding the dress against her now, as she smoothed the skirt with one hand. "It's gorgeous. I love it. And look—I think it's the perfect size too."

"Lucky, huh?" Pink invaded Natalie's features with this compliment for her work. "It's nothing special, really, but I'm glad you like it."

A scoffing sound from Tessa, who was behind them on the stairs. "Don't listen to her. She's actually very talented despite her best efforts to convince everyone she knows otherwise."

"I can tell," said Ama, grinning as she folded the dress carefully back into its box.

"It's just one outfit," Natalie protested. "It's a simple, basic pattern. Hardly proof that I'm some design genius."

"Yeah, but what about the pieces you make for your own wardrobe?" Tessa challenged. "You've gotten plenty of compliments for those in the past. In fact, you made what you're wearing right now, didn't you?"

She pointed to Natalie's current ensemble: a chiffon dress in a vintage cocktail cut, with a hint of shimmer in the dark gray fabric that kept it from being too conservative for the designer's tastes. Ruching on one of its three-quarter sleeves gave it a sophisticated air, while the matching jacket hanging upstairs in Natalie's office would dress it down for the job interview she had that afternoon. If she could land even some part-time work somewhere, it would help keep their new business afloat without confining her to the kitchen at her family's bakery to earn extra cash.

"You made that too?" Ama was amazed. "Natalie, you really are a design genius. You *have* to design Molly's bridal gown," she told her, as if it were the obvious conclusion.

"What? No, that… is not happening at this juncture." Natalie laughed. "Our first client deserves a gown made by a professional— and Bianca definitely wants her to have the best one possible. Not the work of an amateur whose designs have barely seen the light of day."

"Again, exaggeration," countered Tessa. "You're wearing your own clothes, Nat. So is half your family, probably. Me? I have two dresses you've sewn, including one so drop-dead gorgeous that I will probably keep it forever."

"I'm making the wedding cake and I'm not a professional baker," Ama pointed out.

"*I've* never been a professional planner, but I'm coordinating this event down to the last dime we spend for it," Tessa added. "What gets you off the creative hook, may I ask?" She folded her arms, a stubborn gleam of challenge in the stare she leveled at her longtime friend—one that shook a little of Natalie's resolve, judging from the way her cheeks went from pink to pale.

"Let's compromise," Natalie said. "I'll design a mother-of-the-bride dress for Bianca instead. Bianca would look lovely in silk, don't you think? I'm picturing an ankle-length gown with sleeves in a semi-transparent lace… a sort of tapered princess dress, only with modern touches of elegance."

"Isn't that technically the 'grandmother-of-the-groom' dress?" Ama asked. "But it sounds gorgeous, anyway. Bianca is bound to love anything with 'princess' in the design name—although, I think she would rather it was a bridal gown for Molly."

Natalie shook her head. "What did I say? Limited couture for this wedding. Maybe next time will be different. Who knows? Our second client might need bridesmaids' dresses, for instance. No one expects those to be perfect, right? Anything less than hideous will qualify. I can definitely handle that."

Both her partners rolled their eyes at Natalie's words. "Now, I better run if I want a chance of finding gainful employment anytime soon," said Natalie, retreating upstairs to fetch her jacket and purse. "Wish me luck, ladies—if I land one of these, we might be able to pay off our debts to a certain handyman after all."

Chapter Thirteen

"It's just for a quick session," Tessa whispered, as she steered the handyman along the flower stall's aisles. Row after row of hot pink tulips, rose-colored buds, and bright, cheery daisies nodded in the breeze. "We just need to get some samples for the bouquet selection. Natalie's hunting for a florist, and I want to be able to give them some idea of what they're doing before we hire them."

"You said you would keep me in the background," Blake whispered back. "And by the way, are you sure about your friend Natalie being a fashion expert?" He gestured toward his outfit—donned under protest back at Wedding Belles' headquarters an hour earlier.

"Sure she is. That's what fashionable men are wearing these days, okay?" She glanced behind her, seeing a grimace of apology on Natalie's face once again.

"Sorry," Natalie whispered to her. "It was all that was in his size at the warehouse, I swear. It was this or a white tuxedo."

Instead of a suit, Blake was wearing an ill-fitting pair of electric-blue slacks, a yellow polo-style shirt that looked one size too small, and a fluffy white cardigan tied around his shoulders—the best Natalie could do on short notice for this last-minute outing, cobbling together the most casual garments from the warehouse's storage racks and from a box of items that Kandace was "repurposing" in her work. But Blake couldn't wear his flannel and denim, they had reasoned, and since he was out buying building supplies at the time, they couldn't ask to raid his home wardrobe for alternative clothes.

"You look very hip and modern. Exactly like Bianca and Molly would expect a top-notch wedding planner to look."

"I feel like a moron," he answered.

She could agree that he probably did. She, too, preferred his work clothes to this outfit, but it would have to do for today. Even Bianca would have noticed something out of line with a sophisticated wedding planner in faded Levi's and a tool belt.

She stopped to examine a bright florist's bucket packed with freesias in bloom. "Don't worry. All we have to do is take some photos of flowers and figure out which ones will make Molly happy. You'll be back to electrical wiring in no time." She hadn't told him about the plan to keep the floral costs as low as possible, although that was implied by the very existence of Bianca's tin-box fund.

Remember to smile, Tessa willed the contractor silently. He did—although it looked as awkward as he probably felt at this moment. They should have found another wardrobe option, Tessa thought. Didn't Blake say he owned a suit? Or two? Would that be overkill for an outdoor floral stand?

"So many flowers," declared Bianca, who was hovering in front of a display of extremely costly long-stem roses. "How do you choose?"

"Very carefully," said Tessa. "And with Molly's favorites in mind." She glanced at the bride.

"I don't have a favorite, really," said Molly. "I think of colors more than types. I'm pretty much a mixed bouquet kind of person when I buy them at the market. Paolo always brings me roses… but I think he picks them out because they're traditional to give to the woman you love, and he wants to pick the most special bouquet in the shop."

"You deserve it," said Bianca, squeezing her arm. "What do you think is good for a bride as beautiful as Molly?" she asked Blake. "So she won't outshine them so much on her wedding day?" she teased.

"Flowers aren't really my specialty," Blake answered, then received a pinch on the arm from Tessa. "I'll need a moment to think," he amended. He made a show of studying the surrounding blossoms, pretending to look thoughtful while scanning the possibilities.

"I think the freesias are very promising," hinted Tessa. "Or maybe something in… purple," she said, spotting some asters. "Maybe something very light and soft to accentuate Molly's dress." A mythical dress at this point.

"Some of these," said Blake, in return pulling out a handful of the asters. "With some of these, maybe"—a mix of eucalyptus stems, in a soft gray-green—"and maybe a few sprigs of this lavender." He added one or two stalks of it after glancing at the available flowers.

It wasn't a bad selection, Tessa thought, as if Blake had some instinct for this kind of thing; maybe from years of studying paint chips for his contractor's work?

"There," said Blake "It's—"

Don't say "fabulous," thought Tessa. Just this once, she was actually hoping the handyman would be more himself and not like Stefan, who would have sighed with despair at least three times now over the number of wilted buds and imperfect blooms on display.

"—a perfect match for Molly's eyes," finished Blake. With a smile, he held out the mixed bouquet to the bride.

That was the last thing Tessa would have expected him to say. Surprise left her temporarily wordless, even as Molly evidently admired the understated but elegant simplicity of the flowers—which did indeed look beautiful against the bride's eyes.

The cost of these flowers would be nothing compared to the more exotic arrangements Bianca tended to prefer, so they would fit perfectly with the couple's wedding budget. *Thanks, Blake*, she thought. *We owe you this one.*

Bianca seemed disappointed, a frown tugging the corners of her mouth. "They're not too plain?" she asked. "Too—common?"

"I like them," said Molly. "Only... I'm actually sort of allergic to lavender. I wish that I wasn't because this looks really beautiful."

Tessa could hear the disappointment in her voice. "We can find a substitute," she offered. "Allium blooms, or maybe lilac—" She spied some elegant-looking pale purple buds in a nearby pot and reached for them, realizing too late they were orchids, a variety among the most expensive flowers in the florist's whole display. This was a mistake.

"Such little dainty ones," Bianca noticed. "And look—Molly, these *must* be special. Look how much they cost!"

Blake's brow furrowed, and his expression darkened a little. He shot Tessa a look she couldn't quite interpret, because her mind was working quickly to find a way to undo this suggestion. "Not that we have to choose *these*, with a whole market of flowers to explore," she said.

Uncertainty and a little disappointment appeared in Molly's eyes. "These are totally gorgeous, Tessa. But I don't know... they're so expensive."

"Expense is *my* worry," Bianca reminded her. "You pick what you want for your day. These would be a good choice," she said. "We could get big lavender roses on the cake, too!"

"Well, um," Tessa stammered, rushing to intervene. "I don't think we should settle on anything so soon. Not unless Molly really loves it. I mean, orchids are—"

She was about to say "not as elegant as people assume" or "a complete clash with the cake's roses" or some other such excuse, when Molly's phone buzzed. Reading the text message, the bride-to-be gave them an apologetic smile. "Sorry, but we have to leave early. One of my clients needs to move their appointment up by an hour." Taking Bianca's arm, she told her, "Don't worry, we'll find something next time, Gran. I promise."

Tessa sighed. That was a disaster. Bianca now had her heart set on some of the most expensive flowers in the whole market. Maybe Blake could talk her out of it, since it was his opinion that Bianca valued: that of the fake wedding planner.

She put the flowers back in their sleeves. "Obviously, Blake, we'll have to—" she began, then turned to find him unknotting the sleeves of the cardigan from around his neck with a little more force than necessary.

"What are you doing?" she said. "Be careful with that." The fluffy cardigan was expensive hand-carded cashmere, according to Natalie.

"Yeah, we might need it for the next outing," said Natalie, hiding her smile for this joke, although it was technically stolen property Blake was wearing.

"Forget it," he answered. He handed her the cardigan, now wadded up in a cashmere ball. "I have some electrical wiring to repair. And a job that's a lot more important than picking out fifty-dollar orchids."

With that, he stalked off through the rows of market flowers, in the direction of the street.

"What's eating him?" Natalie asked, sounding less amused now. "He looks angry. What did you say to him?"

"Who knows," said Tessa. "He's just being a jerk about helping us out, probably. Maybe the outfit is getting to him. It *is* kind of horrible, Nat."

"I know," said Natalie. "Next time I'll do better. Half the male designers I know wouldn't be caught dead in that ensemble, even the ones who wear leggings."

"I just hope he doesn't catch a glimpse of his reflection before he gets back to the office."

A sudden attack of the giggles swept over both Tessa and Natalie. The contrast between the current image of the contractor in his ill-fitting togs and his usual denim and work shirt was too much—even Blake's good looks couldn't undo it.

"Still," Natalie mused, "anybody that good looking can probably dress how they want and *almost* get away with it. Almost."

"You really think he's that good looking, do you?" Tessa asked, as she toyed suddenly with a loose thread on the cardigan's sleeve. She sounded curious, and something about the skepticism in her voice didn't quite ring true—which Natalie pegged instantly.

"Yes. And so do you," Natalie answered. A knowing smile crossed her lips. "I saw you looking at him when he first stepped out of our powder room wearing that suit. You were working *very* hard to keep your eyes off him. If Bianca hadn't arrived, you would have been as dreamy-eyed as Ama was."

"I don't think so," said Tessa. Dismissively, she insisted, "He's not my type. He's not," in response to the look on Natalie's face. "If I had a type, I would say it's more the... the classical, clean-cut look. Sophisticated and sensitive, probably."

"Like Stefan?" The sarcastic question followed from Natalie.

"No," said Tessa with a scoff of derision. "Just... different from Blake, that's all I'm saying." She put the asters back in their container and fluffed the display neatly, and with a tiny bit more attention than it deserved.

The upstairs wall was in need of spackling and a fresh coat of paint after Blake had covered up its new wiring. Tessa had chosen a shade called "romantic blue" for the color, which was really more of a soft mauve, but looked beautiful on the paint chip.

"What a shame the old wallpaper is ruined," said Ama, as she stirred a paint stick through the color for her office—a shade called "harvest gold" on the paint sample, that reminded her of a turmeric paste her father made at the restaurant. She held it up, watching it drip into the paint can.

"Is it coming off?" she asked Natalie, who had borrowed a wall steamer to remove the water-stained flower paper that had sagged on the walls due to the roof leak.

"Sort of," Natalie answered, as she tossed a torn panel behind her. "At least the stuck part's not coming off in fist-size pieces, like when we peeled it by hand."

New rolls of wallpaper were leaning against the wall that was still painted in its original soft green beneath the bulbous-eyed monsters formed by the water stains. The paper's design was a simple ivory and gold that would look harmonious with the dark green color Tessa had chosen for the room adjacent to her office. For Natalie's own workspace, she envisioned a soft ivory base with a mix of rejected hardware paints for the geometric design that would be stenciled onto it.

All three of them wondered what the handyman would say about the completely un-historic modifications being made to the house's decor. He might be harboring secret resentments for the alterations made by the building's cheap new owners. At least that was Tessa's secret opinion.

Tessa had appropriated Stefan's former office space, where the "romantic blue" was already drying on its first wall. She draped a drop cloth over her work desk to protect it, along with the office chairs she had salvaged from a thrift store. After the walls were dry, she planned to bring in artwork to decorate them, mostly the large photographic prints of flowers in bloom that a friend had given her for Christmas one year. And she had her somewhat more domestic plans for the currently empty room adjacent to it—but she was keeping those to herself until her apartment's lease deadline arrived.

"I wish we could paint the downstairs now," said Natalie, as she turned off the steamer and collapsed into a folding chair. "I wish we could paint over the paper instead of removing it, too."

"Did anybody pick up the paint for downstairs?" asked Ama.

"I did," said Tessa. "The foyer is "pale green mist," and the sitting room is "ghost of romance." I picked up some of those white vinyl birch trees to decorate its walls, too."

"How much did all of this cost?" Natalie asked, wrinkling her brow.

"Not much," said Tessa. Her tone was a little too offhand not to leave the others suspicious that it had cost more than they anticipated. "Image is everything, isn't it?" she said, under the scrutiny of their stares. "I didn't spend the last of our repair fund, don't worry."

Ama dipped a roller brush into the tray and began painting the high walls in her office. "Listen," she said. "Has anybody talked to our fourth partner about the new plan?"

"What plan?"

"The plan to sabotage Bianca's super-expensive wedding dream?" replied Ama. "It can't be me. I think he's spoken to me all of once. You guys are the ones who have spent time with him."

Now Tessa and Natalie exchanged glances. "I guess I should really start removing that wallpaper again," said Natalie, climbing to her feet and muscling the steamer into position.

"Why is it my job?" asked Tessa helplessly. "Natalie is technically the one negotiating with the florist, after all."

"But you *are* the one who came up with the idea," pointed out Ama. A little shower of paint landed on the drop cloths below. "I think you have the responsibility to follow up with him."

"Fine." Tessa dropped the brush into the paint and followed the sound of construction downstairs to the kitchen. "I'll do it now." Better to get it over with, she supposed.

Blake, having resolved the wiring issues, was now trying to patch over the damage to the walls as cheaply as possible; a dust of dry spackling and plaster covered the old linoleum floor. Tessa paused in the doorway, suddenly feeling awkward about this, for no good reason that she could think of.

"Um, hi," said Tessa. "I needed to talk to you about something. Not the wiring." She hesitated, struggling to pick the right words, aware the handyman wouldn't be happy about this topic.

"What would that be?" He grunted as he shifted the stove and oven into its new spot—a tiny secondhand one that, hopefully, was big enough to bake cakes and cookies.

"I just need a quick word on the wedding," began Tessa. "It's a little change in the plans for your 'fourth partner' role. We need you to change Bianca's mind about the flowers."

He stopped his task of balancing the appliance. "Enough," he said. He turned to face her, wiping the grease off his hands with an old rag. "When I agreed to do this, I never thought it would go this far. It's one thing to make someone like Bianca happy by telling her a white lie. It's another thing to rip her off."

"Rip her off?" said Tessa. "Is that what you think we're doing?" She uncrossed her arms, feeling shocked.

"You're not exactly helping her, are you?" he asked. "I saw the pictures of the big cakes and fancy venues you have in mind. And the flowers you showed her at the nursery were probably the most expensive ones there."

"What is it you're trying to say?" Tessa demanded. "That we're cheats?"

"I'm saying that all the money Bianca has to her name is kept inside an old cookie tin—and the three of you seem to think it's bottomless."

Tessa was floored. He actually thought they were stealing money from Bianca? That was ridiculous!

She crossed her arms again. "For your information, we are *not* trying to force those things on Bianca," she said. "We don't even want her to choose them. We are doing what she asks, but we are *trying* to change her mind to spare her savings and her feelings. Believe it or not."

The handyman had fallen silent, though he was not apologetic. Tessa's cheeks grew hot. "I hope it will make you feel even better that the favor I came to ask you was to talk to Bianca over the phone and recommend a florist who had more reasonable prices," she said. "In case you also want to help save Bianca's retirement fund."

She was too angry to look at him, so she stared at the secondhand fridge that was sitting in the middle of the room. A long, awkward silence fell. Blake was the one to break it.

"I can make the phone call." His voice was quiet. "Just give me the number and I'll take care of it."

"Better than wearing another of Natalie's suits in public, right?" said Tessa. With that, she turned on her heel and walked out of the kitchen. If he thought she was angry, so be it. What right had he to make assumptions? Or to be so rude? Of all things, to virtually accuse them of *stealing* from the very person they were trying to help!

"What happened?" Ama seemed puzzled as she noticed Tessa's face. "Are you okay? You look a little pale."

"It's just the red hair," said Tessa, trying to suppress the biting edge to her voice. "Nothing's wrong." *With me, anyway.*

She climbed the ladder in her office and began slapping paint forcefully beneath the wall trim. Anger gave her muscles incentive and energy, although it also caused a lot of mauve paint to splatter on the paint tape and the tarp below.

He's a jerk. Ignore him. He doesn't have a clue who you are or what you're trying to do. Tessa slopped more paint from the tray to the floor. *How do I know he isn't ridiculously overcharging us for the work he's doing on our building?*

She smacked paint on the walls more forcefully. At least he had cared about Bianca in all this. That was the only part that made it seem decent that he had misconstrued their motives. She was surprised that he had cared about someone he had only met a few times—or that he had been paying enough attention to notice any of this. He'd obviously hated impersonating a wedding planner, even though he wasn't as bad at it as she would have predicted.

So he was a nice enough person to care that Bianca might be ripped off by three con artists getting cuts from all these deposits and fees. It still wasn't an excuse for putting his conclusions in such harsh words.

Slap, slap. Paint splattered the last of the wallpaper trim on the opposite wall, which Tessa had hoped to salvage and match in the future. She bit her lip. "Ama, would you bring me a wet sponge so I can clean up a mess?" she called. She stirred her brush in the paint, watching the drip from its bristles swirl among the pool within the bucket.

"Here you go." It wasn't Ama, but Blake who was standing below her, holding out the sponge.

She stiffened. "Thanks," she said snappily. She accepted it and began to wipe away the stains on the wallpaper, making a note to paint the rest of the room more gently.

Blake was still below her. He cleared his throat. "If you need some cleaner for that—"

"Nope. I'm fine. Thanks." She rubbed the last spot a little more forcefully than necessary. "Just fine."

"Or I could get you some mild paint remover—"

"I told you I've got it," said Tessa, as she stretched to wipe away the last micro droplet her eye detected in the sunshine. "Just go back to your work and let me finish—"

Her foot fumbled in search of the next step and Tessa felt her body part ways with the ladder. A shriek of alarm escaped from her lips as she fell backward toward the paint-stained tarps below, only to be caught by a strong grip before she reached the bottom.

Blake was holding her. The muscular arms from beneath his flannel shirt's rolled sleeves were wrapped securely around her, and were the only reason Tessa's sneakers and skinny jeans were not decorated with lavender paint at this moment. They were holding her against a chest that felt decidedly toned beneath that shirt, conjuring the image of those washboard abs in Tessa's mind, despite the distraction of the quick and steady human heart now beating gently against her back.

It was an embrace—that was the definition of it in anybody's mind, including Tessa's own. An embrace that created the intimacy of close eye contact when she turned her head to look at him, meeting a pair of eyes that seemed warmer than their usual steel blue as she gazed into them from this short distance. The frost had melted from their first disillusioning debate.

She had wrapped her hand around his arm in the second afterward—it was more like she was holding him in place than pushing him away. Was it her imagination or could she swear that his heartbeat was faster than normal in this moment?

"I'm okay," she said softly. "You can let go now." She didn't try to free herself as she said this.

"I know."

The distance in height between them was not enough to prevent them from being on the edge of a kiss when she turned her head again. His breath fanned her cheek, the edge of her parted lips. When she tried to right herself on the slippery tarp underneath her feet, she lost traction and her body moved closer to his. Her lips brushed his—that brief contact sent an electric thrill through every inch of her body, because it was almost like a kiss. Lip against lip, brushing against the sandpaper surface of his jaw as she moved aside from it; feeling his own face brush her cheek as he steadied her on her feet again.

"Are you all right?" he asked, a second later. He released her. Tessa let go of his arm.

"Fine." She repeated this word once more, although it was less casual—and far less angry—than before. "Um… thanks, " she said. "Thank you for breaking my fall." She added this hastily in her confusion. She wasn't thanking him for the near kiss. Obviously.

"No trouble." His eyes made contact with hers as she stood up from collecting her sponge off the floor, and Tessa was flustered by this simple glance. Her hand trembled as she placed the sponge beside her paintbrush on the tray. Coming close to breaking a leg—that was the real reason for the strange fluttering inside her, like stray petals caught in the wind.

"You're sure you're all right?" There was concern beneath the surface of Blake's voice, in place of the stiffness from their fight. At least that was the impression in Tessa's mind. "That was quite a fall."

"Well, no broken bones, huh?" She tucked aside a strand of hair that brushed against her cheek, avoiding even the chance she might look into his eyes again. "I'll... I'll just go on with painting the office now. The walls won't color themselves." She made herself busy stirring the paint in her bucket, although it was perfectly mixed already.

"If you need a hand, I have some time." Blake was still lingering in the doorway behind her, his thumbs tucked in his pockets, and his body language as awkward as her own. "I could grab the roller and do the upper walls to save you the trouble... and further accidents involving this rickety ladder."

He shook it a little with one hand, the flimsy aluminum rattling slightly, causing another little drip of lavender paint to shiver onto the drop cloths. "The paintbrush isn't the best choice for working above your head," he pointed out.

"I felt like getting a little exercise," Tessa said, although her defenses were weakening just a little, as the confusion from moments ago churned steadily within. "So you can go back to your work. I'm fine."

She avoided looking in his direction as she began painting—gently—a more accessible part of her future office. It would really help if he would leave now, so everything would settle into its normal place, inside of her and outside.

Blake hesitated. "If that's how you feel about it, I'll go. I just thought I would offer my help. Free of charge, if that's the problem."

That last remark was all that saved Tessa, who had softened enough to actually give his suggestion strong consideration. Now she banished that idea. *Remember what he said before about you,* she reminded herself.

"Feel free to charge for all your services, please," she said. "I should be able to afford them, if I'm ripping off clients with fancy cakes and overpriced wedding venues."

"That wasn't— I was trying to apologize, in my own way," he said, "by offering to help."

"I don't need your apologies or your help, thank you," Tessa replied. If there was any reply from their contractor, she didn't hear it—but it was probably only another derisive noise. Once her heart stopped beating so crazily, she wouldn't care the least bit about his response.

"What was *that* about?" Ama peered inside Tessa's office. "Were you two fighting?"

"Us?" said Tessa. "What about? He's patching our walls, I'm painting them. What would we fight about?" She caught herself painting forcefully again. Her brush slowed, attempting finesse along the side trim.

"I see," said Ama. A funny smile crossed her lips. She tapped her roll of wallpaper against one hand, thoughtfully.

"What?" demanded Tessa.

"Nothing. Nothing at all." Ama drifted back into her own office as Tessa pretended not to pay any attention to this last remark.

Chapter Fourteen

What a silly reaction to a little touch between two humans. Tessa told herself this—with scorn—as she sat behind her desk again, working busily on the latest figures Natalie had given her for the local florist's. It had been a complete accident, those moments of contact with Blake. He'd only been trying to prevent her from breaking her neck.

She shook her head and focused once more on double-checking the numbers for Molly's bouquet options. Helping Natalie choose an affordable florist was her only concern right now, to keep Bianca from buying half the roses in the city to decorate Molly and Paolo's ceremony site.

With lamplight in lieu of moonlight on the street, Tessa locked the door behind her and the handyman for the night. He set down his heavy metal toolbox as he replied to a text. They had said nothing when they encountered each other at the front door, which Tessa felt was for the best.

Blake tucked his phone back in his pocket. "I owe you a proper apology for what happened before," he told her. "If you're willing to accept it."

She glanced toward him. "What?" she said, pretending to be astonished. "You're taking back the insult you levied at me and my business partners by saying we were stealing from a defenseless old lady?" She said it with less sarcasm than before, though. "Are you sure you want to retract that accusation?"

"You're not going to make this easy, are you?" A little smile—a sheepish one—crossed his lips. Tessa believed he really was sorry.

She gave a little shrug. "Did I really convince you it isn't true?" she asked. "I need you to believe that we aren't trying to mislead Bianca about anything besides you being a master wedding planner. We want everything else to be as perfect as possible for her family's big day."

"I believe you," said Blake.

"You're sure?" Tessa quirked an eyebrow. "Because I don't want you to have a guilty conscience for helping us out or anything."

"I'm positive. I think you're probably the best planner for Bianca's family. Even if they had someone else in mind when they tracked you down."

"Thanks." Tessa was surprised—and a little flattered—by this frank endorsement of her skills. Not that he could really mean it, since he hardly knew her. "But you should probably know you're overestimating my talent a little," she said. "Ama and Natalie, they're great, but I'm the weak link in the chain, probably. The least experienced of the three of us, actually."

His brow furrowed. "This is your career, though. You must have some experience in it."

"It's only been my job for a few weeks now," she confessed. "Before now… I was driving around a truck painted to look like a dachshund in a sausage bun. Inflating bouncy castles and haunted houses, and cleaning up neon green cupcake frosting."

"Sounds… awful," said Blake, who then tried to hide his reflexive smile at these images.

"It's all about perspective," said Tessa. "It wasn't my business, or where my heart was, so I didn't like it. But my boss Bill, who started the business, adored it. Even before he had employees to help him, he frosted cupcakes in his own kitchen and biscuit-wrapped mini sausages. He loves kids and loves casual parties, so it was a perfect career for him."

"But not for you," said Blake. "Because... you don't like kids," he concluded.

Tessa rolled her eyes. "Look," she began. "If you're going to make fun of me—"

"Or was it the casual parties holding you back?" There might be a teasing expression on his face, if she could see it better in the lamplight. "You're more the black-tie affair type, I can tell."

"I like both," Tessa said. "It's not that. My heart just prefers helping people make different memories. There's a sign I've bought to hang in my office below all the posters of elegant brides and close-ups of flowers. *Dream Big. Plan Big. Live Big.* I guess that's how I see the world." She shouldered her bag again. "Big, grand possibilities that you can only make happen if you try. And if you stay realistic that not everything can turn out perfectly every time."

She smiled wistfully at the idea that someday, somehow, it would turn out perfectly for her. Even if just once.

"And how will Molly and Paolo's day turn out?" he asked.

"That depends on us," said Tessa. "We don't know yet how we'll handle it, do we?"

"I thought maybe you would say it depends on Bianca," said Blake with a short laugh. "She seems to be the one calling the shots around here."

"But we're the ones who make it real," said Tessa. "To really do our best, we have to be mind readers. We have to figure out the dreams that only the people who love them know—the secret wishes they only tell their best friends. If we're very lucky, then we figure out enough of those impossible details to pull together an event that matters to them. The part that matters is the part that makes it perfect—not the other way around."

Blake lifted his toolbox. "Sounds complicated. Good thing there's three of you to plan it."

"You mean four." Tessa's smile became a shrewd one. "Don't sell yourself short in this field yet, Mr. Ellingham. You may have hidden talents."

"Deeply hidden," Blake replied. "And unless it involves a carpentry project, I'm afraid that's where they'll stay."

"No more pressure," Tessa promised. "From now on, you will be a silent partner as much as possible. After you call Bianca about the florist, that is."

"Promise?" he said.

"Promise," she answered.

"Good," he said. "Because I will hold you to it, Miss Miller."

His voice was softer now. He leaned against his truck, hands tucked in his pockets again, and his tone of voice, along with the way he looked in the lamplight, sent a shiver through Tessa from head to toe. Good thing they weren't standing any closer, she thought—a strange, wild impulse of a thought—or they might be back where they were after the painting mishap, when she landed in his arms. But this landing would be different: a totally intentional, vertical one that would put her back in that strong embrace.

Heat rose in Tessa's face. Suddenly, she was busy searching for her keys, although she had put them in her bag only a minute before. "I expect you to hold me to— I mean, I expect to keep promises that I make people," she replied, in a quick sentence reversal. "So you should. Expect it, I mean."

"Can I give you a ride?" He glanced toward his truck. "Wherever you're going, I can drop you off there."

"Thanks, but I'm good on my own," said Tessa. She wasn't sure if she meant these words solely about tonight's plans, or in a deeper sense. "I have a ride waiting for me. I'll just be going. Goodnight." She waved over her shoulder as she walked away on her own, beneath the glowing streetlights and the decorative building flags swaying faintly in the night breeze.

Chapter Fifteen

The Bloomery was adorably chic, nestled in the newest part of Bellegrove's market district, and a favorite for Stefan's clients who were the extra-picky kind. From antique flower varieties to the latest in award-winning roses, its selection was the most impressively high-end on Natalie's list of possibilities, and, therefore, the least likely one they should choose. So, of course, it was no surprise that Bianca had set her heart on securing their services for her grandson's wedding day.

Natalie had a friend who'd hired them for her wedding the previous summer, and as she informed Tessa in her latest budget estimate, Bianca's biscuit tin couldn't afford a corsage at that place, let alone a bouquet.

"What about Fleur-de-Lisa?" Tessa wondered, glancing over Natalie's other estimates. "They're new and they look pretty reasonable. And they sound fancy enough for Bianca's taste," she added with a grin, as she stirred some creamer into her morning brew.

"Probably," Natalie said. "The manager is nice—I had some design classes with his daughter, actually. They offer great discounts, too, but I spoke to them this morning and they need more notice for an event like this one. They're handling the flowers for some beach resort's big opening banquet, and they're understaffed right now. Maybe we could book them for our next client." *If there is one*, she thought to add, but then decided against it. Even as a joke, it wouldn't seem funny right now.

"So who does that leave us with?" Tessa wondered.

Flipping through her stack of papers, Natalie handed Tessa a brochure, saying, "I'm leaning toward this place for Molly and Paolo's wedding right now. They're fairly new, but they have a good reputation. My brother bought his girlfriend a bouquet there last Valentine's Day, so I know their prices must be reasonable," she joked. "No one is cheaper than Rob, believe me."

"Rosies and Posies?" A grin played around Tessa's mouth as she read the name aloud. "I like that, actually. It's kind of whimsical sounding. Do you think we can get a discount with them?"

"Hopefully. I'm dropping by there later today. It's on the way to my favorite fabric shop, so I'll be in the neighborhood."

She needed to find material for the grandmother-of-the-groom dress she had promised the others she would make for Bianca. Nothing in her own collection had seemed quite right, even though she'd spent over an hour sorting through it the night before. She wanted something subtle but elegant that would complement the colors they were using for the wedding. But first came the flowers, although Natalie wasn't thrilled by the task of "bouquet stuffing"—nevertheless, she found herself standing outside the cozy-looking Rosies and Posies a little before noon.

Something about this place seemed promising to Natalie, since its rosy pink walls made for a warm and inviting atmosphere, while fresh-cut flowers were arranged in decorative pots and vases for attractive bursts of color. But the employee behind the desk wasn't Maxine, the middle-aged shop owner whose profile was featured on the website. Instead, a slender young girl in a floral printed apron was manning the front counter, her olive-toned skin and rich brown hair instantly familiar to Natalie's surprised eyes.

"Gabby?" she asked, seeing the girl's face light up in response. "Ma never mentioned you were in the flower business now! How did you ever escape the pizzeria?" She was only half-joking with her cousin in reference to her family's food obsession when it came to businesses—it was rare to find a Grenaldi in retail who *wasn't* either filling cannoli or dishing up spaghetti.

"I didn't," said Gabby. "Not completely, anyway. I still work the evening shift three times a week at Norelli's. But I'm working here part-time, too, because I've decided flowers would make a nice change. Gotta make room for your dreams wherever you can, right?"

"I know the feeling," Natalie replied, laying her pocket book on the counter where Gabby was arranging a vase of daises. "Although, in my case it's probably Dress for Less that'll be making room for my dreams these days, instead of Kandace's Kreations."

"Kandace fired you?" Gabby's Southern drawl was full of shock.

"Actually, I quit." That was the technical truth, regardless of Kandace's parting shot. "But the reason I'm here is because I've joined this new wedding business," Natalie told her. "Remember my friend Tess? It was her idea, and it's still kind of launching, but it has a lot of potential. I hoped maybe your boss would consider arranging the flowers for our first client's wedding. Is she here right now?" She peered toward the back of the shop, where a curtain was partly pulled back to reveal an office setting.

"Sorry, but no," said Gabby. "She had to help a client with their event downtown today. But I can leave your card on her desk with a note and she'll call you back." She glanced at the business logo on the card Natalie handed her, the rose and bells motif Tessa had requested beneath the gilded lettering. "That's real cute," she remarked. "I like the name, too. It's the kind that sticks in your memory, if you know what I mean."

"Let's hope it has that effect on prospective clients," Natalie agreed. "Mind if I browse a little bit? I'm looking for flowers in lavender and soft greens, mostly," she added, remembering the bride's preference for these during the ill-fated flower market venture.

"Try the pastels," Gabby advised. "They're across from the 'flowers of the sea' display," she added, with a gesture toward a selection of delicate-looking blossoms in blue and white, with seashells interspersed among the vases and pots. "My boss Maxine swears by her selection as the best in the city."

More customers arrived while Natalie was there, several of them regulars judging by the way they spoke to Gabby as she rang up their purchases and took down future orders. And no wonder—the prices were reasonable, the arrangements professional. She could definitely picture a business connection blooming between Wedding Belles and Rosies and Posies. And not merely because Gabby might give her a family discount, either.

As she turned down a row of rose selections, her eye was drawn to a deep-hued blossom in a color somewhere between wine and deep rose. It was striking for its sheer simple elegance, she thought. A perfect color for a dress, even.

Bianca's dress.

The idea came like a lamp switching on in the dark. It was perfect, just the right color for the design she had sketched a few days before, though she hadn't realized it until a moment before. Carefully, she lifted out a single stem from the bunch and carried it to the register, where Gabby was leafing through an issue of *Tea Time* from the register's catalog stand.

"Nice choice," her cousin commented, ringing it up for her. "That's a new variety we got in a couple weeks ago. 'Cheyenne Moon.' Don't you just love the creative names they come up with for roses? We got one in this week called 'Kiss Me Kate.' Oh, and that pink and yellow striped number in the window is 'Cheshire Cat's Delight.'"

"Clever," Natalie agreed. In her mind, she was debating the odds she could get her favorite fabric vendor to match this rose in silk or maybe chiffon. Then she could get to work right away. Bianca's dress would be a gift, of course—she wouldn't dream of charging their client for something she hadn't even requested. It would be payment enough to see an actual client wearing something she had sewn as she celebrated her family's big moment.

Smiling to herself, she tucked the blossom into her bag, its cellophane wrapping shielding it from the work folders inside. "Thanks a million, Gabby," she said. "We'll call your boss about the flowers. I think it could be the beginning of a brilliant working relationship."

Chapter Sixteen

Tessa lugged the cardboard box to the top of the stairs and paused. No one was in sight.

Quietly, she eased down the hall, avoiding the floorboard that always creaked like a squeaky door in a horror movie. A few more yards, and she was safe inside her office, shutting the door behind her with her foot.

That wasn't her real destination, though. Shifting the box's weight in her arms, she opened the door to the adjacent room, the doorknob sticking slightly. It finally swung open to reveal a pile of similar boxes, a makeshift bed in the corner, and a pile of clothes beside the closet. Tessa's clothes.

She didn't mean to lie, really. She just didn't want to worry the others by telling them that she had let her lease expire, and was relying on their business to put a roof over her head. Her new home, such as it was, happened to be the room adjoining her office in a building that was considered worthy of demolition mere weeks ago. No big deal, right?

But, of course, she knew it was. She'd had a hard enough time convincing her mother that she was moving somewhere safe—even though Tessa had emphasized the building's old-fashioned charm and ideal location, leaving out the bits about dry rot, mold, and possibly hazardous floor conditions. Those were only temporary, anyway.

Besides, it was too late. When the lease arrived, she hadn't signed it. No renewal, no apartment. She and her remaining possessions had to move.

Plenty of shop owners lived above their business, she knew. Ama's family, for one. Then again, they had more than one paying customer in their restaurant nightly, something the little negative voice in Tessa's head whispered that Wedding Belles might never have in its parlor.

With a sigh, Ama closed her latest baking cookbook at a recipe for a three-tier Black Forest gâteau which involved an expensive cream filling. None of these were quite right for Molly and Paolo. Expense, size, style—there were plenty of reasons why she didn't feel these were options.

"Ama, did you see it?" Her mother entered with a basket of flatbread for today's lunch menu. She laid the morning mail on the table: a few bills and an Indian-American magazine that Ama hadn't bothered to flip through today.

"See what?" Ama asked.

"The ad. Your papa is so proud of it. He worked hard," said her mother.

"What?" Ama reached for the journal and flipped it open—to the section she used to read in jest with her sisters, the matchmaking ads. "No, no," she groaned.

"What?" Jaidev was reading over her shoulder, along with Rasha, who was tugging her sari-style hostess dress into place with a few extra sari pins. "Hey, he went through with it after all," he said, spotting their family's contact information beneath an ad for a marriageable young woman from a Punjabi family.

"How could he?" said Ama. "I thought I told him I wouldn't meet any of these boys."

"Hush! Your father is proud of that ad," scolded Pashma. "He put some of it on the profile on the web. The computer."

"The internet?" echoed Ama. "He put me on a matchmaking website?"

"Oh, Ama, this is so exciting," said Rasha, squealing a little.

"No, it's not, it's unfair," groaned Ama. "How could he create a matchmaker's profile for me? How could he even begin to write something about me? Does he even know how to upload a photograph?"

"At least he didn't put 'homely' in the ad," pointed out Jaidev, who was trying not to laugh.

"Shut up. It's not funny." Ama snatched the journal away from him and tossed it back into the pile of mail.

"Hey, it's not so bad," he said. "Come on. We've all been there, Ama."

"You could meet a really nice boy," suggested Rasha. "Anything could happen, Ama. What if you meet the perfect guy?"

"From an ad our father posted?" Ama asked hotly.

"It's only for a month." Pashma opened a jar of lentil paste. "It's cheap that way."

"Mom's Rajasthani economy at work," teased Jaidev, as he unloaded packages of meat into the fridge. "She's probably hoping you get married before next month's issue comes out, so Dad won't buy another one."

"Not the ad—the profile," said Pashma, as she reached for some grated carrots and dried tomatoes. "He only keeps it online for a month, unless it brings some nice boys to meet her."

"I don't need an ad to help me find someone. Honestly," said Ama.

"It will be good for you," Pashma insisted. "It will get you into a dress for a change. A real one, not one of those things made out of... of denim or jean or whatever they call it."

"I'm wearing a dress already," protested Ama. "This is a perfectly nice dress. What's wrong with it?" She spread her hands toward her skirt—the funky printed one with the New York skyline, matched with a lace t-shirt today.

"It's nice," said Rasha hesitantly. "It's just... you know... a little subdued."

Rasha's own fashion choices tended to be bright and showy, even when she wasn't in a hostess's sari. Yesterday, she had worn a bright pink blouse with blue and purple flowers printed on it, with sequined denim jeans that didn't have their mother's approval, even with the pink and red flowers bedecking its pockets.

"I like it. I think it's nice," said Ama defensively.

"If you could just wear something a little nicer when you meet a boy," began her mother. "Away from those aprons and all those sugar icings you play with."

"Enough. I don't want help with my fashion choices, and I don't want help finding a husband," said Ama. "Let me make my own decisions, please." She gathered up her books and dropped them into an oversized tote bag printed with a sequined Taj Mahal—a gift from Rasha for her last birthday.

Her family exchanged glances—her brother's was one of sympathetic amusement; her mother and sister's looks conveyed their disappointment and exasperation. Ama pretended to ignore them as she shouldered her bag.

"You're not leaving now, are you?" said Rasha.

"Hey, what about the bread pudding?" asked Jaidev. "You haven't made the milk sauce yet."

"There's some in the fridge, and I sliced the almonds already," said Ama. "I said I was going out for a while to run some errands. I'll be back before the lunch crowd."

She went for a walk, trying not to think about the strict Indian fathers reading her profile as a prospective bride for their sons—or the girls like herself who would make fun of her father's old-fashioned wording for his magazine ad, which did stop short of the euphemism "homely," at least—a word used in Indian culture to imply that she was good housewife material. Jaidev was right about that bit of luck.

She brushed aside a trace of almond powder from her sleeve, and tried to think about the perfect cake for Bianca's family's wedding instead. If this were an Indian wedding, it would be easier—either it would be an American cake dressed up with a sari theme, or it would be finger sweets, traditional Indian desserts. Punjabis love their sweets, and her sister's wedding buffet had been loaded with sweet and sticky *gulab jamun* like Ama made for the restaurant weekly, and other *mithai* decorated with gilded leaves.

The window display in Icing Italia had changed to feature traditional cookies, bones of the dead and biscotti; beautifully white iced *cuoricini* cookies which looked as spicy as gingerbread. There were macaroons, and even a Sicilian cake frosted with chocolate and garnished with almonds, also a favorite ingredient in Indian desserts. A Sicilian puppet was displayed in the window, too, one with a crackly, painted face and the shiny aluminum armor of a miniature knight.

She pushed open the door and entered. An older woman behind the counter was placing several cannoli into a bakery box for a waiting customer. Ama saw Natalie at the other end of the counter, sliding a tray of chocolate-frosted cupcakes into the display cabinet. Her business partner waved at her.

"Hi," said Natalie. "Are you here for some fine Italian cookies? Ma's very proud of that window display."

"Go on, will you?" said the woman behind the counter—a tall, fine-boned woman with dark hair, who had flour stains on her apron. "So I put a little extra effort into it. It pulls the customers in, what can I say?"

"Ma, this is Ama. She works with me at the new event planning firm we're starting. She's from the restaurant down the street, the Indian one. She's a pretty great baker," said Natalie.

"I've seen that place. The one with the big tiger on the sign, isn't it?" said Natalie's mother. "I'm Maria, by the way—that's my son Roberto, and that's Guido in the kitchen." She pointed toward the half-open door, where a thin, deeply tanned man was visible kneading dough at an old table. "Somewhere around here is Louisa, who worries about whether our baked goods are Italian enough for the customers."

"Pleased to meet you," said Ama. "I was out for a walk, looking for inspiration, and thought maybe something sweet would help me figure it out."

"You've come to the right place," said Maria. "Natalie, give your friend something from our best, all right? On the house." She turned to the next customer, who was asking for some macaroons lightly glazed with chocolate.

"What do you like?" asked Natalie. "Chocolate? Pastry? Sweet mascarpone?"

"I get enough sweet milk in Indian desserts," said Ama, smiling. "That's the preferred flavor for them—sweet milk, sugar syrups, and nuts. Lots of rice and wheat puddings."

"If you want something totally different, then try these." Natalie popped a rich slice of cake into a box. "This is Italian wedding cake. It's layered with fruit and nuts—it's so rich that it used to be confined only to holidays, before Italians started serving it for special occasions too."

Ama nibbled a broken edge from it. "Wow," she said. "That's really good."

"I know. My mom makes this every Christmas. I love it," Natalie said. "Maybe it'll help. I mean, it was a pretty popular wedding cake in its time. And Paolo has Italian roots."

"Too bad we can't talk Bianca into this," said Ama, taking another bite. "I could make this. Maybe with lots of berries and two kinds of nuts layered together. And a really light frosting."

"I don't think it's quite elaborate enough for Bianca's tastes," agreed Natalie wryly. "Unless we put some big marzipan doves on it."

"Don't remind me," said Ama. "I just wish I could find something that would make all of them happy. I tried three different designs, and none of them feels right. None of them fitted the wedding's budget, either. Of course, it would help if we had an actual figure to work with."

"I think the figure Tess is recommending is simply 'cheap,'" said Natalie. "But good." She raised one eyebrow. "I still haven't figured out how that's going to help us in the dress department."

"Ninety-nine dollar sales," said Ama. "That's how a friend of mine got an affordable dress. Of course, in my family, you're supposed to be married in something a little different." She thought of her sister-in-law's pink and red sari with its gilded embroidery, from the last family wedding.

She was still sampling the cake as she walked out of the bakery; pausing for a moment she noticed a thin cake on a stand in the window with a doily pattern on it, made with powdered sugar. A rococo-style cake, she knew from an Italian cookbook. The elaborate stencil design had been traditional at Sardinian weddings, where the names of the bride and groom would form part of the decoration.

It was a beautiful design. Just like a doily of the finest lace was covering the top of the spice cake.

"I think I've found an answer," Ama said.

All three of them were in the new kitchen—which wasn't painted yet, although the secondhand fridge and stove were in place, and Blake was installing the stainless steel counters and backsplashes as they spoke.

She turned around the sketch she had made to face Natalie and Tessa. "When Natalie talked about Italian wedding cakes, and I saw the one in the window, something clicked. I thought, why not use those techniques to make something special. So here it is."

Three tiers of sponge, two vanilla and the middle one chocolate, each sliced in half and layered together again with a rich cream flavored with dried berries. There was ivory frosting over the top of each layer, with a fanciful lace pattern stenciled in cocoa powder and gold dust over the surface.

Gold cake pillars separated each sponge tier, and instead of a miniature bride and groom, a few gilded nuts and white-coated raspberries were arranged amongst edible gilded leaves on the top.

"It's still a little rough," admitted Ama, showing them a sketch of an individual slice on a plate, revealing the rich pink and violet streaked cream filling between two layers of chocolate sponge. "But I think it's a start."

"I think it's beautiful," said Natalie. "It's so different. It looks delicate and refined."

"I could do a lace frosting pattern over the sides using a fine-tipped point," said Ama. "I'm thinking we'd leave the sides partially bare—the 'naked cake' look would really accentuate the topmost frosting and the stenciled lace."

"It looks like something Bianca would admire," said Tessa. "How can she not love it? It's way better than the two big marzipan doves on top of a white cake."

"I imagine it with beautifully stenciled spice cookies to match," said Ama. "Maybe some other traditional Italian desserts, and something Irish to round out the sweet finger foods. I think I can find a way to create an Irish tiramisu, sort of—a whiskey-laced vanilla coffee soaking the sponge; a mint cream for the layering. Maybe something with the Celtic love knot motif for some filled cakes or petits fours… cut into bite-size squares." She closed her notebook.

"Can we do it cheaply enough?" asked Natalie.

"If it's me and your family making everything, sure," said Ama. "We can swap the frosting for fondant, even—there's this great cheat recipe that's easy, delicious, and affordable. The cakes are simple to bake. All the flavor comes from the dried berries and the sweet cream."

"My mouth is watering," said Natalie. "I'm sold." She glanced expectantly at Tessa.

"So am I," said Tessa. "So let's show it to Molly and see if she likes the idea. And get Bianca to love it, if we can."

Ama studied her list of ideas. "I know we'll probably need a few more options," she said. "This is finger food desserts only, with no dinner—I know Bianca will worry if there's not a tableful of choices for their guests."

"You sound Italian," said Natalie with a grin. "A full buffet for the wedding."

"There's always something light, like macaroons," pointed out Tessa. "They look pretty on wedding dessert tables."

"Irish macaroons," suggested Blake, as his measuring tape snapped closed.

All eyes were on him. He gave a shrug.

"You know," he said. "Because of Molly's heritage. They could be mint. Or berry flavored. With some Irish cream in the middle." He went back to his work as the three of them stared at him a moment longer.

"That's not bad," ventured Tessa. She looked at Ama.

"No," echoed Ama. "I like it, actually." She wrote it on the list—*Irish macaroons*—deciding not to add a question mark to its end. "I'll go put together a portfolio to show Molly and Bianca," continued Ama, gathering up her sketches. "At least we have one option to show her, finally."

Blake had almost finished installing the first countertop as Tessa rose, the last one to leave the table. She paused. "Thanks for the menu suggestion," she said. "It was a good idea."

"You don't have to say that," he answered. He shrugged his shoulders. "It was just an idea off the top of my head. I think a *real* wedding planner could do better."

"No, I like it," insisted Tessa. "I just didn't realize you were paying that much attention to the details. Or that you knew anything about desserts."

"Maybe I've done more in the kitchen than just rewire appliances and install countertops," he added, as he placed a level on the counter's surface. "Maybe I've read a cookbook or two in my time. Ever think of that?" He glanced at her. She couldn't tell if he was serious or joking. Not that it mattered, because she got the point—that he was trying to help them out in whatever way he could.

"That's how I got started in this business," she answered. "Not a cookbook, but an open magazine. Some perfect party... I don't remember what it was or where it was... just that I looked at the picture and thought, 'I want to make that real.' You know, make it happen in real life, a beautiful party full of lights and food and fun."

Blake didn't say anything in reply, but she could tell he was still listening. He picked up a screwdriver from his toolbox but didn't use it for anything, merely held it in his hand as she talked.

"When I grew up, I couldn't shake the idea. That picture in my head—it stayed with me all that time. I pursued different, sensible ideas for a while in college, but all roads I followed just led back to wedding receptions and engagement parties and all kinds of celebrations."

The dream had never vanished. Unlike the secret dreams of a personal happily ever after from Tessa's past, the desire to make people's special moments as memorable as possible had blazed brightly through every obstacle—even through the tiny eyeholes of the stinky T-Rex mask at Party 2 Go.

She lifted her planner's notebook and tucked it under her arm. "Did you want to be a— a handyman when you were a kid?" She knew the correct term was probably "master carpenter" or "building contractor," because he did more than fix leaks and rewire appliances. There was an art to what he did for the buildings he worked on, judging by his portfolio. The rest of the proof was in his words and passion for it.

"Let's see." Blake tossed the screwdriver aside, reaching for his carpenter's pencil. "I wanted to be an inventor when I was young. In fact, I built a time machine in my family's garage when I was eight." A brief, quick smile came and went. "A cardboard box and some old pipes, it seems. It was powered by materials from our recycling bins."

"Sounds sophisticated," Tessa answered. "Just where did you travel in your device?"

"Everywhere," said Blake. "Colonial times, the Civil War, the Wild West. I liked history better than most classes, so I had lots of inspiration. Outer space... future cities. In a way, my childhood fantasies ended up coming in handy in my real future, by the time I grew up." The screwdriver pried aside a small blemish in the plaster, letting the steel panel fit tightly against the wall. "All that history paid off, anyway."

"For the houses you work on," Tessa guessed. "You need it for restoring their past, right? That's why your truck is so full of... stuff. Nice stuff," she added, in case he mistook her tone for labeling all the antique corbels and iron railings as junk.

She knew what a corbel was now, thanks to the internet.

"I go to local estate sales and auctions," Blake explained, rummaging around his toolbox for another implement. "If there's a house or business being demolished in the area, I try to find out if there's anything worth salvaging before they pull it down—fireplace mantels, stained-glass windows, old armoires. I find new homes for them when they fill a gap at another place I'm restoring. It's usually easy to tell when a piece is right for a certain atmosphere."

"Wow," said Tessa, impressed. "So you're like a... a house surgeon, in a way. You rebuild the missing and damaged parts."

Blake lifted an eyebrow. "I've never had it put like that before," he answered. He tossed the screwdriver into the toolbox again.

"This looks great, by the way," she said. She touched the surface of the counter, stroking the smooth metal. "And this is compliant with city code, right?"

"Health inspectors won't be able to complain," said Blake. "I got you the best deal that I could, after arguing with the guy at the salvage yard. Hopefully, that won't turn out to be the last good deal I ever make." His smile was one of irony.

"It won't," promised Tessa. She moved her hand at the same moment Blake reached for his hammer on the counter. Their fingers brushed. Tessa felt a sudden jolt through the tips of her own, her mind imagining a blue spark leaping between them. Electricity.

A pause. "I should put some sealant behind this," said Blake, clearing his throat. He reached for the tube of caulking—located on the opposite side of the counter from Tessa's hand.

"I should go back to work myself," said Tessa. She took a step backward, almost stumbling over his toolbox in her sudden decision to retreat from his workspace.

"See you later." He was too busy with the counter's seam to look at her again as Tessa hurried to her office without replying.

Chapter Seventeen

Tessa slid the copy of *Brideshead Revisited* next to a set of volumes on decorating, then stood back to admire the effect. The shelf was a little crooked, true. But she could fix that if she borrowed a hammer and nails from Blake's vast collection of tools downstairs. Maybe in the dead of night, when he wasn't around to notice.

Or remind you how attractive he is, she thought, remembering that moment in the kitchen last night. It wasn't the first spark between them, either. She might never feel the same again about ladders, for instance, though she would certainly try to block that particular incident from her memory.

In the meantime, she could distract herself by sprucing up her new home, such as it was. Having more of her favorite things on hand would make it seem cozier in no time. Or so she told herself, as she hung a mirror on the powder room door. Her reflection revealed a few cobwebs in her hair from poking around the old dresser in search of a space for her linens.

Her lips formed a wry smile at the sight—before letting out a shriek of surprise as the bookshelf gave way under its new burden. Hardbacks tumbled to the dresser below, tipping over a box full of cosmetics, which scattered everywhere in seconds. The broken shelf banged against the wall, scuffing the old paint that Tessa fully intended to replace.

"Is someone in there? What's going on?"

The door popped open, and Natalie stuck her head inside. Her eyes grew wide at the sight of Tessa's belongings scattered amid a sea of cardboard boxes. "What happened?" she asked, stepping forward to help.

"Ummm... nothing. I've just been sorting through some stuff," Tessa replied, shoving her hairspray back in the box, along with several tubes of lipstick and a curling iron. "You know, basic organization," she added, stacking the books into a pile beside the dresser.

"Isn't that the loveseat from your apartment?" Natalie pointed to the cushy piece of furniture partly hidden beneath a stack of dry cleaning. "These are your bunny house shoes, too. Pretty causal for the office," she said, dangling the grubby but cherished footwear in one hand, the bunny's whiskers drooping slightly. "What's going on, Tessa? Because it looks like you're sleeping here or moving your stuff in, or something."

"Sort of. I mean, it's more convenient since I've been putting in so many late nights and..." She trailed off as Natalie shook her head with a stony look of accusation.

Tessa took a deep breath. "Okay, so technically, I *am* living here," she confessed. "But it's only because I really need this business to work, and I'm saving every penny I can to make that possible. It's just temporary, so don't worry. And don't mention it to Ama right now, okay?"

"Mention what to Ama?"

Their other business partner had appeared on the scene, her smile a little confused as she glanced at them through the door. "Sorry to interrupt," she told them, "but a photographer phoned Tessa on the business line earlier. I didn't know you were up here, so I had to take a message. What happened, by the way?" she asked, nearly catching her foot on a strand of twinkle lights Tessa had left just inside the door.

"Did the previous owners leave this stuff behind? I don't remember seeing any of it when we moved in."

"It's Tessa's," said Natalie. "She's decided she's going to move in here."

"Really?" Ama looked a little shocked. "Wow. That's really… brave of you," she said, after searching for the words a moment.

"That's one way to put it," said Natalie, though in a tone that suggested "stupid" or "reckless" might have been a more suitable description. But she didn't say either of those aloud, which Tessa was grateful for, since it gave her an opportunity to change the subject.

Tessa turned back to Ama. "Tell me what the photographer said. Does he need me to call him back? I gave his receptionist all the details so hopefully—"

"He's booked already. Until fall, actually."

Of course he was, Tessa thought. All the really reputable ones had been booked weeks in advance. She had contacted just about every photographer and studio listed in the local yellow pages at this point. Except for one, a little studio called Special Moments that photographed "life's occasions big and small," according to its webpage. She decided to visit it in person, since she was running an errand in that part of town later on.

Special Moments was located in a tiny brick building squeezed between the Hummingbird Cafe and a shop that sold musical instruments. Another customer was exiting the building as Tessa approached, their tiny Chihuahua dog dressed in a little summer outfit. It yapped furiously at the sight of Tessa, while its owner apologized and said, "Hush now, Mitzi!" to no avail.

No one was behind the front desk when Tessa arrived, but a young woman in a maternity blouse and jeggings emerged from a curtained-off room a moment later.

"Well, howdy there! I didn't hear you come in." A smile accompanied her friendly sounding Southern twang as she consulted a binder in front of her. "Are you my husband's ten-thirty appointment? He's getting the film ready now, so we can take the photo as soon as you and the little fellow are ready. Or is it a girl?"

"Who?" Tessa asked, feeling confused.

"Your dog," the woman said. "A poodle, isn't it? My husband, Alan, made the appointment, but he wrote something that looks like 'poodle' here. Or Pomerat." Laughing, she added, "My husband's handwriting is practically encoded. Which breed is your dog, incidentally?"

"Actually, I don't have a dog. Or an appointment," Tessa admitted. "I wanted to talk to your husband about a possible job, though," she began, eyeing the photo gallery on the opposite wall. It was filled with portraits of small dogs that reminded her of the one she had encountered on the way inside: dogs in Halloween costumes and Santa suits; dogs in funny hats and handmade sweaters. Dogs in tam-o'-shanters and tartan, even.

Wait a second. Were all these pictures of dogs? Maybe she had gone to the wrong address. But the name above the door had been the same as the website she'd visited—which hadn't mentioned anything about being for pets only in its description of life's photographic moments.

"I'm afraid we're not hiring right now." This from the photographer, who'd overheard Tessa's last remark and misunderstood its meaning. He wore a friendly smile as he joined his wife at the desk, a pair of reading glasses propped on his nose. "My wife Callie and I run the studio together and there's not really enough work for an assistant.

But if you leave us a contact number, we'd be happy to consider you for a future position."

Tessa shook her head. "That's not what I meant. You see, I'm an event planner for a new firm in town, and we're hoping to connect with a local photographer for our client's wedding day."

"A wedding." The photographer exchanged a glance with his wife. "I've never been hired to photograph one of those before. Well, except—" He jerked his head in the direction of one of the portraits on the wall: a pair of Yorkshire terriers dressed as a bride and groom, complete with a little bone-shaped tie for the tuxedo.

"They were a lovely couple," Callie recalled, lips twitching into a humorous smile as her glance met Tessa's. "They've already started a family, I heard. Six puppies in all."

"Very impressive," said Tessa, grinning in spite of her disappointment. Another photographer crossed off her list; a big, fat question mark in its place for how to find a suitable candidate now that she had exhausted the local talent. "Well, I'm really sorry to have bothered you," she told them.

"Alan," the woman said, turning back to her husband. "Show her the other photos you took."

"Other photos?" Tessa stopped, glancing back at him. "Do you have a portfolio of some other work you'd like me to consider?" *Please say yes*, she thought.

"Sure. Absolutely. Come this way," he said.

Tessa followed the couple to a doorway where a curtain was pulled aside to reveal a very different collection of images from the one she had just viewed: photos of weddings and big, cheerful celebrations, confetti raining down on one event; fireflies glowing in the atmosphere for another. Laughing faces and smiling eyes from life's events both big and small, captured in stunning color, black and white, and even old-fashioned sepia.

"These weren't professional jobs, I'm afraid," he said, waving a hand at them. "Just photos I took for friends and family. But I like to think it's my best work," he added, with a grin that proved he was modest enough to think it might not be, if she happened to disagree. Tessa didn't, of course. They were brilliant. Clearly, his best talent was a hidden one.

One in particular stood out for her: a wedding on the beach, the bride and groom running hand in hand along the shore as well-wishers threw confetti in the air. Wind whipped their hair, their faces alight with laughter and excitement. It was as magical as anything you could see in a magazine, only this was genuine. These were real people experiencing real happiness on the best day of their lives. It was breathtaking.

"That's one of my favorites, too," Callie said, noticing her smiling at the photo. "He's good, isn't he?"

"He is," Tessa agreed. "Really good. So why aren't these photos on display up front so the customers can see them?"

"Oh, you know how it is," Alan said with a shrug. "These were just taken as a favor to family and friends. And it seems like folks don't take your work seriously unless you're getting paid for it. I keep 'em in the back. No one's ever asked to see them until now."

"You know," said Tessa, "I might be able to help you out there."

"So he'll take the wedding photos for just a flat fee? That's amazing," Natalie said. She was paging through the folder of copies the photographer had given to Tessa for their clients, looking at the amazing snapshots of family weddings.

"Yep. A really reasonable one, too," said Tessa, who was perched on the arm of the loveseat, since Natalie had taken the only part of the cushion not covered in dry cleaning. "Since he's an undiscovered talent, he's willing to charge a lesser fee in exchange for the exposure, I guess."

"Kind of like us," Natalie joked.

It kind of was, Tessa thought. Although she didn't have a second business to fall back on if her big creative leap didn't work out. "By the way, how is the job search going?" she asked Natalie, since the subject was on her mind.

"It's over, for now. You're looking at the newest part-time employee at Dress for Less," said Natalie. "The finest in discount clothing and retail." She sighed and took a sip of her coffee. "At least it'll pay the bills until something better comes along, right? And if I get bored, I can always quit and go back to Ma's bakery."

"Congratulations," said Tessa, clinking her mug against Natalie's. "Between that and Ama's cookie business, at least two of us will be fairly solvent."

"And you're contributing your rent money to the business, I suppose," Natalie said, glancing at their surroundings. "Are you really sure about this, Tessa? Giving up your apartment, kicking your long-time job to the curb. You've burned a lot of bridges for this, so to speak."

"Bridges that were leading nowhere," Tessa reminded her. "At least now I have a chance of finally getting someplace that I really want to be."

Or losing everything she had, including her dreams. But that was something she preferred not to think about just now.

Chapter Eighteen

"You'll come, won't you?" said Tessa to Blake, as he adjusted the new stainless steel panel behind the stove. "I think it would mean a lot to Bianca… and to the business's future. And Natalie already picked out a suit for you to wear."

"Not electric blue," said Blake, with a warning glance over his shoulder.

"How do you feel about salmon pink?" she asked. His gaze grew chilly, until she smiled. "Kidding, kidding. It's Versace, and very traditional. Very gray."

"Gray is good," said Blake.

"So you'll be there?"

"How can I refuse?"

Bianca had invited the staff of Wedding Belles to her place, insisting on having them all meet with Paolo and Molly over dinner. Tessa was trying to imagine tiny little Bianca preparing a meal for seven people, and wasn't sure this was a great idea, but Bianca had insisted this was what she wanted.

"Come in, come in." She ushered them into her home, a beaming smile on her face. "You are in time. The fish soup is hot and the seafood will be ready soon."

"It smells good," said Natalie, sniffing the air. "Very rich and tempting."

"It is a good Norwegian soup," said Bianca. "A real 'chowder' as you would say. There is fish and sour cream thickening it with the eggs." She took their coats. "Paolo, pour some aquavit for a toast."

"Aquavit? Not Italian wine?" said Ama, as she removed her pashmina scarf and sat down beside Molly on the sofa. "That's kind of a surprise."

"This is Gran's drink," said Paolo, pouring some small glasses. "Growing up, I ate a lot of Gramps's food, since he was the cook. But when Gran cooked for love, it was always the northern country's dishes."

"Tonight we are having my soup, some crab and baked fish, then some roast mutton with spinach and nettles and potatoes to the side. I have made some horseradish sauce and tomato butter if you wish for some spice—"

"Horseradish and tomato butter?" said Blake, trying to look intrigued and not repulsed by the concept. "A new choice of condiments for me."

"You eat horseradish with fish," explained Paolo. "Like Italians eat red sauce with pasta," he said, grinning.

"Don't worry," said Molly. "I'm as clueless as you are when it comes to national dishes. Paolo was the first person who told me that the Olive Garden was about as Italian as SpaghettiOs."

"I love the Olive Garden, too," confessed Ama, giving Molly's arm an empathetic squeeze. "And SpaghettiOs."

Blake looked as if he agreed also, but he didn't say it aloud. The reputation of Stefan would not include confessions of eating canned pasta, Tessa thought, and she was grateful he was making an effort to stick with the image; right down to the suit Natalie had borrowed for him—a very attractive gray, as promised. And Blake looked more than a little attractive in it, as Tessa had anticipated. She did her best, however, not to notice.

"Trust me," Paolo told the others, "I only know because Gramps loved his food. Me, I'm happy with a Chicago deep-dish pizza. But in my family, food equaled heritage for the most part."

"That's something I can identify with," said Ama with chagrin. "I've eaten a lot of *makki di roti* and tandoori in my time. I was the only girl at my lunch table who'd never eaten a turkey Christmas dinner or had a Thanksgiving pie. Even for birthdays, all the desserts were made with *ghee* and sugar syrups when I was a kid."

Tessa peeked in the kitchen. Bianca, wearing a frilly apron over her pink summer dress, was stirring something in a big soup pot. Steam rose from the oven when she opened its door and checked on a fish lying in a roasting pan with wedges of lemon and some onions. The fish still had its head, Tessa noticed with surprise.

"Can I give you a hand?" Natalie asked, pushing the kitchen door open wider from behind Tessa.

"No, no," said Bianca. "I am fine. Go talk to the young people. Go," she said, shooing them away from the door. "It will only be a little longer."

Dinner was like a Swedish *smorgasbord*, only consisting of Norwegian dishes. Platters, bowls, and trays were passed back and forth at the table, while Paolo poured cool glasses of water and samples of sweet apple brandy for his grandmother's guests.

Glancing at each of them around the table, he said, "I'm glad all of you could make it tonight. You've done so much for us, making the wedding special. And not... well, making too much of it." Here, he avoided his grandmother's gaze, although she was busy telling Ama about the mutton's seasoning.

"We're doing our best," said Tessa. "So long as you're happy, we're happy."

"So long as it's the best, *I'm* happy," declared Bianca. "Only the best for the two people I love most." She lifted her glass to the young couple at the table. "I am so glad that Mr. Ellingham told me about the best flower shop. They have a pretty bouquet for Molly that made her happy."

"He told you about the flower shop?" Tessa glanced at Blake, who was eating his mutton with more polite table manners than the way he consumed his lunch-hour sandwich during the renovation work. He smiled at her over his wine glass, with a subtle wink that was quick enough that no one else would notice it.

"Of course I did," he said. "I'm always on top of things, right? Only the best for our clients."

"Yes. I mean... you had said you planned to, of course," she said quickly. " I just didn't realize you took care of it already." For a moment, Tessa held Blake's gaze from across the table. Something felt easy and natural about this mutual link, until the loud clank of someone's silverware jarred her back to the present moment. Quickly Tessa turned her attention elsewhere by heaping some more horseradish on to her plate—not her favorite, but it was the handiest serving dish in reach.

"I can't wait to show you the designs for the cake," said Ama to Molly. "I think you'll like it. It's something different, but it's really pretty. We think we can build a theme around it for your wedding dessert table, with the cookies and the macaroons, and a few Irish treats I'm creating."

"That sounds like a lot of food for only a few guests," remarked Paolo.

"What do you mean 'a few guests'?" asked Bianca. "You will have all your friends there, and all my friends."

"But Gran, why?" said Paolo with a laugh. "Molly and I don't have a lot of people who are dying to come to our wedding—"

"Says you," retorted his grandmother, with a grasp of English semantics that surpassed her usual standards. "Everybody who knows you thinks you and Molly are nice people. The people who love you will want to see your happy day."

"We'll see," said Paolo. But Bianca frowned.

"I have done the invitations already," she announced. "The print shop near the grocery, they took them off the computer for me. The ones that Molly had put there," she added, referring to the template Molly had been working on for the wedding invitations. She had shown it to Tessa when they had tea at Bianca's apartment—a pretty but simple design with a floral branch like a woodblock print. Molly planned to print them off at her own home using a special gloss paper from her design supplies, but she kept a copy on Bianca's rarely used laptop in case she needed to work on it during one of her visits.

To think Bianca had actually taken the laptop to a print shop and explained to them about the template for the invitations—she must be more technologically savvy than Tessa would have imagined.

"But Gran," Molly was saying, "you couldn't have mailed them. We don't even have a place picked for the wedding yet. I left that part of the invitation blank." She and Paolo were exchanging anxious glances as the rest of the guests waited to hear Bianca's reply.

"I took care of that, too," Bianca said with a dismissive wave. "I went to that place I showed you, the place with the ceiling like starlight? It was just as beautiful as the picture. They told me we can have the wedding *and* reception there! So it is all taken care of now."

The NiteLite. Tessa's heart sank, remembering the steep prices she had promised Paolo they would never accept. Keeping her voice as calm as possible, she asked their client, "How many people did you invite, Bianca?"

"Oh, plenty," Bianca said, as if to reassure them. Turning back to Paolo, she added, "I sent them to all the names on your list. I had the people from the neighborhood, and your cousins, too. They will be so happy for you, just like I am."

"But—but that must be fifty or more, Gran," said Molly worriedly. "We weren't going to mail all of those. Some were just going to be extras for passing out to my clients as samples."

"Well, I needed them all," Bianca insisted. "I put the money in the postman's box and he brought me plenty of stamps. I put them on the envelopes while I watched the game show on TV. I thought the whole time what a lovely surprise it will be for both of you."

She was beaming and clearly expected her grandson and Molly to share her enthusiasm. But their silence and worried glances told her otherwise and her smile seemed to vanish as she told them, "It doesn't make you happy, though. I thought you would be so pleased."

"Oh, Gran, why didn't you wait?" said Paolo. "How will we ever pay for a place like that? Or enough food for so many people?"

"You don't worry about that," said Bianca. "I worry about it. I'm the one who is going to buy those things for you."

Tessa could see the frustration in Paolo's face; Molly's expression was equally upset. "You know how we feel about you paying for the wedding," said Paolo, after a moment. "It's not right. Molly and I have a little money set aside, and that's what we're planning to use."

Bianca's face lost its color. "But I told you," she said. "I told you I was going to give you the wedding. You said you would let me."

"But I meant just *some* things for it," said Paolo. "Not Molly's dress, or big reception halls. I meant small stuff, because we can't afford anything more."

"Please, Gran," said Molly. "We appreciate that you want to do this for us, we really do. But it's time to face the fact that we can't afford much more than this dress and the cake."

Bianca slapped her napkin down on the table. "I can pay!" she said forcefully. "I have saved for this—I have saved my money—your grandfather has sacrificed and saved for this day—"

"He sacrificed and saved so you could be comfortable during your retirement," protested Paolo. "That's what his pension is for. I don't want it spent on frivolous things for me."

"Your wedding day is *not* frivolous," said Bianca. Her voice trembled. "Not to me. It is important and should be celebrated. It won't come again, Paolo. You will only have this chance. It should be more important to you than it is to me. So I am going to use the money to pay for this day, whether you want it or no."

"It's a tin box of change, Gran." For the first time, Paolo's voice rose. "It won't pay for luxuries—it won't pay for half the things that you want. And I won't spend all of my and Molly's savings to do it, Gran. That's final."

As if realizing he was too emotional, he fell quiet. "I'm sorry," he said. "Gran, I didn't mean to upset you. I'm just trying to protect you."

Bianca shook her head. "You don't understand how important it is," she said.

"I do, believe me," said Paolo. "I'm sorry. I think—I think I need some air." He laid his napkin on the table and rose. "Excuse me, everybody." He offered an apologetic smile, although his heart wasn't in it.

"Paolo, wait," said Molly, but he had already left the dining area. "He's just a little tired," she explained to everyone. "I'll go talk to him. He'll be back as soon as he's had some time to think." She patted Bianca's hand. "It's okay. Everything will be fine." She followed Paolo from the room.

Blake cleared his throat. "Maybe we should go," he suggested. "Give your family some space—"

Bianca shook her head. "Stay," she insisted. "They will come back in a few minutes. Paolo... he is just afraid for me. No matter how I tell him not to worry, he does anyway." Her hands shook too as she lifted her silverware again.

Tessa felt reluctant to leave, as did everyone else, since it would only embarrass Bianca to have everyone disappear from her table. Blake picked at the vegetables on his plate, while Natalie pretended momentarily to study a picture on the wall. Ama pushed a smile to her lips.

"This spinach and lentil dish is really delicious," said Ama to Bianca. "Could I have the recipe?"

Before the meal was finished, Paolo and Molly had returned, both with polite smiles for the rest of the dinner guests to conceal their obvious worries. Tessa wanted to pull them aside and assure them she could fix this somehow, but there was no opportune moment for it. She didn't want to hurt Bianca's feelings if she overheard them, either. It would have to wait until tomorrow, when feelings had cooled off for all parties involved.

Nobody talked about the cost of wedding venues for the rest of dinner, as Bianca served dessert: sweet berries and whipped cream piled high in cut-glass bowls. Instead, Molly talked about her latest client's design, and Paolo told stories about his grandfather first teaching him to make pasta, which led to plenty of stories about family and food.

"You must come again," said Bianca, pressing Blake's hand between her own. "I want to hear all about the good wedding ideas you have for my Paolo and Molly. You have said so little tonight—you are so quiet when you are working, Mr. Ellingham."

"A wedding planner's brain works that way," said Blake, after a moment's pause to absorb her remark—no doubt searching for words that wouldn't sound either moronic or egotistical. "You have to think of your clients every second until they're happy."

"That is good." She patted his hand before letting him go. "You are so very talented. Stella's son's lovely wedding must have made you very proud as a planner."

"I..." Blake caught Tessa's eye. "I think the credit goes to the team, not the person who's supposedly the lead. They're the ones who inspire the best ideas." With one last smile for Bianca—and, for a brief second, Tessa, too—he crossed the threshold to the hall outside.

"Thanks for the recipe," said Ama, tucking it into her pocket. "Even my mom might like this one, and she never likes anything that isn't home cuisine." She stepped aside as Paolo slipped on Molly's coat and gave his grandmother a goodnight kiss before leaving.

Tessa was the last guest left. She was stacking the plates from the table, scraping the last of the fish and the vegetables onto the last one. "It was really nice of you to have us to dinner," she said. "You went to a lot of trouble, cooking all these dishes for us."

"No trouble," said Bianca. "Though I have not cooked so much in a long time. Only when Paolo sometimes comes to dinner—but he has been a busy young man for a long time now." She snuffed the candles in the table's centerpiece. "He thinks I am making too much fuss over this wedding, perhaps, but someday he will understand. When he is my age and looks back, he will understand it was worth it."

"Maybe so," Tessa said.

But right now, if she were Paolo, she would regret ever trusting Bianca—or the Wedding Belles, for that matter—with any part of this wedding.

Chapter Nineteen

"Natalie, could you restock the pink and red camisoles by the window display? We sold out yesterday, but there's still a few in the back."

"Sure, Allyson." Natalie gave her new boss a smile on her way to the back room.

Her job at Dress for Less had its perks, namely that it was part-time, leaving plenty of room for class and her work at Wedding Belles. It was also insanely dull for the most part, and the stock room was both dank and a little creepy, though Natalie wasn't as weirded out by the half-dressed mannequins as the rest of her coworkers—unless she was helping do inventory at night. Then it felt like they might suddenly come to life and try to strangle her, like the villains in a scene out of a *Doctor Who* episode.

Retail. That was the bottom level in the fashion industry, a veritable nightmare for half the people she knew from the design world. Right now, every one of them would say she was crazy for leaving Kandace, despite her awful designs.

Her phone buzzed as she searched the shelf for the camisoles. Pulling it out, she checked the screen to find a new message from Tessa:

No refund. Meet me at office ASAP.

No refund what?

The venue. Said no.

Great. Just great. So Molly and Paolo were stuck with the big, expensive wedding venue Bianca had booked without their permission. Natalie let out a sigh and pocketed her phone again, grabbing a stack of camisoles from an open cardboard box. She arranged them in the window display, where a fifty percent off sign drew the eye of two teenagers passing on the sidewalk. Dress for Less definitely had more business than Kandace's shop.

"Heading to lunch, Natalie? A couple of us are going to that pizza-by-the-slice shop, if you want to come," her coworker Ramona offered, as she and the new cashier clocked out of the break room.

"Thanks, but I have plans," Natalie answered, shouldering her tote bag. A few bridal magazines were sticking out of the top, along with a folder full of clippings and sketches. She tucked them out of sight before anyone could ask about them, making her way to the exit as she checked the time on her phone again.

"You picked up gelato?" Tessa sounded incredulous as Natalie unpacked the carton from its brown paper bag. "I text you for an emergency meeting and your first thought is gelato? Tell me how that's possible."

"Why not?" Ama said. "I brought fresh-baked gingersnaps. Although, I'm not sure how they'll taste with Strawberry Delight," she added, studying the label on the carton Natalie had bought on the way there.

"How can you two be focused on sweets at a time like this?" Tessa demanded.

Natalie and Ama exchanged glances before saying, almost in unison, "Comfort food."

"It's kind of a tradition in big, close-knit families," Natalie added, by way of explanation. "Someone's happy; you feed them. They're sad; you feed them. They need some advice—"

"You feed them," Tessa finished, rolling her eyes. But she was smiling now, though it was only a tiny one. Natalie suspected she had cried earlier that morning, since her eyes were a little bit red, along with the tip of her nose. Tessa would claim it was allergies if she asked her, though, so it seemed better to pretend she didn't notice.

"So what now?" Ama asked, once they had settled into place on the various kitchen stools and chairs. Blake had a few errands to run, apparently, so their building was free of construction zone chaos for a change.

"Now," Tessa answered her, "we hope against hope the NiteLite has a sudden change of heart. Though I'm not sure the manager actually has one of those, so that's probably not happening. To them, it's a done deal."

"Did you tell them it was tantamount to robbery?" Natalie asked, digging a spoon into her gelato with ferocity. "Taking advantage of sweet, well-meaning customers like Bianca is hardly a great advertisement for your supposedly swanky business."

"He claims she was insistent about what she wanted," Tessa replied. "Knowing Bianca, I couldn't really argue with that part of that story."

Ama shook her head. "Poor Molly and Paolo are probably wishing they had eloped by now."

"I'm starting to wish it, too," Tessa sighed. "Believe me, I tried every argument I could think of, but the manager wasn't budging. All

I got was an offer to cancel their reservation. And that didn't seem like the smartest move, since Bianca had paid a twenty percent deposit."

Natalie's eyes widened. "You're telling me she actually paid that much? I can't believe she had enough to cover something like that, honestly. I mean, can you even fit that much money into a biscuit tin?"

"She probably emptied her checking account for it," Tessa guessed, crumbling a gingersnap in frustration. "If she even has anything left, it's probably just the change in a biscuit tin. We have our work cut out for us if we're going to keep our promise to Paolo about protecting his grandmother's savings before he and Molly tie the knot."

"Speaking of Paolo," said Natalie, "how did he take the news?"

Tessa groaned at the memory of her phone call with the would-be groom. "Not great. He got really quiet for a while and just when I thought we'd been disconnected, he said they would find some way to pay for it. He sounded really upset. I feel so guilty this even happened."

"Why? It's not your fault Bianca went behind everyone's back to surprise them," said Natalie.

"Maybe it is, though," said Tessa.

The other two just stared at her. With a shrug, she pushed her bowl aside and said, "Think about it. If I had just found the right venue for their wedding, none of this would have happened. But my instincts have been off this whole time. I'm not picking up the signals that tell me how to make this event as meaningful as possible for Molly and Paolo. I might as well be throwing darts at a board when I'm making suggestions for their wedding."

She let out a sigh and mumbled, "If only Stefan hadn't taken that job in Paris."

"Are you kidding?" Natalie laughed. "He would have bankrupted them by now, planning 'Cinderella's Wedding: Part Two.' Rolling right along with every one of Bianca's air-castle dreams. We can at least save them money on everything else, even if the venue is out of our control now."

"That's true," said Ama. "We're getting them a great deal on the food and flowers so far. And that photographer you found sounded really promising."

"He is," Tessa assured them. "He's really talented, based on the work I saw. It's just me who's the problem."

"What about me?" Natalie countered. "I haven't found the right dress for Molly yet. I've searched every boutique in town and everything is either the wrong style or the wrong price so far."

"We both know how you could solve that."

Natalie's face grew hot with this sly accusation from Tessa. She spooned another bite of her rapidly melting gelato. "I'm making Bianca's. Deal's a deal."

In truth, she had already finished the dress for Bianca—she just hadn't found the guts to show it to their client yet; something she acknowledged with a twinge of guilt as she hung a dress with a similar lace bodice on a rack at the clothing store that afternoon.

She had an appointment to view sample bouquets with Maxine at the flower shop as soon as her shift was over; then came homework for classes and more online browsing for possible wedding gown options. Tessa's words on this last subject had been unwelcome today, but Natalie couldn't deny they were also a little bit true.

Tessa was so stubborn sometimes. Then again, her friend had planned to use Stefan as a human shield between herself and the world of wedding planning until dumb luck had shoved her front and center in their new business. Natalie, on the other hand, intended to go on hiding behind the skirts of someone else's designer dress, at least until she felt confident that her future was *not* selling clothing at a retail store.

After work, she walked past the window display for The Bridal Closet, a short distance from her new work site. In the past, she had pictured one of her own gowns among their row of couture designs, where a prospective bride might spot it and know it was just the right one. Years later, that same bride might pass it on to her daughter, or even her granddaughter, the dress adopting the different pieces of their family history as they passed it down the line.

An awfully traditional notion, she thought, with a crooked smile— for someone who was a little tired of traditions and old-fashioned ideas. But it was just a fantasy—the dress and the dreams associated with it.

Natalie turned toward home again in the twilight, her tote bag swinging softly against her side.

Chapter Twenty

The light on the answering machine was blinking when Tessa came through the door, a grocery sack in each arm. The handyman was at lunch, Ama was working in the restaurant, and Natalie was at class. So no one was there to hear the shriek Tessa let out when she played back the message from the manager at the NiteLite.

Pulling out her cell phone, her fingers raced over its keypad, composing a quick text to Ama and Natalie. A few minutes later, both her business partners had joined her at Wedding Belles headquarters. Natalie wore a look somewhere between panic and excitement, as she asked, "They really canceled Bianca's reservation? But how? Why?"

"Something about a leak in the cooling system flooding their building last night," Tessa explained. "They've had to cancel all their major events for the next few weeks until their ceiling is replaced—so they're giving Bianca's deposit back."

"That's good, at least," said Ama. "Now Molly and Paolo won't have to pay thousands of extra dollars in wedding bills."

"And Bianca can use it to pay for more practical stuff, like groceries and utilities, for a while," Tessa said with a smile.

"Yeah, but… what now?" Natalie glanced between them, brow furrowed. "We have just weeks to find new places to host the wedding *and* the reception."

"For fifty people," Tessa added, her initial enthusiasm for the concept starting to fade as reality set in. "We could definitely have a problem with that."

"Plus, the invitations already went out with the NiteLite as the venue address," Ama reminded them, chin resting on her hands in contemplation.

Oh, right. The invitations.

"We can fix the invitations, I promise you," Tessa assured Molly and Paolo as they sat across from her in the Wedding Belles parlor later that day. Blake was on a supply run, so they didn't have to worry about blowing his cover—although Tessa almost wished he was there for moral support at least, since both Ama and Natalie had had to leave for other obligations.

"Amended invitations will be sent out as soon as you settle on the new locations," Tessa continued, keeping her voice upbeat and confident. "And I promise you that I will personally contact each of the guests on your list to ensure they're aware of the change in plans."

"Thank you," said Paolo. "We really appreciate that, believe me. But…" He glanced at Molly, the two of them communicating some unspoken thought. Her fingers reached for his, linking together on the sofa.

"We're kind of worried about the timing," Molly admitted. "It's just so last-minute, having the reservation fall through. Even if it wasn't the right one, it was the only one we had. And if we have to postpone the wedding now—"

"What?" Tessa felt the color drain from her face with these words.

"We don't want to," Paolo assured her. "It's just gotten more complicated than we thought it would be. Gran is pretty disappointed about losing the NiteLite, and we didn't exactly have a 'Plan B' for if it fell through."

"That's what I'm here for," Tessa said. "And Natalie and Ama—and Mr. Ellingham," she added, at the last second. "Let the four of us be your contingency plan. We can fix this for you."

"Can you?" Molly looked as if she wanted to believe this, although her smile was still a little uncertain. "We would both be so grateful if you could. We really don't want to postpone our wedding if there's a way around it."

"But if we have to cancel, we have another plan," said Paolo.

Elopement, Tessa thought. The one way to save Bianca money, for the two of them to have a quiet, private ceremony with no frills… and no one to make them serve a five-layer cake afterward.

"You won't have to," Tessa replied.

She sounded utterly confident as she spoke these words. If they could just hear the beat of her heart, though, they would know she was terrified in this moment. Because, as much as Tessa wanted to keep her promise to them, there was no "Plan B" right now. And if they canceled this wedding, all three of them knew how monumental Bianca's disappointment would be. But only one person in the room knew how devastating it would be to the Wedding Belles themselves.

There was nothing standing between this disaster and themselves. Except three very determined women, and one handyman who couldn't plan a wedding if his life depended on it.

"What about the rose garden? Molly sort of liked that idea, right?" Natalie asked.

She was busy hemming a skirt in a cotton fabric that sported a cute Mexican-style flower print, perfect for summertime. But her model for this project, Tessa, was having a hard time holding still as they discussed possible solutions for their latest crisis up in Natalie's sewing room.

"That's the problem," Tessa said. "Molly 'sort of' liked a lot of our suggestions. I want this to be something she loves, though. Her and Paolo both." *And Bianca*, she added silently, since it went without saying. All three of them knew Bianca would have to be happy with the wedding they planned if it was going to be a true success, at least in the eyes of Paolo and Molly. It wasn't just about the price now.

"All of us want it to be that way," Natalie agreed. "But I have to be honest, Tessa. If even Molly and Paolo can't figure out what would make this their dream wedding, then how are you supposed to know? I think you're being too hard on yourself."

"No, you're being too easy on me because I'm your friend," Tessa replied, grinning a little in spite of her worried mood. "As a wedding planner, I have to make each client's event the best it can be. You wouldn't sell a dress to a client if it wasn't the right fit, would you? Of course not. And I can't do that with someone's wedding day, either. It has to be perfectly tailored just for them."

"Hold still," Natalie scolded. "I'm having trouble pinning this skirt."

"Why can't you have Ama do this after her cookies are done?"

"Who do you think this is for? I don't want her to see it early." Natalie reached for another pin. "Hold on, I have a sequin hanging by a loose thread."

They went in circles with more suggestions for the wedding venue. Beautiful gardens and churches, the park with its canopy of oaks and dogwood blossoms; even the beach. None of these seemed like the right fit, though. Something was still missing.

By three o'clock, Natalie was off to class, the finished skirt tucked safely in her backpack to show to Cal later that day. Tessa slipped back into her jeans, which seemed boring in comparison to the skirt's bright flowers and sequins. There were similar squares of fabric stacked on top of the old trunk where Natalie kept ribbons, lace, and other supplies for trimming garments. A few dress patterns and colored pencil sketches were strewn across the nearby desk, where a gift box tied with a simple lavender ribbon drew Tessa's eye.

The dress for Bianca. She recognized it instantly from Natalie's description: the delicate lace sleeves and silky fabric in a classic cut. Her friend had finished it days ago, yet here it sat, still waiting to make its debut in the world. Just like the other dresses she could see hanging in the partly open closet, so many of them familiar to her from when Natalie first sewed them years ago.

Would they stay hidden away forever? The idea was a painful one, since it meant her friend's talent would stay hidden, too. And what about this one? Natalie hadn't made a move to deliver it. But Tessa was certain that Bianca would adore this dress, if she just had the chance to see it.

Poor Bianca. She would be devastated if the wedding really had to be postponed. Despite their differences on just about everything else connected to this event, she and Bianca shared the same goal: a beautiful, unforgettable wedding day for two very deserving people.

Maybe that would be enough to see it through, Tessa thought. Tucking the gift box beneath her arm, she slipped from the room and shut the door behind her.

Chapter Twenty-One

Tessa had to knock twice before Bianca answered her apartment door.

"Come in, come in," she said, waving Tessa inside with a smile. "Will you have some tea?" she asked. "I make some every day at this time. You like peppermint? I have some lemon, too."

"Peppermint sounds good," Tessa said. The television in the living room was on mute, some kind of game show on the screen. Bianca ushered her into the kitchen, where she took two teacups from a cupboard overhead. Tessa set the gift box she was carrying onto the table as they waited for the kettle to boil.

"For me?"

"For you," nodded Tessa. Bianca wore a puzzled smile as she lifted the lid for the box.

"For the wedding," Tessa explained. "Natalie—Ms. Grenaldi—thought you might like to wear it." She didn't mention who had made it, however.

"Such a pretty color," Bianca exclaimed, holding the fabric up to the light. "So rich, too. It is like the wine my husband used to buy. He liked to cook with wine, my Pietro. Imagine—a dress for me. I will look stylish—like a princess at the wedding."

She was smiling, a look of delight on her face. "I will try this on when Molly is here," she promised, placing the dress carefully back in its box. "I cannot wait. Tell Ms. Grenaldi I thank her. So very nice of her."

"It was her pleasure," said Tessa.

"Tell her to find a dress for Molly—she is so good at this. If she can do so well for me, what will she do for the bride? She worries too much about the price of things instead of finding the best one." She patted Tessa's arm. "Tell her that we trust her. Maybe she won't be so worried while she is looking."

"I'll do that," Tessa said, hiding a smile as she wondered what Natalie's reaction would be to this piece of news. Disbelief and then denial, probably.

"Come, come," said Bianca, lifting the teacups and proceeding to the living room. "Sit down." She patted a cushion before the low coffee table where both cups rested, steam rising from the tea within. She turned off the television set, the brightly colored game show background vanishing.

"You know," Tessa said, as Bianca handed her a cup of tea a few moments later, "I realized when we met that you weren't really Italian, but I keep forgetting. I guess it's the name."

"Bianca?" her hostess said. She laughed. "My husband gave it to me. Italian for 'white,' he told me. He liked it—a name for the girl with such fair skin. I had milk skin back then. Fair hair—no dye to cover the white," she added with another laugh. "Bertha Auganes from the country of Norway. Only I was not the stout farm girl they pictured, but a skinny little thing who couldn't lift the heavy baskets."

"Who were 'they'?" said Tessa. "Your husband's family?"

"His village." Bianca placed her cup on the table. "I came there as a hired girl. An adventurer, because I had nowhere to go. My father was killed in the war. My mother, she had a bad heart." Here, Bianca pressed her hand over her own chest. "She told me before she died... told me to make a new place in the world. To be brave and find a better life than they had known."

Tessa realized that Bianca was even older than she had previously imagined her to be. The fighting that had killed her father was World War II; Bianca must have been at least a half-grown child during the 1940s.

"So I went south—following the harvests," she continued. "First I worked on a friend's farm, then the farm of one of my mother's distant cousins. They told me about a village where a friend stayed in Italy during the war, where you could live cheap as a boarder and work in the vineyards when the crops were ready. No cold winters of darkness and snow, but sunshine even in winter. It sounded so beautiful that I decided to go."

Bianca took a long sip from her cup. "It wasn't like the pictures," she said. "It looked so dry and dusty. And I was poor and could only speak a few words of Italian from a little book that my cousin gave me. The work was hard—the family was afraid I was too little to be any good at it, though I showed them it wasn't true. I cried to go home every night... but then I met Pietro."

"Your husband," Tessa prompted. She had forgotten her own tea while listening to Bianca's story, and the liquid was tepid when she tasted it.

"He was strong. Not handsome, but so funny. Such... 'good humor' is the words. He taught me better Italian; I taught him some words in Norwegian. And then he was going away to America. Three days—and he wanted me to come with him."

"Three days?" echoed Tessa.

"No, no. He had been planning to go away long before that," said Bianca. "Only he didn't tell *me*. He didn't know he wanted to marry me, see, until it was almost too late. Then everything must be rush and scramble so we can get on the boat and go to the other side of the ocean. We ended up here... well, a few streets away from here," she corrected. "We had two rooms, and he had a job at a factory."

Tessa had placed her tea aside now, although she wasn't quite ready to leave. "Tell me about your wedding, Bianca," she said.

Bianca snorted. "That day," she said. She shook her head. "It isn't worth telling. All went wrong. It was just a quick ceremony so we could get on the boat. It's nothing you want to hear about."

"I do," insisted Tessa. "I think it's important. Maybe it wasn't perfect, but it was still important."

Bianca put her cup on the table. "I show you," she said. She opened a drawer in the dining room buffet and took out a tin similar to the one that held the precious wedding funds. From inside, she took a photograph and showed it to Tessa.

"My wedding," she said. "No dress, no nothing. That little building behind us is the church—not much left after the war, either," she explained.

A small group of people stood outside of a plain stone building: the woman in the middle wore a neat print dress with a lace shawl around her shoulders, and a few ornaments in her hair. Beside her was a taller, darker man in a suit, smiling for the photo. She recognized the two of them from the photo of Bianca's first day in America.

"His uncle took the picture," said Bianca. "They gave the camera to us as a gift. It cost a lot of money... I don't know which person in the family chose it, or bought it." She laid the tin box on the table and moved aside a couple of magazines in order to sit on a nearby chair. "We had to hurry to pack our things. Pietro's mother was crying as she fixed the food we ate—you know, I do not remember if anyone danced at our wedding dinner. I can remember nothing but the thought of the boat, and if I would be sick aboard it... and missing my home." She smiled. "It was so sudden."

"The shawl you're wearing in the picture is beautiful," said Tessa.

"Paolo's mother loaned it to me," said Bianca. "It was green—for good luck. In Italy, green is important for weddings. The print of my dress didn't have any, since it was... yellow, I think." She frowned. "In Norway, it is different. In the old days, you wore the costumes—folk dress, they call it now. All the bright embroidery, and the pretty needlework on the apron. The women in kerchiefs, and the bride in her special crown. You march to the church—march to the music of the fiddle with all your family and friends. Like a big parade."

"I guess you didn't have any of your family or friends at the wedding, with the short notice," ventured Tessa. "Did you not have any of your traditions?"

"I had the crown," said Bianca, smiling. "That much I did have. It was Pietro's doing."

She lifted from the tin a stiff piece of fabric and cushioning that resembled a flat pillow, or two doilies with cardboard sandwiched between them. From its sides dangled lots of prism pendants, their faux gold frames now tarnished. Two ribbons hung from either end.

"It ties underneath the chin," explained Bianca. "It is worn like a hat, with the prisms dangling around the brim. This is a poor imitation, but it was all he could do."

"Pietro made it for you?" said Tessa, amazed. She turned the crown in her hands, examining the old stitches now loose around the stiff, yellowed lace doilies' edges. Some beads had been sewn around the perimeter of the hat, now missing except for a few pearl ones here and there.

"He did," said Bianca, nodding. "With ornaments from a fancy lamp and two lace napkins of his grandmother's. He was terrible with a needle and thread! Some of the beads came off in the church, even—I could hear the threads pop as I walked to the altar. But he did it because I had told him that I would wear one if I were at home. A headdress instead of a veil. In Norway, we don't have to hide from evil spirits under a veil, the way they do in Italy," she added jokingly.

"Of course, I wore both on that day," she continued, after a pause. "Paolo's mother loaned me the lace shawl and I wore it over my head, over the headdress. He said it looked pretty when he lifted my bride's veil back, behind all those little tinkling crystals. 'You look like a princess,' he said. Such nonsense, because I was wearing only a plain dress that I had sewn a few days before."

"I think it's sweet," said Tessa softly. "Especially that he tried to give you one of your traditions for the wedding."

"I think he thought of it because I cried so," said Bianca with a chuckle. "I was a very tearful bride some days before we were married. I knew when we were on the boat, we wouldn't come back. We would leave it all—Italy, Norway, all our family and friends. But I couldn't stay without him."

In the tin, Tessa saw a handful of other souvenirs—old Italian and American coins, a postcard or two, even a candle stub. A photograph of Bianca and Pietro in the snow, then standing in a building courtyard where some half-hearted shrubs were planted, a blurry figure on a bicycle riding past. *Our first home in the Brentwood*, read the shaky line written on the photo's back.

"So you see why I want Paolo and Molly to have more for their wedding," said Bianca. "I don't want it to be so hasty and have such makeshift things."

"But you understand why they're worried," said Tessa. "They don't want you to give up everything."

Bianca patted the tin on the table. "I have plenty of money in the box," she said. "He shouldn't worry. I will have it all taken care of."

Tessa shook her head. "You have to make some concessions for him, Bianca," she said. She took her client's hand. "Trust us. We can give all three of you a special celebration without spending a lot of money. It's our job to find a way to do it, so open your mind beyond just big and grand options. If we can make the wedding a special celebration all about Molly and Paolo, that's what matters."

"But can you do it where it will not feel small?" asked Bianca worriedly. She clutched Tessa's hand in return. "Where they will not look back and wish for better?"

"Trust me," repeated Tessa. "We can."

Chapter Twenty-Two

"Another change of plans," announced Tessa. "We're going to add something special to Molly and Paolo's wedding. A little something for Bianca."

As she spoke, she opened the tin of mementos, which she had borrowed from Bianca the day before. She lifted out the crown and showed it to them, along with the wedding photo, sharing Bianca's story about the quick wedding in the Italian village decades before.

"I think some element of this has to be included in Molly and Paolo's big day," said Tessa. "It's a part of Paolo's heritage that deserves to be honored. If this wedding is going to be about celebrating traditions, we can't miss the chance to add this one."

Bianca could be at peace then, Tessa felt. In a way, it would be celebrating her own union sixty years ago, because her story would be part of it, too. A way of bringing to life the wedding she wished for, and the kind of weddings that people like Paolo and Molly would experience if they were surrounded by old traditions and a big family circle.

"What is this?" Natalie examined the crown, trying to disentangle the crystal prisms from each other.

"A Norwegian wedding crown," said Tessa. "At least, that's what it's supposed to be. Bianca's husband made it for her to wear on their wedding day."

Collective gasps of "awww" came from both Tessa's partners. "That's so sweet," said Ama. "He made this?"

"He did. And it was the one part of Bianca's story that really mattered to her," said Tessa. "I think it was the only bit of that day which was really hers. Her and Pietro's celebration was missing all the usual hallmarks for both their cultures, but we won't let that happen to Paolo and Molly's day."

"I've been working on a list of Irish and Italian themed treats for the reception," said Ama. "Besides the 'Irish tiramisu' idea, I've added shortbread cookies because they're popular in Ireland—and I thought we could add a Celtic knot design to the top using icing."

"Green is important both in Irish culture and Italian weddings," said Tessa. "Maybe we can do something with that."

"Perhaps we should find out what would have been important for Bianca's wedding in her homeland," pointed out Natalie. "You know, like the church she would have chosen, or some ceremonial tradition that's part of the event."

"I think the biggest hurdle is finding a place for the reception—and maybe the ceremony," said Tessa. "We can use the church for the ceremony, but you heard what Paolo said about the reception."

"Maybe the ceremony is where they can honor Bianca with something instead," suggested Ama. "Her story, her traditions—we can bring together all three cultural elements somehow. Irish, Italian, and Norwegian."

"Let's figure out how to do it," said Tessa.

"We can get a great deal on this place for the reception, trust me," said Natalie. "That's the beauty of having connections in the city. It's an ideal space with a beautiful little landscaped outdoor terrace that should be in bloom for the wedding."

"How do you know them again?" Tessa asked.

"A friend of my mom's. The owner used to work at a Neapolitan restaurant my cousins own." She crossed the street as the walk signal appeared

She and Tessa entered the doors of a spacious Italian restaurant, its atmosphere low lit despite the sunshine coming through its front windows. The employee behind the seating host's podium smiled.

"Hey, Natalie," he said. "Long time no see. Come to check out the terrace room?"

"I have," she said. "This is my business partner Tessa Miller, by the way. She's the event planner for this wedding."

"Nice to meet you," he said, leaning across to shake hands. "I'm Rick. I run this place these days."

"Thanks for offering us such a great break on the deposit," said Tessa. "Our client will be really grateful. It's so generous of you."

"Well, Nat practically qualifies for the family discount around here," said Rick. "Brayden would probably kill me if I tried to charge her the usual price. Anything for Natalie, he would say."

"Who's Brayden?" asked Tessa.

A sudden flash of embarrassment reddened Natalie's cheeks. "Nobody," she muttered quickly.

"He talks about you so much that it feels like it's only been days since I caught up with you, not weeks," continued Rick to Natalie. "Tell him to keep his mind on his work sometimes, will you? Oh, his mom says 'Hi,' by the way—"

"Do you want to see the banquet room now?" said Natalie to Tessa.

"Sure," she said. "But who's—?"

"Come this way." Natalie seized Tessa's arm and pulled her in the direction of a set of French doors on the opposite side of the dining room. "It's right through here."

The private dining room featured a long banquet table and chairs—the latter could be removed, Natalie pointed out, and the table could be moved back and shortened to allow more room for guests to circulate. The room was big enough that a musician or a small trio could provide entertainment acoustically, especially if the terrace doors were open. There was even a small patio seating area with a wrought-iron table and two chairs, and an old stone bench near the hydrangeas.

"It's really nice," said Tessa, admiring it from the open French doors leading to the garden's paving stones.

"There's an Italian trio who plays the restaurants on weekends, if Paolo and Molly are interested in hiring them for the reception," said Natalie. "Their rates are pretty reasonable. But I've looked up a couple of acoustic Irish bands who play traditional airs and love songs, and they seem promising. They have websites with some digital live tracks we can screen for Paolo and Molly."

Tessa snapped some photos with her smartphone. "We'll have to bring them here to confirm if they like this spot," she said. "But I think it's definitely the top contender."

"Now for the ceremony," said Natalie, tucking her hands into the pockets of her jacket. "Will it be the church or somewhere else?"

"I've looked at the church and it's nice," said Tessa. "But I think I have an even better location."

The place Tessa had in mind was blocks away from the restaurant, in a part of town that was once considered Little Italy before some major renovations in the neighborhood a decade or two ago. Now the buildings were part of a chic downtown apartment complex with a historic feel to the brickwork and the intricate latticework on the old fire escapes leading down to the enclosed landscaped courtyard.

"An apartment yard?" said Natalie. "It's nice, Tess... but don't you think it's a little weird?" She glanced at Tessa quizzically, then at their surroundings. The smooth, paved area was softened with simple green spruce shrubs, and mint green sedum plants crawled along the decorative stones in the flowerbeds. There were succulents in hues of violet and jade, and sprigs of light, feathery flowers like sea foam poured from the antique ornamental urns placed along the walls of the surrounding buildings. Near the far end of the yard, planted in a circular stone bed, was a sapling tree with beautiful cascading branches.

"I found the address on the back of Bianca's photo," said Tessa. The building on the right is the one where she and Pietro first lived when they came to the city... back before real estate prices skyrocketed and it became a trendy place to live."

"Are you kidding?" Natalie asked, turning to her with astonishment.

"No, I'm serious. This garden was inspired by a traditional Italian villa's landscaping, in honor of the immigrants who used to live here— families like Bianca's. The tree is actually an imported sapling from Italy, a cold-hardy one," she said. "I talked to the managers of the buildings and it *is* possible to get a permit to host an event in this garden."

"What are you thinking?" said Natalie. "An open air ceremony?"

"Maybe. We could set up chairs, and have the ceremony near the tree," said Tessa. "It would be reminiscent of Bianca's past, the wedding she and Pietro had. I think this could be the tribute that Molly and Paolo would like to give her."

"What about the church?" asked Natalie. "You did say it was nice."

"Neither Molly nor Paolo was really committed to having the ceremony there, though," said Tessa. "I think they're open to exploring other options, especially if we can work out a really inexpensive deal for this site. It's definitely big enough to accommodate their guests. It would be easy to rent chairs and seat people—we could put up some kind of arbor for Molly and Paolo to stand under, maybe. We can even roll a carpet to it from the courtyard's entry gates—which would be perfect if a limo is dropping off the bride, by the way."

"Okay, I can see it," admitted Natalie. "There's definite potential in this location. But do you think Bianca would go for it? She doesn't tell the story about her wedding except as a cautionary tale."

"I think the only reason she doesn't want to celebrate Paolo's heritage is because those traditions are associated with her own make-do wedding, and the fact that Paolo's father didn't bother to honor them either," said Tessa. "If we can bring them to life beautifully, I think it will really mean something to all of them, in the same way as we're doing with the foods for the buffet and the reception site."

Natalie snapped a photo on her phone. "I guess the best way to find out the answer is to ask, right?"

Ama had been busy that morning working on the menu for the reception, and the table in the new kitchen back at Wedding Belles was covered in sketches and photos printed out from the internet. She cleared them all aside for the cake tasting with Molly and Bianca, however, so only a bakery box from Ama's Sweetheart Treats business was on the table, with a single layer of her wedding cake design inside.

"What do you think?" she asked, as she placed a slice before each of them. "I think we'll need three layers, since you're obviously expecting more guests than before," she added, "so I thought maybe the middle one would be similar to this, only with chocolate."

She crossed her fingers under the table as Molly poked a fork through the soft, white cake, split in half and filled with a generous layer of cream streaked with berry juice for a marble effect. Dried cherries and blackberries, and chopped walnuts and almonds studded it beautifully—at least that's what Ama hoped.

"Mmm," said Molly. "This is really good. I like it." She glanced at Bianca.

"I was kind of inspired by the traditional Italian wedding cake," said Ama. "The pattern on the top is from a rococo-style design, worked in with sweetened gilded cocoa powder." She waited as Bianca tasted it.

"Oooh, so sweet," she said. "The berries and nuts—Pietro's mother made one a little like this for Christmas, I remember. Only hers was heavy and spicy… this is so light. It's like an angel's cloud." She smiled.

Inwardly, Ama breathed a sigh of relief. "Okay, then," she said. "Let's talk about the Irish-inspired macaroons I have in mind." She reached for her book of sketches, eager to begin this plan.

In her office, Natalie gathered her books for her business class. "I texted you my photos of the courtyard," she called to Tessa. "I've gotta go." Hurrying downstairs, she crossed her fingers that she wasn't too late to catch the bus to her class.

"We do our best in the business world to face realities even as we face customers," Professor Bender explained, as he wrote on the chalkboard *Remember your test on Tuesday!* "Don't let yourself be fooled into thinking you can satisfy everyone all of the time."

Would they be able to satisfy Bianca in the end? Natalie pondered the possibility that it could all backfire as she took the bus to her family's house after turning in her latest assignment. No princess dress, no five-tier cake—would Bianca suddenly realize that Molly wasn't arriving at the wedding in a glass Cinderella carriage, with fireworks after the ceremony?

Tessa had better be right about the traditions mattering more than the price tag. It wouldn't look great for their business if Bianca's unhappiness spilled over to taint Paolo and Molly's feelings about the wedding. After all, reminders of her homeland and the wedding-celebration-that-wasn't could still spin into disappointment. She could almost imagine Bianca pulling a last-minute change by opening charge accounts at expensive boutiques to buy Molly's gown and order a six-tier Bavarian cream cake.

At her mother's house, a different sort of cake was waiting for her on the kitchen counter: a leftover wedge of spiced coffee cake studded with almonds and brown sugar. It was too tempting to ignore. She broke a piece off one edge and poked it into her mouth.

"Shouldn't you wait for dinner?" her mother chided her, as she poured a cup of coffee for herself. "If you're not in a hurry, I'll fix you something. Your uncle left some of his tortellini in the fridge." She gestured toward it; the fridge's surface was covered in Italian menus and family photos.

"I can't stay, Ma. I have a hundred things to do for the wedding," said Natalie. "Plus, I have a paper to write for my class. I just came by to pick up the stuff I left on the living room coffee table a few nights ago."

"You staying for dinner?" Her brother entered the back door, shrugging off his firefighter's jacket.

"Are you *ever* at your own place?" Natalie asked him.

"I gave it up. I'm always at the fire station or here," he said. "Didn't Ma tell you that already?"

"Leave me out of this," said their mother, holding up her hands. "You two should talk to each other. He's your brother, Natalie. You should call him."

"Why isn't it his responsibility to call me?" retorted Natalie.

"Oh, hey—that reminds me," said Roberto. "There's a guy I work with who wants to meet you. Can I give him your number?"

"Roberto, you know how I feel about setups," said Natalie warningly. "I hate having somebody build up some expectation about me, and then he gets sprung on me at the last moment."

"Come on, it's one date, sis," said Roberto. "You'll like him. He's pretty good looking, he's good at his job, he's not a criminal. He's your type."

"You should go out with him," Maria urged her. "He could be the one. He sounds better than these man-boys you've been dating the past few years."

"There is no 'the one,' Ma," said Natalie. "All I came here for were my sketches, not a date. I can find one of those myself." She tucked a bakery box with the rest of the cake under her arm, then retrieved her paperwork from the untidy stack on the coffee table.

"When are you going to take a relationship seriously?" Maria asked her at the door. "I worry about you. You're going to miss your chance for love if you're not careful."

She framed Natalie's face with her hands, looking into her eyes with worry. Natalie knew how her mother felt about her views on life. She was serious about her studies, serious about her career, even about her family… but never about matters of the heart. That just wouldn't do in Maria's mind.

She kissed her mother's cheek. "I'm fine, Ma," she said. "I don't need anybody." With a smile, she opened the door and stepped outside before Maria could argue with her.

Her phone suddenly beeped with a text from Cal. He was still hinting about her finding him a job away from Kandace's studio of chaos… for instance, if she ever opened her own design studio. Suddenly, that didn't seem like the same pipe dream from weeks ago, when she was pinning the demented harlequin skirt around one of Kandace's mannequins. She was a long way from her designs being showcased, of course—still, it felt like a more realistic goal now than her mother's plans for her to finally settle down with someone.

Why wait for something that wasn't going to happen? True love just wasn't reality; it was a fairytale. Natalie couldn't see a self-sacrificing, handsome, devoted Prince Charming materializing on her doorstep… if her current love life was any indication, casual relationships were something most guys preferred anyway.

And it wasn't like her parents had some magic story, was it? Her father once joked that their marriage might as well have been arranged by the culinary gods—her mother was the passionate one with a head for business; her father from an easygoing family of bakers, pasta makers, and daydreamers.

So maybe Tessa was right about other things being more important right now than love. Now, if only she could end her serial addiction to dating and having fun… like that would ever happen! Natalie rolled her eyes at this idea.

As the evening bus taking Natalie home rolled past the Tandoori Tiger, an engagement party for a different sort of arranged marriage was taking place in the restaurant's dining room, beneath the glitzy lanterns and flower lights that Ranjit loved so much. In the kitchen, Ama's sister-in-law Deena hurried to gather another tray of spicy roast chicken and *masala*-seasoned potatoes.

"Ama, you *have* to see the bride's sari," she said, as she lifted the tray with one hand. "It's this parrot green shade that would be *perfect* for you."

"Really? Let me see." Rasha was peering through the kitchen door's crack. "Oh my gosh, it's gorgeous," she said. "That's so much prettier than the one I wore for my engagement party. It was such an ick shade of yellow."

"I liked you in that dress," protested her husband, who was stealing a sticky rice ball from his mother-in-law's tray of finger foods—before his hand was slapped away.

"Men know nothing about fashion," his sister-in-law informed him.

"So we've been told," said Jaidev, as he arranged flatbread slices on a tray. "Where's the lentil paste?" he asked. "Ama, what did you do with my bowl? It was right here where you put this coconut *barfi*."

"I moved it over by the rest of the *masala dosa*," she answered. "Don't panic, all right?"

"Ama, come look," insisted Deena.

"No, thanks," said Ama. "I've seen plenty of Indian fashions in your wardrobe." Her sister-in-law's collection of hostess saris for the restaurant featured every color under the sun, to Ama's mind.

"Where is the rest of the food?" said Ranjit, pushing open the kitchen door.

"Out, out," said Pashma. "Go host. Jaidev is bringing it."

While her family argued about the flavor of the lentil paste, Ama slipped outside the kitchen's back door, catching a breath of fresh air away from the smell of frying oil and the lingering odor of garlic, blackened chicken, and *masala*. The sounds of the wedding party's festivities were quieter out here—she pictured them as the sounds of Paolo and Molly's future celebration in another week.

Would there ever be one for her? Not that she wanted a loud commemorative celebration of sitar music mixed with pop tracks and her family's loud friends dressed in Bollywood fashions—no, not that part, really. But the falling in love part... that was something she did want.

She hugged herself and sighed. Maybe somewhere out there was her destiny in the form of another person, thinking the same thoughts as he stood on his apartment balcony, or sat on a building's steps. Only she was beginning to think he wouldn't be dodging a loud, culturally vibrant family like her own. He would be longing to escape something else, and the two of them would build a new life together. Hand in hand, they would shake off old expectations and limitations, fingers intertwined as they seized the future.

That was a really beautiful picture. *If only it would become reality*, she thought, as she gazed up at the stars, barely visible in the city haze.

The back door banged open. "Ama, where is the red chili paste?" asked Rasha. "You were the last person to use it."

"I'll come find it." Ama followed her back inside.

Across town, beneath the same starlight and streetlamp glow, the Wedding Belles' new headquarters was dark except for two lights burning, one on each floor. In her office upstairs, Tessa was surfing the web for inspiration for their clients' ceremony. Her office still smelled of fresh paint, so she propped the window open with a half-empty can of trim paint to let the breeze circulate.

Norwegian wedding traditions. Norwegian villages in the Voss region. Traditional Irish desserts. She downloaded some photos to her phone, scrolling past the ones she had taken earlier of the possible venues. Studying one, she released a sigh of expectation. It was up to Molly and Paolo now to determine if any of these choices were the right ones.

Blake was screwing the outlet plates around the sockets in the kitchen as she came downstairs. "You're working late," she said, leaning against the doorframe. "Shouldn't you be home right now?"

"I work late on lots of jobs," he answered. "Besides, I'm trying to finish this one in a day or two."

"Move on to more profitable clients, eh?" said Tessa. "I guess we're not your most lucrative contract, are we? No guarantee we can afford those fancy Victorian light fixtures, or whatever."

A short laugh came from Blake. "Let's just say I'll be asking for half up front on my next job," he answered. But he was joking, Tessa thought. "Shouldn't you be at home, too?" he added.

I am home, would be the honest response. But Tessa didn't feel like imparting that particular secret right now. With a shrug, she told him, "Like you, I prefer not to leave until the job's done. I was actually checking out some ideas for the wedding. I found some pictures of Bianca's village church where she would have married if she had stayed in her home country. It's really pretty." She showed him a photo of the Lutheran church's hand-carved woodwork and old-fashioned pews on the screen of her phone.

"Pretty," he agreed. "That wooden altar is a nice piece of craftsmanship."

"Isn't it?" said Tessa. "Especially that ornate floral pattern across its front. It would be amazing if I could locate a similar piece for Paolo and Molly's ceremony. I'm sure they would love to pay tribute to that part of his grandmother's past, especially since it didn't have a chance to be part of her own big day. But apparently antique, hand-carved Norwegian altars like this one are hard to buy, even online."

"This is Norwegian farming country, right?"

"You remembered," she said. "Yeah. Bianca talked about her past a little when I visited her the other day. She said some things about missing her homeland. When she and Pietro moved to America, she knew she'd never see it again, probably, just like he would never see Italy again."

"That would be tough," said Blake. "Not seeing your home again. Or your family." He turned back to the socket he was screwing in place, giving the hardware a few more twists. "She probably felt some regrets, even if it was worth it."

"I'm hoping to find a way to give her a little piece of it back," said Tessa. "That's what we're working on right now. I think I'm going to talk to Molly and Paolo and see if they have some ideas."

"Better take along some suggestions," said Blake. "I don't think they've given any of it much thought. This whole wedding was Bianca's idea… if it hadn't been for her, they probably would have eloped like his parents."

He'd been paying more attention to Molly and Paolo's story than Tessa gave him credit for. She felt surprised. "That's what happens when you don't have anything solid to anchor you, like traditions or family ties, I suppose," she said. "Or a lot of money to impress your friends," she added jokingly.

"I wouldn't want a big wedding. All those champagne bottles and chocolate fountains—that's not for me," said Blake. "I think I'd want something small and simple. A girl who didn't want all the flashy, perfectionist details."

"You know, it's not the money or the size that matters," said Tessa. "You can make a wedding feel intimate and still have a big crowd… and a little flash, too."

He shook his head. "I'd expect that remark from a wedding planner," he said.

Tessa raised her brows. "What does that mean?" she asked.

"What? It's your job. Of course you like the big splash," he said. "That's what you do—you even liked it when you were a kid, you told me."

"You make it sound like it's the same as wanting some tacky affair meant to make guests green with envy," said Tessa, suddenly indignant. "It's nothing like that, I assure you." She was bristling slightly, as if he had suggested she was the kind of girl who only liked glitz and black-tie events with printed invitations.

"I didn't say that it was. All I said was you seem like the kind of girl who prefers things a little fancy," he protested.

"You don't know me well enough to know *what* I like," said Tessa. "But it's just in your nature to make assumptions like that, isn't it? Goodnight, Mr. Ellingham." She marched up the stairs, letting her office door slam shut behind her with more force than necessary, ignoring the handyman's protesting defense.

To think she'd actually mistaken that tiny spark between them in the kitchen for anything but static electricity. It simply proved what she had already learned: that moments like that were imaginary.

Chapter Twenty-Three

The dress was the last big dilemma.

Natalie had paged through catalogs and visited friends' boutiques, shopping for a dress that would match both Molly's beauty and Bianca's expectations. It was a disappointing search, because none of them were good enough. The sleek modern designs were a little *too* sleek and would wash all the color from Molly's fair skin in such stark shades of white. The princess gowns she reviewed were far too plain—for Bianca's standards, anyway.

They needed something different. Something unlike what was in the shops. In the end, Natalie could think of only one thing to try.

"What are you doing home at this hour?" Roberto checked his watch. "Don't you have a date tonight?" He set his late-night sandwich on the counter as Natalie closed the front door.

"Don't they ever feed you at the fire station?" asked Natalie, on her way upstairs.

"I have a big appetite," her brother answered. "Anyway, you didn't answer my question."

"Not tonight," said Natalie. "I'm looking for something I left in the stuff stored in my room."

"You mean Ma's second guest room, right?"

"Eat your sandwich," Natalie answered.

She searched through the drawers of an old dresser before remembering the box in her closet. There was the green dress that Kandace had rejected, lying on top of a heap of garments and sewing supplies. She closed the flaps of the box these lay inside of, labeled "finished projects," and lifted it in her arms, kicking a pile of old hangers back inside the closet before she shut the door.

"So what did you tell your date tonight?" said Roberto, when she came back downstairs with her armload.

"I told him I had a headache," said Natalie. "You know, the same thing all your dates used to tell you whenever you called them."

"Funny, sis," he said. "Ma left some macaroons in a box for you in the kitchen. Oh, and she says to call her about dinner on Sunday."

"Can't make it. Got a thing at work," answered Natalie, opening the front door by squeezing the box against herself. "You can have my macaroons, 'cause Ama gave me some leftover dessert from her restaurant."

"Ma's gonna be upset when she hears you're not coming."

"Like I've never eaten her lasagna before," said Natalie, scoffing. "Tell her I have a big date."

"Yeah, that'll cheer her up. You wasting time with some jerk who won't become her next son-in-law."

"Funny, bro." She pulled the door closed behind her with one foot.

In her studio at Wedding Belles HQ, she rummaged around for the right shade of thread in her sewing boxes after rolling out a bolt of fabric. She needed her good scissors, too. She slipped her pincushion on her wrist, and began working on the garment spread over her worktable, one which, thankfully, looked decent for something stored in a folded garment bag for ages.

Tessa claimed Bianca had loved the dress she made for her. Natalie only hoped she hadn't exaggerated the elderly woman's feelings to spare Natalie's own, because that wouldn't do her a favor in this case. Her hand shook a little when she picked up the scissors, forcing her to take a calming breath. *Relax, Natalie. You've done this a hundred times before.*

At least it wasn't a design for Kandace she was working on. She thanked her lucky stars that it wasn't the Wendy blouse made with see-through lace and trimmed with dozens of pink bows that Cal had texted her a picture of earlier in the week, along with a caption expressing his distaste for the finished product.

The first dress she'd ever sewn was still hanging in the closet at home. Even with all its flaws—including a pouched-out side seam—it was still better than her former boss's first creation, she was willing to bet. She could picture Kandace's now—some weird patchwork skirt decorated with mini skulls. Or maybe a chenille sweater shaped like a caterpillar's bumpy body. Her superior "I'm an artist and you're not" attitude probably convinced her home economics teacher that it was brilliant.

The needle slipped easily through the fabric in quick stitches. Natalie smiled to herself, as the fabric shimmered in the moonlight like an ivory stream.

"Now, this may be a little different from what you pictured," Natalie said to Bianca. "I know it's not the same as the dresses in some of your pictures, but it's really unique. One of a kind. And I think… maybe… it's special enough for Molly."

Bianca nodded. "I want to see it, then," she said. "If you think it's what Molly would like." She lifted her chin, tugging the sleeves of her faded sweater more neatly around her wrists as she glanced toward the curtain drawn across the neighboring room.

It opened, and Molly stepped out, adjusting the folds of her own outfit, a dress pinned to fit her. "What do you think?" she asked Bianca. She turned in a slow circle, showing the dress from all sides.

"How do you feel in it?" asked Natalie, in a voice that suggested she wasn't dying to know, necessarily—which couldn't be further from the truth.

"I feel amazing," said Molly. "I've never worn anything like this before." She glanced in the mirror again, as if she couldn't tear her eyes away from her reflected image. *The best sign of all*, Natalie thought.

The fabric was somewhere between champagne and ivory in the daylight. The bodice featured ruches, with the sleeves gently off the shoulder, and an asymmetrical waistline, the skirt gently flaring to a train; no crystals or sequins or pearl beading. It was simple, but soft and elegant, the fabric shining in the light.

At first, Bianca didn't say anything. Molly smoothed the skirts with her hand. "What do you think, Gran?" she repeated. "I think it's really beautiful. I like it so much better than the one I tried on a few days ago."

Natalie waited. Bianca had put her hand over her mouth when Molly emerged from behind the curtain. As she gazed at Molly, her eyes had begun to glitter softly. At last, she spoke.

"It is... so beautiful," she said. Her voice trembled. "She looks lovely. Just like a movie star."

"Do you think so?" said Natalie. "I know it's different from what you were searching for, but I thought maybe you would like it. It really looked like something perfect for Molly."

Bianca nodded. "We will take it," she said. "If Molly loves it, we will take it."

"I do," said Molly. "Same answer to the dress as Paolo. A definite yes." She broke into a smile at this point, as did Bianca. The elderly woman rose to her feet and took both of the bride's hands in her own. She squeezed them tightly, her beam as wide as Molly's.

"I can get you a great deal on it," said Natalie. "The designer hasn't had much exposure, so it's practically cost price."

"We must take a picture." Bianca was removing an antiquated film camera from her purse, turning on the flash button. "For your wedding album."

Natalie snapped photos of Molly, then of Molly and Bianca together. "Let's talk accessories now," she said. She stepped aside to retrieve her catalogs, leaving Molly and Bianca admiring the dress in front of the mirror. In the doorway behind her, she found Tessa watching.

"That's a gorgeous dress," said Tessa. "Molly looks great in it."

"I thought she would," said Natalie. "When I saw it, I thought she would look like an angel: it wouldn't wash out her color, it would look elegant with or without a veil. It was just what she needed."

"It's yours, isn't it?" Tessa said.

Natalie stood before the bookshelf in Tessa's adjoining office, her hand pulling out one of the bridal fashion catalogs. She didn't say anything, pretending to look for something inside one of the issues.

"I would know one of your dresses anywhere, Nat."

Natalie shrugged. "It's a bridal version of my best reject from the Garland Boutique downtown, once upon a time," she said. "They almost put it on the rack, but no dice. And it definitely wasn't ugly enough for Kandace. So I thought I'd find somebody who appreciated it."

"Cost price, though," said Tessa. "You're selling yourself short, Natalie. That dress made Molly look amazing. And I know it took courage for you to show it to anybody."

"Maybe a little courage," said Natalie. "I can think of worse sacrifices than selling someone a dress that's been in storage for a year." She hid her smile as she gathered up two more catalogs to peruse with their client.

It had taken more courage than Natalie was admitting; they both knew. After all the snide comments Kandace had made, it couldn't have been easy to show her work to a customer as picky as Bianca—especially a dress that was anything but the princess's ball gown Paolo's grandmother had pictured.

Tessa squeezed Natalie's arm as she passed her in the doorway. "I'm proud of you, just so you know."

"Call it the first brave step to my future as a designer," said Natalie. "Now if I can only find a matching veil and some hair ornaments to crown Molly, then my part in this deal will be fulfilled."

"Believe me, it already is," said Tessa.

Natalie rolled her eyes. "Whatever," she said. The little gleam of pleasure in response to this praise was buried deep in Natalie's eyes, but it was still there if someone looked closely.

"Who wants to talk veils?" asked Natalie, holding up a catalog as she entered her office again. "Tiaras, head garlands, simple clip ornaments—we have lots of options to explore, ladies."

"Coming," promised Molly, who couldn't get enough of her reflection in this dress, like a girl trying on her first formal. Bianca was still smiling as brightly as if her future granddaughter-in-law were wearing a Versace gown and not an obscure designer's concept.

Natalie's phone buzzed. On the screen was a text from Cal: *Miss u more every day. Kandace's latest dress STINKS btw!!* He sent a picture of a sketched baggy garment embellished with mini gauzy Tinker Bell wings hanging off its shoulders.

Even while basking in her success, Natalie couldn't help recoiling a little from the image on her screen. There was no doubt about it: Kandace's latest line was definitely destined for the store's bargain rack.

Chapter Twenty-Four

The flowers for the wedding were simple and affordable, but beautiful. Rosies and Posies had created a bouquet of lavender shades and soft greens for Molly, featuring lots of roses as well. There were no bridesmaids, so the only other flowers were to decorate the two big urns on either side of the courtyard tree, and two centerpieces for the buffet table.

"*If* the courtyard meets with their approval," Natalie pointed out, as they made a list of extra supplies for decorating the chosen venues. "They haven't seen it yet. And I definitely sensed skepticism in Bianca's voice when you told her you found an outdoor spot that would be perfect."

"We'll see," said Tessa. "But in the meantime, I want to be prepared. The two big arrangements can be used at the church instead if that's the venue of choice. And if we get a really nice garland we can decorate an arbor for them to stand underneath during the outdoor ceremony… or we can use it to decorate the church altar instead."

"How good a deal will this florist give you?" Ama asked, as she checked her oven's timer. She had a dessert order for a bar mitzvah to finish: a set of shortbread cookies in the shape of the popular cartoon characters from *Transformers*.

"Really good, thanks to my cousin Gabby," Natalie answered. "She got her manager at the flower shop to give us a 'friends and family' discount. *And* its owner Maxine promised she would hold some extra lavender roses and baby's breath in case we need something more," she said.

Tessa checked her to-do list again. "Nat's already taken care of the permits for the restaurant, of course, since Paolo and Molly both approved it—"

"—and the cake is a 'go,' of course," said Ama. "But I'm not sure about my tiramisu. I think I need a second and third opinion."

"Do you have samples?" asked Natalie.

"Of course." Ama produced three little glass bowls from the fridge. Each contained layers of whiskey-vanilla infused ladyfingers with a sweet coffee syrup and a mellow mint cream. Both Natalie and Tessa tasted it.

"Not bad," said Natalie. "I like it. It's different from my mom's tiramisu… it's kind of like a trifle, actually."

"Would chocolate on top be too much?" asked Tessa—receiving a resounding "yes" from both her partners.

"I'm thinking of switching to the Irish macaroons instead of this," said Ama, opening her notebook. "Oh, and did I tell you about the cool Norwegian wedding cake?" she said. "It's tradition there to serve these flat bread layers, sandwiching them with sweet cheese, cream, and syrup, then cutting them into squares." She showed them a photo in a cookbook called *Traditional Norwegian Recipes*.

"They kind of look like tortillas," said Natalie, wrinkling her nose as she read the recipe. "The cake itself sounds kind of bland. I mean, slathered in flour and griddled?"

"It's to make it perfectly white," explained Ama. "It was part of the tradition, when white flour was a luxury. But what if we changed the recipe to make them a little lighter, more like a crepe, for instance, and then layered them in stacks with the traditional ingredients? We could serve them in little clear bowls so you could see the layers."

"I like it," said Tessa. "Can you make it work?"

"I think so," said Ama. "So if we have that, the cookies, the macaroons, the sugared almonds and the wedding cake, maybe the tiramisu—" Here, a sudden spout of smoke from the oven cut Ama's list short.

"My bar mitzvah cookies!" She threw open the door as a blue flash emerged. Acrid smoke filled the room and the three of them coughed loudly. The shrill *tweeee!* of the smoke alarm followed.

"What happened?" said Natalie between hacking coughs.

"I don't know," Ama said, gasping for breath. "I had it set to the right temperature—"

Blake appeared in the room. "What happened?" he demanded, echoing Natalie's words.

"I don't know—cookies in oven—" Coughing smothered the rest of Ama's statement as she poked at the oven's interior with a spatula, trying to rescue her baking tray.

Blake pulled a flashlight from his belt and peered inside the oven. "The element's burned out," he said. "It must've had too many miles on it already." He fanned some smoke away with a towel, then reached up to lift the smoke detector from above the stove and end its persistent *tweeee*.

"What do we do?" asked Tessa. She avoided Blake's glance as she spoke, since she hadn't quite gotten over the sting of their last conversation. His assessment of her career—and her personal character—was anything but flattering. If it weren't for the fact that burned-out elements sounded fatal to an oven's operation, she wouldn't be consulting him at all.

"You'll have to get a new one and install it," said Blake, as he reset the alarm. "Until then, your oven is out of commission. Meaning no cakes, cookies, or anything else."

"That's not really an option for us," Tessa replied, feeling a little bit peeved at his casual attitude. "I know our work may seem frivolous to you," she added, remembering his words the other night, "all flash and glitz—but I'm afraid it's necessary to keep our clients happy."

"What are you doing?" Natalie hissed. "We need his help to fix it."

But Tessa did not relent. "If you're too busy, I'm sure we can find someone else to repair it. But if you happen to have the time between more important projects, we would appreciate the help." She crossed her arms with this defiant speech.

For a moment, the handyman seemed speechless. Then, he turned to Natalie and said, "I'll have to look up the model number. Until then—"

"We'll make do," Tessa finished, fanning the smoke toward an open window with a copy of Ama's cookie recipe. *With what?* mouthed Natalie, although Tessa ignored her. The handyman nodded, then popped the smoke detector back in place and left without another word.

"Way to go," snapped Natalie. "You want to tell us why you just sabotaged our chances of getting our oven up and running again?"

"He wasn't taking it seriously," Tessa said with a shrug. "He would probably drag his feet on doing it, since it's not vital to the building."

"Well, I hope someone takes it seriously," said Ama, scraping her burned cookies into the trash can. "I can't make appetizers for fifty people without an oven. The one at my family's restaurant isn't an option, really, unless I want to bake Molly and Paolo's wedding food in the middle of the night." A little note of panic crept into her voice.

"Same for the bakery," Natalie said. "You want to wrestle my Uncle Guido for kitchen privileges? I can tell you now that you'll lose."

"We'll get this one repaired in time," Tessa said, less sure of this now that the reality was sinking in. Perhaps she *was* a little short tempered with the handyman—but he could have been nicer about her job, too. Maybe she could smooth it over.

But she didn't see Blake again for the rest of the day. His absence hovered in the back of her mind, growing from a slight annoyance to something more like worry. He obviously had errands to run, or something. No reason to google "oven repair" and try to locate and install the missing element herself, as if she had ever done more than tighten the screw on a door handle. No reason to think she had another crisis of conscience on her hands with just days left until the wedding was scheduled to take place.

No reason at all.

Chapter Twenty-Five

The noise was a shuffling sound, followed by a thump. Tessa rolled over on her side in the summer's heat, sweltering beneath the cotton sheet. Another noise. She chalked it up to her neighbor who worked the late shift at a warehouse, until her sleepy brain remembered that she had no neighbors anymore.

She bolted upright. Her gaze fell on the clock on her bedside drawers. *Two thirty-three.* From downstairs came another thump, and the low whine of scraping metal. Tessa's heart pounded.

Creeping from beneath the sheet, she pulled on her robe and seized her phone from the dresser. Should she call the police? Tell them there was a break-in and to hurry, possibly bringing a SWAT team? Lock her door, and the door to the neighboring room, and the one that led to the adjacent powder room—for heaven's sake, didn't *any* room in this place have total privacy?

She took a deep breath. It was the pipes, maybe. They could be thumping, because the plumbing was bad, right? Or the fridge might be having one of its noisy fits during a cooling cycle. She was imagining things because she was alone late at night in a huge, creaky old building.

She shivered and pulled her robe closed. Her door was open, creaking slightly as she poked her head into the hall outside. Nobody was there, and the doors to her partners' offices were closed, as were those of the washroom and the empty rooms still in need of work. She felt the worn carpet cushion her feet as she crept toward the stairs, arming herself as a precaution with a heavy decorative curtain rod that was awaiting a pair of gauze drapes in her private apartment.

Please don't creak, she begged the spiral staircase. Its steps were warm beneath her feet, and silent until she reached the midsection, where the whole unit swayed a little due to some kind of warping in its structure—Tessa had forgotten the exact words the contractor used when trying to explain it. She waited for it to settle, heart hammering again, before she took another step.

Relax. Nobody was listening. There was nobody here, just because she imagined it. Probably it was a dream, the way you dream about people calling your name just when you're dropping off to sleep. Or somebody had slammed a car door on the street beneath her window— that was a good explanation.

The latest thud from downstairs was unmistakable. Tessa jumped, and the curtain rod fell to the floor below, where its impact was muffled by one of Ama's geometric area rugs. Tessa's shaking hand scooped it up again as she crouched in the shadows, one shaking finger trying to dial the emergency number on her phone. Unless the refrigerator had fallen over on its own, that noise had been made by a human.

Still crouching, she inched toward the front door, and that was when she noticed a light from the kitchen. The thief turned on a light? That seemed counterintuitive in the world of stealthy criminals. Plus, what were they doing robbing that room in the house? Nothing of value was in there, unless they wanted to steal Tessa's old toaster with its one working slot. But if Ama left her industrial mixer here—

Fear of creaking floorboards should have stopped her, but Tessa was now creeping toward the kitchen door, standing ajar. Her hand tightened around the curtain rod. There was a siren function on her phone, and a recording of savage guard dogs barking, and either one of those might send a thief running—especially one who'd discovered there was nothing available but canisters of flour and sugar.

The thief was in the oven. Literally. It was the reason Tessa lost her senses entirely and pushed the door open in disbelief, at almost the same time the upper half of her intruder emerged from its mouth. He started at the sight of her, dropping his screwdriver as the shriek escaped Tessa's lips, the curtain rod clattering to the floor a second time as she swiftly closed her robe around her short satin nightgown.

"Mr. Ellingham?!" she demanded, in shock and embarrassment.

"I'm sorry!" he said. He averted his gaze, face red with embarrassment. "I didn't know anybody was here... it's two in the morning—"

"I *know* it's two in the morning," she snapped. "What are you doing here, sneaking around our building in the dead of night?"

"What are *you* doing here?" he countered.

"I live here," she retorted, then repented of this a second later. "That is—I've been spending some nights... staying here for a period while I finish some... some things." She gazed loftily at the ceiling, trying to sound casual about this explanation.

"You live here?" he said. He sounded surprised, and a little skeptical. "Where?"

"Upstairs," she said shortly. "There's plenty of room." Not that it was any of his business where she lived or what she did. This was her building, after all.

"This place is a death trap as it is, but it must be a hundred degrees up there," he said. "You must be living in an oven." Tessa became aware that her hair was sticking to the layer of perspiration on her face, and that her robe was clinging to her as well. It was a thin robe made of filmy lavender silk, which is why she pulled it more closely around herself now, to hide the view of her short nightgown. Why couldn't she have had a premonition about this incident and slept in nice baggy pajamas despite the heat?

"Anyway, what are you doing here?" she repeated.

"Your partner Ama gave me a key," he said. "I… uh… had a late pickup outside the city, and I was in the neighborhood… so I stopped by to finish something, because I need to start on those cabinets tomorrow…"

"And you left your screwdriver in our oven?" said Tessa. Blake's story petered out at this point. Tessa saw a metal grate lying on the floor a few feet away, scorched and charred on the outside. There were black stains on Blake's hands too, and a newly opened manufacturer's plastic sleeve lay crumpled to one side.

"You were fixing our oven, weren't you?" she said. Blake looked evasive.

"Look, I… I happened to have a spare one handy," he said. "It was the same model, so I thought I would let you have it. It happened to be in the back of my truck too—by sheer coincidence, I assure you."

Surprise filled Tessa completely. "You shouldn't do it for free," she said. "We'll pay you. We were going to hire you to do it."

"You hadn't asked me," he said. His tone was slightly gentler. "I thought I would do it as a tiny favor, no strings attached." He picked up his screwdriver and closed the oven door.

Obviously, he hadn't been driving around with a spare oven element that just *happened* to fit their appliance, and they both knew it. If she weren't so embarrassed that they were practically accepting charity from the contractor—Blake's pity manifesting itself in his secret midnight repairs—then she would be desperately thinking of the right words to thank him. Instead, she studied her toes rather than looking into his eyes; maybe because he seemed so embarrassed for getting caught in the act. Because he didn't want the thanks or the credit—or because he knew how embarrassing it was for her and her partners?

"We'll still pay you," she said.

"Whatever you want." He put his tools back in their metal box. "But it was fifteen minutes of my time. I've spent more time brushing my teeth before. But if you insist…"

A tiny smile crossed Tessa's lips, and she dared to steal a glance in Blake's direction. "You really don't have to feel sorry for us," she said. "For a new business, I think we happen to be doing fairly well in terms of coping with our limits. Other than the little maneuver involving you," she amended quickly. "But other than that, we have things perfectly under control."

"You living here, therefore—"

"—is purely business strategy," said Tessa. "I'm consolidating my expenses and maximizing my capital's investment. The other partners are doing the same thing… in their own way." Natalie quitting her job at Kandace's hadn't been helpful the first few weeks, but it also couldn't be helped, given Kandace's nature.

He snapped closed his toolbox. "So what happened to the partner I'm pretending to be?" he asked. "He decided to streamline his capital for a different purpose?"

"Stefan was more of a… figurehead," Tessa replied vaguely. "I'm sure he would have invested some money. Probably." She hesitated. "His contribution was more about bringing a certain image or—or panache—to the business."

"Like his reputation?"

"Exactly. Stefan was considered very good at what he did. A lot of people *loved* the events he planned at his last place of employment. Some people called him the best young event planner in the business, which is exactly why people like Bianca hire him." Tessa had given so many speeches like this one about Stefan's reputation that she delivered it on autopilot. She could write the bio for his new website—except she didn't know French, and Stefan would prefer more dynamic and flattering language when being described.

"I notice you point out that a lot of 'people' thought this," said Blake. "Call me crazy, and maybe I've been misreading the signs whenever you talk about him, but I've developed the impression that you're not really one of those people. You don't think he's the genius the rest of these people do."

Tessa's toes traced a line in the floor's dust. "Stefan and I just have different taste, as I said before," she said. "He likes everything to be dramatic and impressive down to the last detail—which is great, if that's what your client wants," she clarified. "Only... he had a slight tendency to dismiss any ideas his clients had that didn't fit with the image. It was sort of a dictatorship for Stefan, not a partnership with the client, when it came to creating the event. He tended to step on other people."

It was true. Stefan was a dictator when it came to his ideas and his style, and had mowed over meeker clients whose taste hadn't been perfection in his eyes. Tessa would rather die than make a client cry by crushing something they really wanted.

"He sounds like a real asset to the business," said Blake dryly.

She shook her head. "He was successful and available," she said. "Having someone like him would prevent us from failing. That's what

I thought. It would have been horrible to work with him, but I told myself I could put up with it."

"Why were you planning to try?" said Blake. "I know you said you're new at this, but you've worked for event planners before. It's not like nobody in the city would trust you—it just might take a little longer to find someone the first time. You talk to people confidently, honestly, and professionally, which is how a good client relationship begins."

"Because I have no confidence in myself," said Tessa. "I'm scared. I was too scared to try on my own, which is why I stuck with a job going nowhere, and left my dream in my notebooks and a savings account until I just… broke."

The words had tumbled out of her, ones too honest to share with a stranger. She was crazy, confessing something like this to Blake without hesitating. Why wasn't he looking at her like a mad person, instead of listening with that honest, thoughtful expression? There was no boredom in those bright blue depths, no laughter, not even a hint of a smirk that betrayed a lack of surprise for the truth behind her decisions.

"It's not a big surprise, is it?" she said. "Look at me—even when I was finally brave enough to take the leap, I still wanted a safety cord. Natalie is so right about me. I would've hated every moment of being second to Stefan, even while telling myself I was living my dream. There's not a chance he would have ever let me really help a client. He probably would have vetoed my every suggestion." A short, bitter laugh escaped her as she imagined it as reality. Natalie and Ama would have hated it, too. They probably would have been glad when the partnership collapsed—which, as likely as it was even now, would have definitely happened with Stefan in the mix.

"I didn't think that," said Blake. "I never thought you didn't have skills, or that you didn't have the confidence. Maybe that you went after this guy for his reputation a little too eagerly... but we all have those moments when we grab onto something to stay afloat. It's human. Sometimes we can't help it."

"That's nice of you to say, given that it dragged you into our client's relationship," said Tessa, with another hint of a smile, one that couldn't help itself. "I think you have the right to be a tiny bit scornful of my weak moment."

"You always have to jab people just a little, even when they're being nice to you, don't you?" He smiled knowingly, as he lifted his toolbox and climbed to his feet.

"Not always," said Tessa. "I'm one of those people who's only contrary with people I know." *Know well* being the implication, she realized. She was saying that she was comfortable around him, and it was this confession that made her feel uncomfortable at precisely this moment, as he stood across from her.

Standing in a hot kitchen in her thin, clingy robe, across from someone who looked so rugged and muscular... their eyes met for a moment, and Tessa's brain lost track of both her thoughts and all the warning bells in her head about this scenario. Her breath quickened a little, and in Blake's eyes she saw a series of emotions; which, though she couldn't quite identify them, caused the blue to deepen and burn with a softer fire than before.

Tessa sucked in her breath and glanced away to study the faded wallpaper. Blake gathered up the torn plastic cover and the old stove element, adding them to his pile of construction debris. "Do you have a fan upstairs?" he asked her.

"No," she said. "I have one of those cooling units that fits in the window."

"Is that enough to make it tolerable?" he asked. "Heat rises."

"It's broken," Tessa admitted, as if he hadn't guessed already. "It wasn't the bargain I thought it was."

"Maybe it just needs a little adjustment," he said. "You can't stay up there in that heat, especially if you can't open the window now. You'll smother. These mini heat waves are killers."

"I can't ask you to fix it," said Tessa. "I'll open the window in my office."

"Did you ask me? Let me take a look at it and see if it's fixable, at least." He brushed past her and entered the foyer, then climbed the stairs. She followed him, trying to keep her robe closed at the same time.

"The space is sort of messy—it's really not that bad, the heat—" It hit them like a wave before they reached the top of the stairs, and Tessa let her argument die, although she was still desperate to stop him before he opened the door to her private apartment. Rumpled sheets, clothes thrown over the back of the old love seat from her apartment, shoes and books scattered—it was a college dorm room the day before the frantic clean for inspection week. A picture of Tessa and her mom on graduation day was on her dresser, and a baby photo of her father holding her hung on the wall beside a magazine photo of a tent decorated with star lights, a milling crowd of happy guests beneath it.

"I've been planning to tidy," she said. "It's not much to look at, I know." She swept a few garments that she would prefer *not* to be seen underneath her business jacket, and straightened a framed print hanging crookedly on the wall: a shower of rose petals falling on a bride in a courtyard.

"So who's looking?" Blake set his toolbox down and opened the cover of the cooling unit.

"You are. You're in my space. It's not like you won't notice it." She sat down in the chair, on top of a business dress and a planner's notebook.

"I'm sure it'll look terrific after you pick out a bargain paint color. Pumpkin orange or maroon red or something else that makes a statement." He opened a small valve on the unit, then screwed it closed again. He tweaked one of the wires leading to the power button.

"You're making fun of my taste," said Tessa.

"Only because you won't take it seriously." His screwdriver tightened something, then he popped the front in place again. He pushed the plug into the wall and switched on the unit. Tessa felt the miracle of cool air fanning her, even from across the room.

"Better?" he asked.

"Better," she said. He could probably hear in her voice how much, even if she hadn't closed her eyes while basking in the luxury of the cool breeze—better than any south-coast seaboard wind turned stagnant by city steam, and the heat rising from the buildings around her.

"I'll go," he said. "I need some sleep. You do, too." He closed his toolbox again and rose. She forgot about the breeze and turned around hastily in the chair as he entered the hall.

"Thank you," she said. She meant for everything, and not only for her broken window unit coming to life again. She meant for his covert attempts to fix their oven without a charge, as if shaving a few dollars from his next bill could make all the difference in the world to their future.

"You're welcome." He smiled at her. "See you tomorrow."

"See you then."

"I'll lock the back door behind me. Don't worry about that. I'll leave your friend's key on the table, so you don't have to worry about it, either."

"I wasn't," she said. She had forgotten all about it, actually.

His smile became a smirk. "So you claim." Tessa rolled her eyes.

She heard the sound of his boots crossing the foyer, then the kitchen floorboards. Hugging a throw pillow against herself, she listened quietly until she couldn't hear anything else downstairs, and knew that Blake was gone for the night.

She wasn't tired anymore. With a sigh, Tessa switched off the lamp and sat in the dark, thinking as the cool air began circulating through her room.

Chapter Twenty-Six

The next afternoon, Tessa arranged to take Molly and Bianca to see the courtyard, after borrowing a friend's car. "I think you'll really like this location," she told them.

"I wish that you had shown it earlier," said Bianca worriedly. "All those people—what if it's some place too small? What if they come and see it and the rest is pretty and the site is plain?"

"Gran, I told you, we decided to trust Tessa and Blake's choice. I said they could surprise us," said Molly. "They've done such a good job, it's the right thing to do."

The unconventional thing to do was more like it, Tessa thought—but it was the only way to keep Bianca from choosing a venue herself.

"When I saw this place, I could really picture a wedding on site," said Tessa. "Flowers, chairs for the guests, maybe even a red carpet leading to the altar, so Molly can walk there in style."

"From a limo car," chirped Bianca. "This neighborhood is familiar," she added. "I haven't been here in a long time. There was a grocery on that corner. And a little bakery over there that sold day-old pies and bread." She pointed through the window for Molly, in the direction of a wireless service store.

"I think the place we're going will seem familiar, too," answered Tessa.

She parked the car across the street from Bianca's old building. As the grandmother climbed out, Tessa could see a look of puzzlement on her face. Molly helped her cross the street to the stately old buildings with a stone wall between them, the iron gate leading to the sidewalk unlocked for Tessa's benefit by the left-side apartments' doorman.

"I think…" began Bianca. "I know this… is it…?"

"Look, Gran," said Molly eagerly. "Isn't it pretty? It's like a cool little Italian garden." She led Bianca inside, a smile of pleasure on her lips as she admired the landscaped courtyard.

Bianca looked at Tessa. "What is the address of this place?" she asked.

"It's your old building," said Tessa. "The Brentwood. That's why it seems so familiar. It's not likely you recognize it as it is now—it's changed a little with the times."

Astonishment filled Bianca's eyes. "I remember," she said. "This courtyard—there were laundry lines across those windows, not all these fancy metal frames on the stairs. Children drew games with chalk on the pavement… and there was a little shed where the building's carpenter kept his things…"

"You lived here?" said Molly. "That's so neat." She held up her phone and took a photo. "We have to show Paolo this. He won't believe it. Isn't it incredible?"

"It looks so different," said Bianca softly. "I don't know… I don't know if this is the place we should have the wedding." She shook her head a little.

"I hoped you would think about it," said Tessa. "This place is just like you. It found a new life… but it still remembers its past." She broke a sprig off one of the spicy evergreen shrubs and held it out to Bianca. "I thought maybe it was time to remember what you loved best about your wedding in Italy."

Bianca took the tiny evergreen branch between her fingers. "These didn't grow here when we came to this place, Pietro and me," she said. "But I remember the smell. Some like this grew outside the olive grove Pietro's family owned. I used to meet him there sometimes, in the afternoon." Her voice had grown even softer than before.

"Think about it," said Tessa. "I think Molly looks pretty excited about it, though." Molly was talking on the phone, presumably to Paolo, who had probably already seen the photos his fiancée had taken of the courtyard. Tessa stepped back, letting the three of them admire it on their own for a while.

"I guess we'll have to wait for them to call us with the verdict on Bianca's approval," said Natalie, sitting in Tessa's office a few hours afterward. She was watching as Tessa tallied the total costs for the wedding, trying to wrestle the budget's numbers into still smaller ones.

"It wasn't a mistake to choose it," said Tessa. "I don't think it was, anyway."

She had had a few feelings of regret since this afternoon's outing. Had she stirred unpleasant memories for Bianca, somehow? Bittersweet reflections about leaving her European homeland for another life? Maybe that wasn't something for this wedding to either celebrate or heal.

"There's a place down the street from the bakery that sells garden supplies," said Natalie. "I'm going to call them and price a lightweight garden arbor tonight. Something we can assemble really easily, that won't leave any damage in the courtyard. Hopefully, my cousin will have set aside some nice flowers to dress it up a little—those things look pretty plain on their own."

"Just no fluffy tulle sashes, okay?" said Tessa. Her phone rang and she answered it as Natalie left. "Hello?"

"Tessa?" She recognized Paolo's voice on the other end.

"Hi, Paolo," she said. "Is everything okay?"

"I just wanted to call and let you know that we really like the courtyard for the site for the wedding. We really appreciate you finding it... and that's exactly what we want, so long as it doesn't cost too much," he added.

"It won't," said Tessa. "I already appealed to the heartstrings of both buildings' managers. They've agreed that it's fine, so long as we have permission. And I can take care of that this week."

"Thanks," he said. "I wanted to say again how much I appreciate this. I never would have thought of choosing a site special to my grandparents' story. Gran never would have told me about it in a million years... I don't think she even considered the possibility of retracing her and Gramps's steps when Molly and I tried to think of places from the past."

"I hope she's okay with choosing it," said Tessa.

"She can't get over how much it's changed," said Paolo. "It's not the glamorous site she pictured, of course. I think she's a little disappointed we're not getting married in some grand cathedral, though—even the church's stained glass wasn't quite what she had in mind," he joked.

"Before we're done, Paolo, I think she'll see it as more than just a pretty courtyard where kids used to park their bicycles," said Tessa. "I can't promise you that... but we will do our best."

"I know you will. Tell the rest of the staff we're grateful, okay?" said Paolo.

"I will." Tessa hung up the phone.

"Guess what?" she said, peering into Ama's office, where Natalie and Ama were laughing over an internet video on Ama's phone.

"What?" said Ama, as the two of them looked up.

"Bianca isn't sulking," hinted Tessa.

"No way! She liked it?" said Ama.

"Are you serious?" said Natalie.

"I just had Paolo's personal seal of approval," said Tessa. "We're moving forward with the plan to set up Molly and Paolo's ceremony there."

"But what does Bianca really think?" said Ama. "She has her heart set on paying for a dramatic wedding. I can't see a garden outside of her old apartment building being what she had in mind—especially since it probably won't cost all that much to stage it there."

"We'll have to do our best to prove that it's exactly what it looks like—the perfect place for this wedding," said Tessa.

Natalie and Ama exchanged glances. Tessa thought she sensed a little doubt between them. "So," said Ama. "Who wants to try my version of *brudlaupskling*?"

"I'm having sixty chairs delivered to set up rows on either side of the aisle," said Tessa on her phone, as she walked past the chic little couture fashion store which had taken over the former grocery in Bianca's old neighborhood. "That's ten rows of chairs on either side, with three in each row… plus, we have the guests stationed on the fire escape balconies above for the big surprise."

"How did you pull that off?" Natalie asked. "I thought the residents would be weirded out by the idea."

"Simple. I appealed to their romantic side," said Tessa. "All it takes are a few willing people to make something happen. Anyway, if you could pick up the aisle carpet sometime today, I would really appreciate…" The rest of Tessa's request died away as she opened the courtyard gate and stepped inside.

There, in front of the tree's ornamental bed where the arbor should go, stood a wooden altar. It was hand-carved with flowers across its front, and ornamental scrolls traveling down its supports, with a rough, handcrafted, artistic beauty. A light finish gently darkened its wood.

"Natalie, where did you find it?" said Tessa. "It's gorgeous! Tell me it didn't cost more to rent than buying one of those wire garden arbors."

"What are you talking about?" said Natalie, confused. "I didn't order the arbor yet. The shop was closed by the time I finished booking the limo."

"You mean you're not responsible?" Tessa snapped a photo of it and texted it to Natalie's phone. "It looks so much like the one in the picture I found online of Bianca's village church. All that really gorgeous woodwork… it's practically identical." This one even looked antique, although well preserved.

"It wasn't me," said Natalie. "I've never seen it before, I swear. Wow, though. Whoever owns it probably didn't get it cheap."

"I have to call you back," said Tessa. She hung up the phone and walked closer to the altar. What was it doing here? And could they rent it for a fee?

Someone behind her cleared his throat. "I brought it here," said Blake. He stood at the gate entrance, hands tucked in the pockets of his jeans. "I thought it might be a nice touch. For Bianca's sake especially."

"You found this?" clarified Tessa. "How? Where?"

"I had some free time," said Blake. "I remembered the picture, so I contacted a few antique dealers I know. One of them specializes in woodwork and had some imported items from European churches, and from some old Scandinavian communities in America. From there, it just kind of fell into place."

"Things like this don't turn up just anywhere," she said.

"Pennsylvania," he said. "That's where I found it. I drove there, picked it up in my truck, and did a little work to it."

"You drove all the way to Pennsylvania for this?" Tessa was awed.

"It's not all that far," said Blake, in the dismissive tone of someone who drives a lot. Tessa guessed that the "junk" in the back of his truck must have come from all over the Eastern seaboard.

"So simple," she joked. "Anyone could have done it."

"He shrugged and said, "It was nothing a little sandpaper and woodwork experience couldn't fix."

"This is beautiful," said Tessa. "Really special. This"—she paused, words failing her— "is so much more than any of the rest of us could have done for this wedding."

"Not that." Blake shook his head. "But I was happy to do it."

"I don't know what to say. It's incredible," said Tessa. "When you said you'd help us, I never meant you had to do anything this extraordinary… just say a few words to reassure Bianca that she had an experienced wedding planner on her side."

Blake's smile was a little sheepish. "I'm not sure I accomplished that very well. But maybe this will help make up for it."

"I think she'll be very impressed by this—more than by the advice of event planner Blake Ellingham," said Tessa, hiding her smile.

"Let's hope so," he answered.

Tessa turned back to the altar. "In the meantime, I guess I had better find a safe place for this until the wedding," she said.

"I've got that covered. The apartment next to us is letting me store it in the basement," he said. "They've got a locked cage down there for keeping

valuable furniture safe. I just wanted to see how it looked in the yard first."
He wheeled a hand truck from against the building to lever one end of the
altar, strapping it in place. "Plus, I wanted you to see it and be impressed."

"Being the over-the-top, glitzy wedding planner that I am?" said
Tessa, lifting one eyebrow.

"Don't push your luck, Miss Miller. I could have this altar back in
my truck in two minutes' time."

"Sorry. Please don't do that," said Tessa. "I was only kidding." Her
lips threatened to form a smile again, but she managed to keep it inside
until Blake was busy lifting the altar to move it.

"Tessa, where did you find it?" The voice belonged to Molly, who
had just arrived with Bianca and a friend. They were staring at the
altar in Blake's possession.

"I didn't, actually," said Tessa. "The credit belongs entirely to Blake.
He contacted a few friends in the antiques business and found the
closest match he could. He even did the restoration work necessary to
make it beautiful in time for the wedding."

"You did?" said Molly. "It's amazing—I can't believe you went to
all that trouble."

"No trouble," he assured them. "And no extra charge. Consider it
my gift—to all of you."

"Ah, my! It looks just like one I remember as a child," said Bianca,
clasping her hands together as she examined it closely. "Just so. I used to
run my fingers along its carving like this—always afraid that someone
would tell me not to do it. Playing with God's furniture." She laughed.
"Children can have such funny ideas."

"I had no idea you had so many contacts," said Molly to Blake. "I
never realized how handy it must be in your work to know people who
can find this kind of stuff—make the past real again."

Neither did I, thought Tessa.

"You are a man of many talents," said Bianca. "First you help plan the wedding, *then* you help find flowers for Molly... and now you make the altar look so beautiful for her big day. What more could we ask?"

Blake's face had turned a deep crimson. "It was nothing, believe me," he answered. "Add some flowers across the top and it'll look as good as new."

"It already looks great," said Molly. "Are you sure we need flowers?"

"Maybe just a simple garland," said Blake, studying the altar. "Just a little something to offset the wood's simplicity. Add some greenery, maybe, since green is traditional for both Irish and Italian heritage. It won't detract from it; it'll actually enhance it—with the right choice, that is. Which will be up to Tessa here, who's the expert." He glanced at her, and Tessa felt a strange, pleasant tingle at these words: her as the expert. Those words hadn't come from a real fellow wedding planner, but they felt good all the same.

"It'll look *fabulous*, I'm sure," said Tessa. She touched Blake's arm lightly. A warm smile crossed his lips in return. Flustered and confused suddenly, Tessa turned away, focusing on her clients again. "Let's go over the layout for the chairs and for where Molly and Paolo are going to stand," she said.

She pulled out her plan for the ceremony to show Molly and Bianca, using a pencil to point out the position of the altar and the spot for the musician who would play the song for Molly's wedding march. Behind her, she knew that Blake had made his exit through the side door before any more questions could be asked of him—about flowers, or anything else.

Chapter Twenty-Seven

"I can't believe he did that for us," said Ama. "What are we going to pay him? I mean, this is a lot more than just fixing some bad wires and putting the light switch plates back on. Even than installing the new oven element."

"We'll have to figure out something," said Tessa. "I don't know what—we're already in debt to him through next year, probably. Unless, of course, we land some really rich customers between now and then."

"I think we'll need better advertising to achieve *that* goal," said Ama. "Hand me that icing bag, will you?" she said, lifting another Irish spice cookie from her platter of unfinished ones.

The days leading up to Molly and Paolo's wedding had been filled with last-minute details and adjustments. The closer it came, the more nervous Bianca became about the big day, especially on the morning of the wedding.

"What if it rains?" she said. "It is an outdoor wedding. Everyone would get wet—what would we do?"

"We have a backup venue," Tessa reassured her. "The church will let us move the ceremony to their sanctuary if the weather takes a turn for the worse."

"Some people say rain is good luck, but I don't know," said Bianca. "Maybe we should put brooms in the trees."

"Brooms?"

"It wards off the rain. An old superstition. A friend of mine did it long ago when she got married. No rain that day, only sunshine, even though there were such big gray clouds in the sky!"

"I think we'll be okay without the brooms," said Tessa gently.

The Irish and Italian cookies and the mint and chocolate macaroons were perfectly nestled in wax paper, awaiting transport to the venue, along with the miniature dishes of Ama's new *brudlaupskling*, made with thin sweet wafer layers, a thick cream and mascarpone sandwiched between them with a sweet berry syrup.

"I think that's everything," said Ama, who was rushing around with an apron covering her pumpkin-colored salwar kameez. "The real challenge is getting the cake to the restaurant, and assembled, without having it collapse into an utter mess."

"I'll help," said Natalie, who put an apron on over her pink cocktail dress before she lifted the bakery boxes of cookies. "Is that a new dress?" she said, noticing the sparkly embroidery covering the top and trousers of Ama's formal outfit. A pair of matching gold flower clips pinned her hair back from either side of her face.

"It's not mine," said Ama, as she lifted two more boxes. "I borrowed it from my sister, who loves clothes. My only dress-up dress needs a trip to the cleaner's." She noticed her reflection in the glass panes of the window and hesitated. "Do I really look okay?" she asked doubtfully, making a slight face. "This isn't exactly my style."

"I think it's beautiful," said Natalie. "Come on. We have to go. Let's be careful with the cake, since there's no backup for it." The rear hatch of her brother's Land Rover was open, letting them stack the boxes inside and brace them with some padding that Natalie had brought along.

"Where's Blake?" said Ama, lifting the box containing the bottom layer of the cake. "If he grabs one of these, we'll be done."

"He's not here today," said Natalie. "He does have other jobs besides ours. And Tess is at the reception site, double-checking the setup. We're supposed to meet her there, then we're going to the Brentwood courtyard to check the ceremony's setup."

The fourth partner was expected to come to the wedding and reception. After all, it would seem pretty odd to Bianca and her family if her beloved wedding planner didn't show up for the event he'd supposedly worked hard to create. But Blake had never promised to be there in so many words. Technically, his pseudo-partners knew, their agreement was only good up to the wedding day, which meant he was free to resume his carpentry-only duties.

"I left a suit on the back of the door," said Natalie to Ama, as if reading her mind. "Just in case." A nice tuxedo, freshly "borrowed" from the stash at Kandace's. She had persuaded Cal to discreetly pick it up for her, with promises in return of tickets to next season's Broadway road tour of *West Side Story*.

"Be careful with that tiny box," said Ama, as she lifted the last armful. "That's the gilded decoration for the top of the cake." She locked the side door of Wedding Belles behind them.

"Let's get this show on the road," said Natalie.

Despite Bianca's fears, the wedding day dawned perfectly. Five minutes before the ceremony was scheduled to begin, the limo arrived outside the courtyard's gates, and the driver helped out Bianca first, who looked astonished at the sight of guests filling the chairs, and the altar decorated with sprays of flowers. On the fire escape balconies above, several of the couple's friends were seated, waving to the groom's grandmother.

"I still can't believe she actually convinced people in these buildings to let strangers sit outside their windows," muttered Natalie, from her place near the back of the bride's side of the aisle.

"Love gets people to do strange things," said Ama.

Tessa had been waiting just outside the gate for the car to arrive. "Ready?" said Tessa. She took Bianca's arm to help her to her seat in the front row. "You'll want to see Molly come down the aisle in a moment."

A moment passed before the bridal music began, and the bride emerged from the car, her bouquet in hand. The dress looked even more stunning in daylight. In place of the traditional veil and flowers, Molly wore a gilded coronet set with several crystals and pearl beads. It had taken some extra search time—and a few minor alterations by Tessa, using some pearl beads and jewelry pins—to make sure it was worthy of the makeshift Norwegian wedding crown that had inspired it.

As the violinist played a soft classical number, Molly walked down the red-carpeted aisle. She paused at its end before the wooden altar wreathed with pink roses and pale green boughs, the spot where Paolo and the minister were waiting. Natalie blushed as a few hushed, admiring whispers about the dress circulated from the back rows after Molly had reached the altar.

From the sidelines, Tessa, Natalie, and Ama watched as the bride and groom exchanged their vows, then shared a kiss. Cheers erupted as the newly married couple followed the red carpet to the waiting car afterward, and from above, a shower of pink and white petals descended as the balcony guests began tossing the contents of their baskets. They landed on the happy couple, their guests, and the red carpet, in a soft, whirling flurry carried on the breeze. Tessa hoped that the photographer had snapped that moment from the limousine's open sunroof, as she had requested. It would make a fantastic image for the couple's album.

"It was like snow," said Bianca. "Snow falling from the rooftops. And Molly—she looked as beautiful as the actresses you see on the red carpet, just as Paolo said. More beautiful—she looked like an angel."

"That she did," said Paolo, beaming at Molly beside him. Reaching down, he gently brushed a stray petal from Molly's blonde hair, her coronet's stones glinting in the sunlight as they posed for one more photo.

The reception was already underway by the time the bride and groom arrived with Bianca. Tessa, who had arrived before the guests, was relieved to see that the cake had been transported in perfect shape, and was standing on its pillars in the middle of the table, as the restaurant's staff arranged the buffet trays of cookies, the Italian wedding cake, the macaroons, and the sugared almonds. Two large flower arrangements flanked Ama's three-layer creation in the middle.

"Do we have enough champagne chilled?" Tessa asked the server who was pouring glasses for the first toast—outside, the limo was dropping off the bridal party at the front door. In a moment, they would make their grand entrance for their guests.

"There's plenty standing by," Rick's waiter assured her. "When you're ready, the band will play the wedding march to announce them." An acoustic trio with a guitarist, a violinist, and a bassist were providing the musical entertainment, from Italian love songs to Irish dance tunes. It was the perfect compromise, Tessa had decided.

A second round of cheers came from the guests as the bride and groom entered the room. Toasts followed, the cake was sliced in a photograph-worthy moment, and the candied almonds began vanishing at an alarming rate from the buffet table as Tessa kept an eye on napkins, champagne glasses, and dessert plates.

She smoothed her green party dress with one hand. Thus far, everything had gone perfectly except for a few little things, such as a broken folding chair that turned out to be an extra one, and a brief fumble with a macaroon by one of the guests that left crumbs on the carpet. As for her clients, they looked so happy—as if it really had been the wedding of their dreams.

"So far so good," said Natalie quietly, as she circulated with another iced tub of champagne. "Have you seen Ama?"

"I think she's being chatted up by somebody," answered Tessa. "Who knew that being part of a wedding's staff could be such a great social gateway?" The baker was currently cornered by an eager, chatty friend of the groom, who was not put off by her shy expression of obvious reluctance. Clearly, he wasn't her type… unlike the handyman Blake, Tessa reflected. Not that it mattered, of course.

"You know what they say about weddings and romance," said Natalie. "At least he's cute. And at least she doesn't have a date to complain about her drawing someone else's attention."

"*You* didn't have a date, which surprised me," said Tessa.

"I didn't feel like inviting any of my paramours to share in the joyous occasion," answered Natalie, with a toss of her head.

As Tessa sneaked a candied almond from the fresh dish on the table, she spotted a familiar figure among the guests. Tall, dark, handsome, and wearing an Armani tux that resembled the kind of garments Natalie borrowed from the warehouse… wait—it wasn't—?

"Hi," said Blake.

"Hi," said Tessa, trying not to sound as shocked as she felt.

"I found this on the back of a door at the office," he said. "I thought it might be the sort of thing a distinguished wedding planner would wear. Or maybe a handyman who wants to look nice for a friend's wedding." He smiled. "The tie's crooked, though. I can never seem to get it right."

"I think it suits you that way," Tessa replied. "It's a good combination." She tried hard to suppress the heat creeping into her cheeks now.

"Are you here alone?" he asked. "No date for the big day?"

The blush made its escape before Tessa could hide it. "As a matter of fact, I thought it would be more appropriate to stay focused on the event in a professional capacity. So I came alone."

"So did I," said Blake. "A stunning coincidence, don't you agree?"

They both laughed—awkward and nervous, Tessa thought. She tried hard to keep from blushing again.

"I didn't think you'd come," she said. "I mean—when you didn't show up at the wedding. I was going to tell Bianca you were busy with the next client already."

"I didn't want her to be disappointed," he answered. "But I figured that the big moment belonged to you alone. The real wedding planner and all. I didn't want to steal that glory by accident."

Again, Tessa felt surprise. It hadn't even crossed her mind that everyone automatically looked to her today instead of to Blake, recognizing her true role for the first time—or that the handyman would realize it. She hadn't imagined that he would avoid coming for any reason other than escaping his role as the fake wedding planner.

"Thanks," she said. "It meant a lot to me, truly. It's my first wedding to plan, and it was nice to be the person everyone asked for help, and not just their assistant."

That's how it would have been with Stefan, truthfully. Natalie was right: Tessa would never have planned an event on her own so long as he was part of the business. But with Blake instead, it had been her guidance and expertise that led them in the planning process. Some of the moments they shared had felt almost like a real partnership, at times. *If* he had been a real event planner, and not merely pretending.

The musicians had struck up a soft, steady love song that Tessa's mind couldn't place at this moment as she gazed at the handyman. A few guests were dancing near the band. Blake held out his hand.

"A quick spin?" he said. "Just so we look like we're enjoying ourselves?"

Tessa managed to hide any roses that might be trying to bloom in her cheeks. "I suppose it's only right that Bianca sees the expert wedding planner Blake Ellingham blending among the guests," she said.

"You don't have to call me that anymore, remember?" he answered, as his arm encircled her back. His mouth was now close to Tessa's ear. "We're no longer business partners after today." His free hand took hold of hers, encircling it, too. "Just 'Blake' is fine."

"Just 'Tessa' is fine as well." Leaning against him, she realized her body was tense; not with discomfort, but nervousness. Her heart was beating fast inside her, the fingers touching Blake's almost trembling, like the symptoms of someone falling into a deep attraction: the first stages of her old romantic crushes. *You're being very stupid and impulsive right now*, she told herself. It must be the tux he was wearing. Or the atmosphere. Weddings made people wish for romance and magic, didn't they?

"Do you think this wedding turned out to be a success?" Blake asked her. "The way it was supposed to be in your mind?"

"I think it's been pretty unforgettable so far," said Tessa. "In a good way," she added. "Of course, sometimes we can't tell the difference until time has passed. Then, sometimes, we see the good parts instead of just the parts that didn't turn out like we imagined." She remembered the fondness in Bianca's voice at the memories of her last-minute haphazard wedding, despite her disappointment over the missing traditions and celebration.

"No disasters today," said Blake, looking around him at the guests dancing, the rest laughing and talking as they mingled. "The wedding couple and Bianca must be happy about that."

"They look happy," agreed Tessa. From where she and Blake were dancing, she could see the bride and groom sharing their slice of cake, smiling into each other's eyes—and not for the benefit of the photographer capturing the moment. "That's what every wedding planner wants to see when they look at the couple whose big day they planned," she said, watching them as Blake was doing, too.

"The romance that made it happen," said Blake. "You see more than just the big, beautiful event you planned when you look at the two of them, don't you? You're looking at why it was all worthwhile."

He was right. That remark expressed perfectly what she felt at this moment, gazing at Molly and Paolo in their happiness. It surprised her so much, this understanding of her work, that her power to reply was momentarily stripped away.

"Here he is," said Bianca, who had spotted them now. "I must thank you. The altar was beautiful, the flowers were beautiful… it was a day that Molly and Paolo can be so proud of all their lives." She clasped Blake's hand in one of her own, and Tessa's in the other. "How can I thank you both?" Her glance was fixed on Tessa more than Blake now, as if, somehow, the grandmother realized at last who had truly planned this day for her grandson and his new wife.

"It was our pleasure," said Tessa. "All of us." She met Blake's eye with a tiny smile. "I know I speak for Natalie and Ama, too."

"I want to thank them also," said Bianca. "It was all so nice. Just as you said it would be."

"I'll be recommending you to anybody I know who's looking for an event planner," said Molly, as the happy couple joined them. "You really did make this day perfect."

"And you kept Gran from spending every dime she had, too," added Paolo, as he hugged his grandmother close. "Even if she did insist on paying for Molly's dress and the limo in the end."

"I would pay for more, if you would stop being so stubborn," said Bianca.

"We want you to save your money for yourself," said Molly. "You need to live on your pension, not pay for champagne for us. And whatever's left in the tin will help you out with bills, too."

"Oh, I spent half of it already," said Bianca, waving her hand dismissively. "Since you wouldn't let me pay for the whole wedding, I got you something else. Two tickets for your honeymoon and a nice hotel. Next week, when you take time off from work, you can go."

"Gran, we're just going upstate for a few days," said Paolo. "We don't need your money for that."

"Upstate? That's not a honeymoon," scoffed Bianca. "I got you a proper one. To an island resort." She fumbled with the catch on her purse, then produced two plane tickets in an envelope. There was a reservation slip tucked inside for an exclusive resort on a Caribbean beach.

"Gran!" said Molly, her mouth dropping open. "How much money did you spend?"

"How could anybody let you do this with only a few hundred dollars?" asked Paolo. "It's a scam, Gran."

"*That's* all you thought I had?" said Bianca. She laughed. "No, no—I have lots more. Your grandfather Pietro—he had life insurance. So I saved the money so I can buy you a wedding… but when you said 'no,' what else can I do?" She shrugged her shoulders. "I wasn't going to waste twenty thousand dollars."

Twenty thousand? Paolo and Molly exchanged glances of shock. So, for that matter, did Tessa and Blake. All this time in Bianca's tin, the cash from her husband's life insurance policy had been waiting, easily worth more than double the money spent for today's wedding.

"What?" said Bianca. "Why do you all look so surprised?"

In response, they all laughed.

"A toast to our first successful event," said Tessa, lifting her glass. "And may the next one be just as wonderful."

"I'll drink to that," said Natalie, who brought her espresso cup to clink against Tessa's water glass. Ama chimed in, with a paper cup bearing a local teashop's logo. "We couldn't have asked for a better first client than Bianca."

The cake was gone and so was the rest of the food, leaving the reception's room bare, except for a few stray flowers decorating the table linen. All three of the Wedding Belles' official partners sat at the empty table as one of the restaurant's waitresses coiled the vacuum cleaner's cord and wheeled the appliance out of the room. The French doors stood open, letting in the evening's breeze from the terrace garden outside.

"I guess this definitely means we're up and running," said Natalie. "Time for me to apply some of my serious business skills to our operation's plan."

"And your needle to some more dresses," said Ama slyly, as Natalie pretended not to hear.

"We have to pay our handyman for fixing our leaky roof, too," said Natalie, casting a glance toward Blake. He was leaning against the terrace doorway, polishing off a slice of wedding cake from a plate.

"Don't worry. I'm not planning to sue you before your business succeeds," he told them. "We'll work out a payment plan of some sort. You can mail me five dollars a week until you've paid your bill."

"I think it might take too many years for us to pay you that way," said Tessa. "But there is something else we can do." Here, she met the glances of her two partners, both of whom gave silent nods of agreement.

"I'm afraid to ask." Blake was smiling, but they could detect his suspicion about where this was leading.

"We could offer you a partnership," said Tessa. "A stake in our business. You'd receive a fourth of our net profits from everything we earn."

"I already have a business," said Blake gently. "And it's not as a wedding planner, or a consultant, or whatever this is. The last thing I want to do is take anything unearned from you—"

"You can take it if we're insisting on *giving* it to you," said Ama.

"You deserve it," said Natalie. "You really helped us out, and not just by fixing our broken building—"

"Which, by the way, we can't afford to pay you for just yet," Tessa reminded him. "So we'll need all the help we can get in order to pay that bill."

"I won't have anything to contribute," he protested. "I can't just stand around in a suit or a tux, trying to look like I know what I'm doing in front of your clients."

"But you could help us in other ways," said Tessa. "When it comes to locating something special like that altar—or choosing a historic venue for hosting weddings."

"Or you could just hang around at all our meetings and look good in a suit," added Natalie. "That would make us happy."

Was it a mistake, or was Blake blushing now? "I don't know." He shook his head.

"You won't be pretending anymore. And you really don't have to show up at any of our events, if you don't want to," said Tessa gently. "You can be a silent partner. And you can always quit sometime in the future, and we'll pay you back. Somehow," she added.

"Then again, there might be lots of things you could help us with," said Ama, stressing the "might" in her statement. "You obviously have an artistic eye."

"True," said Natalie. Blake's face had reddened even more in response to these suggestions about his "fourth partnership" including actual contributions.

"It's up to you, of course," said Tessa, who was more serious now. "But we really are sincere. We want to do this for you. We need you. At least, you would admit that our crumbling building needs you," she amended, though she wasn't thinking about the help he had given to their kitchen and second-story floors. But she wasn't sure he would admit to the value of the other ways he had helped them.

Blake had begun to waver. "I don't feel completely right about this," he said, rubbing the back of his neck. "But I wouldn't object to being paid for the work I've already done, if you don't mind."

"Of course," said Natalie.

"And if that means sticking around… I can do something to help you out on the side, probably. Just for a little while," he added. "At least long enough to patch up some of your building's worst problems."

"Think of all the beautiful handiwork you could do around the place," coaxed Natalie. "And you'll be earning money just for being there."

"We'll call you our consultant," said Tessa. "How does that sound?"

He sighed. "I'm really going to regret working for you three, aren't I?"

"That depends," said Tessa. "You might really have a flair for the business." A playful smile accompanied this statement. The handyman rolled his eyes. A look of reluctant resignation crossed his face—no words of refusal came in reply to Tessa's offer.

"I'll be in the garden," he told them. "Rethinking my decision to agree to this, if I'm smart." His three new business partners glanced at each other as he stepped outside, watching him mull it over in the garden.

"You think he can live with this?" Natalie asked.

"Wait and see," said Ama. "I think he could really surprise us."

Tessa glanced toward the figure in the garden. "I think you're right," she said. "He's already surprised us a few times, hasn't he? There's something a little different about him. He didn't stick around just to spackle our walls for mere pennies these last few weeks." The unexpected facets of the contractor's personality promised more was yet to come. He could be sensitive, almost charming at times. If she wasn't careful, she might find herself thinking about all of this more often than she should, too.

"Here's to happy endings," said Natalie, lifting her cup. "For Paolo and Molly, for Bianca, and for all the future events we plan."

"And may we all find our own," added Ama.

As her partners sipped the last of the champagne, Tessa stepped outside to the terrace, with two champagne flutes in hand, approaching the contractor leaning against the terrace's little table. "Here," she said, handing one of the glasses to Blake. "It's the last of the bottle. We're drinking a toast to the future, so you should join us."

"You don't need me for that," he said. "You fixed your future on your own. All I did was strictly what I was asked to do."

"I think we do," said Tessa. "At least to fix our leaky roof and bad pipes. But... also because we owe you a lot more for what you did for us."

"Not that again," he said, groaning. "Will you stop thanking me?"

"That's kind of hard to do, after everything you managed on our behalf," she said, crossing her arms. "Becoming The Wedding Guru... finding that amazing altar..."

"I already told you. I'm happy to be paid for my regular work in your building," he said. He smiled at her, and his voice became gentler. "Let's leave it at that. Although... I would like a crack at finishing that little room downstairs that needs new wainscoting. If you want to say 'thank you' properly."

"You *are* impossible to work with," declared Tessa. "Unbelievable." She shook her head, and leaned to kiss Blake's cheek in a tender gesture—only he turned his head at that exact moment, and her lips made contact with his own in a kiss.

Quick, light, and almost accidental... but Tessa felt electricity in the second her lips touched his. Was she imagining things, or did his lips actually *return* the pressure—reach for her own in the second before she broke from that touch in her surprise?

She gazed at him, wide-eyed, too surprised to find the words. In Blake's eyes was a look that might be amusement or amazement, but certainly not unpleasantness. A hint of a smile appeared in them, and Tessa felt her lips mirroring his.

"I should—go back inside," she said, when she found her voice again. "See if the girls need some help." She set her glass on the patio table, but couldn't help glancing back once more at their fourth partner before she went inside. Their eyes met again and Tessa felt an emotion both familiar and forgotten: a mixture of passion, hope, and excitement. The same feeling she used to get daydreaming about her future, and how she would spend it making other people's perfect moments come true. Looking into that clear blue gaze, Tessa felt this might be a perfect moment for her, though—and maybe, just maybe, others were in store for the future.

Electricity. Chemistry. Whatever else it might be, she hadn't been imagining things when she felt it in Blake's arms before. Maybe that kind of magic—the romantic, inexplicable kind—wasn't as crazy as she believed after all.

A Letter from Laura

"Everybody loves a wedding," the old saying claims, and in my writing career, I've dreamed up several wedding scenarios, from perfect vows to romantic disasters. But *One Day Like This* has been something new and unique for me, and I hope that, if you enjoyed the world of Tessa, Natalie, and Ama as much as I did, you will sign up below for notifications about upcoming releases. Your email address will remain completely private, and you can unsubscribe at any time.

www.bookouture.com/laura-briggs

Thank you for joining my characters on this adventure in their fictional hometown of Bellegrove, a city with historic atmosphere, cultural flavours, and a little Southern charm to boot. It's a promising setting, I hope, for more romantic stories yet to come as Tessa, Natalie, and Ama learn to navigate the sometimes-complicated world of wedding planning and the complex scenarios in their own love lives.

I also hope that if you enjoyed this book, you will leave a review sharing what you loved about their story. To learn more about the series, please join me on social media using the links below—I look forward to sharing with readers soon the exciting romantic sequel in this series!

Thanks for reading,

Laura Briggs

www.facebook.com/authorlaurabriggs/

twitter.com/PaperDollWrites

paperdollwrites.blogspot.com/

83232051R00168

Made in the USA
Middletown, DE
10 August 2018